Beyond the Horizon:
A Life of Discovery, Innovation, and Resilience

CARMINE BIANCARDI

Disclaimer

This is a personal memoir based on the author's experiences, memories, and interpretations. To protect privacy and comply with confidentiality agreements, certain names of individuals, organizations, and projects have been changed or fictionalized.

Any resemblance to real persons, living or dead, or real institutions and projects is purely coincidental unless otherwise noted with permission. In some cases, composite characters or events have been used to represent broader truths while maintaining narrative coherence and ethical discretion.

Dedication

To my daughters, Rebecca and Thelma,
and to my beloved wife, Corinne,
who left this world far too soon after a brave fight with illness.

My family has been my steadfast crew through calm waters and the
fiercest storms.

And to all who walk the path of illness, loss, and uncertainty—
May you draw strength from endurance and find peace in the safe
harbor of hope.

Acknowledgment

This book would not have been possible without the unwavering support, love, and guidance of many extraordinary people.

First and foremost, I thank my daughters, Rebecca and Thelma, for their endless patience, love, and encouragement throughout my life. Your strength and resilience inspire me every day. To Monica Castiglioni, my companion and steadfast supporter, thank you for standing by my side through adventures, challenges, and moments of reflection.

I owe a profound debt of gratitude to my parents, Melita Magnano and Biancardi, whose values, courage, and love of the sea shaped the man I am today. Their lessons in perseverance, integrity, and curiosity continue to guide me. I also wish to remember Zia Luisa, my father's sister, whose care and presence enriched my childhood and supported our family in countless ways.

To my siblings—Nuccy, Maria, and Sergio—thank you for your love, encouragement, and support through both good and difficult times. To all those who have been close to me throughout my life, your friendship and presence have been invaluable. I also acknowledge my second wife, who, even though our marriage did not last, supported me when I needed it most.

To my mentors, colleagues, and friends across the fields of maritime engineering, naval architecture, and historical research—

especially those within the Royal Historical Society (RHS), the Society of Naval Architects and Marine Engineers (SNAME), and the Royal Institution of Naval Architects (RINA)—thank you for your inspiration, collaboration, and encouragement throughout my professional journey.

I am grateful as well to the academic institutions I have had the privilege of collaborating with, including Università Parthenope di Napoli, Italy; the Australian Maritime College, Tasmania, Australia; Stevens Institute of Technology, Hoboken, USA; the U.S. Merchant Marine Academy, Kings Point, USA; Manhattan College, New York City, USA; the University of Glasgow, UK; and others, for their support and partnership in research, education, and maritime innovation.

I wish to acknowledge my professional experiences at METTLE and STR Europe, along with my collaborations with the European Commission and European Parliament, as well as other companies and institutions, for shaping my career, fostering innovation, and enabling me to contribute meaningfully to engineering, research, and policy development.

I am deeply thankful to the medical teams at CHU Pasteur in Nice and the Tzanck Institute on the French Riviera, who cared for me during my two kidney transplants, and to all healthcare professionals who have supported me along the way. Your skill, compassion, and dedication have allowed me to continue pursuing my passions and sharing my story.

I also wish to honor the friends, teammates, and mentors from my sporting life—basketball, rugby, sailing, and beyond—who taught me lessons in strategy, resilience, leadership, and the power of teamwork. Each of you has left an indelible mark on my character and perspective.

Finally, to the readers, explorers, and cruise guests who inspire me to share my experiences and the history I cherish—thank you. Your curiosity and enthusiasm breathe life into these pages.

To all of you, past and present, near and far, I am profoundly grateful.

Carmine Biancardi

Table of Content

About the Author

Carmine Biancardi is a Chartered Engineer, academic, and Fellow of the Royal Historical Society (UK), the Royal Institution of Naval Architects (UK), and the Society of Naval Architects and Marine Engineers (USA). Since 1990, he has been a Licensed Chartered Engineer, recognized internationally for his contributions to research, innovation, and leadership in naval architecture and marine engineering. Over the course of his distinguished career, he has led pioneering R&D projects, published influential work, and guided both students and professionals in shaping the future of maritime design and history.

Born on the small island of Procida, Carmine developed an early and enduring love for the sea, ships, and the maritime traditions of his community. That passion led him to the Nautical Institute of Torre del Greco, where he trained as a marine captain and mastered disciplines ranging from celestial navigation to ship stability. His professional path carried him from cadet officer voyages across the Mediterranean to becoming a respected voice in international naval engineering circles.

Carmine has also built a long academic career as a university professor, teaching in countries including Australia, the United Kingdom, Italy, Japan, the United States, Cyprus, and Malta. His work in higher education has influenced generations of students and researchers, combining rigorous scientific knowledge with practical experience and a cross-cultural perspective.

His life, however, is not defined by professional achievement alone. Twice a kidney transplant recipient, he has faced the fragility of life head-on—enduring the struggles of illness, the long waits for a donor, the isolation of recovery, and the resilience required to return to health. He has also known the pain of personal loss, including the death of his first wife to cancer. Yet these experiences, rather than diminishing his outlook, have deepened his sense of purpose, gratitude, and determination to live fully.

Alongside his academic and engineering accomplishments, Carmine has pursued a lifelong love of sport and adventure: serving as a basketball referee at national and international levels, playing rugby, sailing as an accomplished skipper, and competing as an athlete in multiple disciplines. These pursuits, like his professional and personal life, reflect a commitment to teamwork, strategy, perseverance, and the courage to face challenges both on land and at sea.

Today, Carmine continues to share his knowledge and passion as a lecturer, engaging audiences around the world with history, world affairs, destination storytelling, and personal reflections. His talks connect the technical with the human, blending scholarship with narrative to both inspire and inform.

This book brings together the many strands of his life—the sea, science, history, resilience, and family—offering readers a deeply personal yet universal journey through hardship and triumph. It stands as a testament not only to a career of distinction but also to the enduring strength of the human spirit.

Preface

The scent of salt and sun-baked earth still lingers in my mind, a vivid memory from my childhood on the island of Procida. This book isn't just a simple retelling of events; it's a journey into the lasting impact the sea and my family have had on shaping who I am today. Growing up on that small Italian island, life was always tied to the rhythms of the sea—the ebb and flow of the tides, the struggles, and the triumphs of the people around me.

The fishing boats bobbing gently in the harbor, the fresh scent of fish just caught, and the sounds of children playing in narrow, sunlit streets are memories that go beyond mere nostalgia. They are deeply woven into the story of my life. These memories are not just fleeting moments but part of the very foundation of who I am. Through this book, I want to explore how my family's story has shaped my journey, a legacy passed down over generations.

My father, a World War II veteran who served in the Italian Navy, is a symbol of strength and resilience. His experiences shaped him in ways that would define not only his life but the lives of those who came after him. My mother, a devoted Sicilian nurse, taught me the meaning of love, care, and sacrifice. Together, they built a foundation of strength, resilience, and unwavering commitment to family. Their stories, combined with those of my entrepreneurial grandparents and my siblings, create a rich tapestry of family, community, and hard work.

As I reflect on these memories, I want to capture not just the specific time and place I grew up in, but the universal themes of love, loss, strength, and the human spirit. The sea, the island, and the people around me all played a part in shaping who I am today. Through this story, I hope to connect with others who, like me, have been shaped by their roots and the ties that bind us to those we love. This is a story of family, community, and the powerful force of the sea—a story that I believe will resonate with anyone who has felt the pull of home, of history, and of the people who shape us.

Chapter 1: Procida – The Island That Shaped My Spirit

It was one of those perfect, sun-drenched days in Procida, the kind that seemed to stretch on forever. I remember running along the narrow, sun-baked streets, feeling the salty Mediterranean air cling to my skin. The sound of the old wooden boats creaking in the harbor reached my ears as I made my way toward the water, their sturdy frames swaying with the rhythm of the sea. Even as a young boy, I felt that pulse deep inside me—an unspoken connection between myself and the ocean.

I was just a child, barely old enough to tie my shoes, but I remember the first time I stood at the edge of the wooden pier. My eyes were wide with wonder as I watched the fishermen haul their catch into their boats, their hands working with practiced ease. The sky above was a clear, dazzling blue, and the water shimmered beneath me in every shade of turquoise imaginable. Procida—its colorful buildings stacked like a patchwork quilt along the jagged coastline—felt like it was alive. Every inch of it seemed to breathe with the pulse of the sea.

But it wasn't just the view or the boats that captivated me—it was the sea itself. I'll never forget the first time I truly understood its power. I was at Chiaia Beach, the golden sand stretching out before me like an endless promise, when a wave came out of nowhere, knocking me over. The cool water swallowed me up, tugging me beneath the surface for the blink of an eye. For a moment, I felt small—scared even—but before I could fully grasp the fear, the sea pulled back, leaving me soaked but unharmed.

I stood up, brushing sand from my skin, and I remember laughing—because something inside me had shifted. The sea wasn't just something we played in—it was something much bigger. It was alive, with moods and mysteries of its own, and from that moment on, I felt that it had a place in my heart, a place that I would always return to.

From then on, the beach was my home. Every day, I ran along the shore, my feet sinking into the warm sand, racing with the other kids to the water's edge. We spent hours pretending to be pirates, sailing on imaginary ships, diving into the waves, and letting the cool water wash over us after the heat of the sun. There was something about the rhythm of the waves that made everything feel right—simple, pure, and full of possibility. It was where we were free, where our dreams were as wide as the ocean, and the sea was always there, ready to carry us away on some new adventure.

But there was more to Procida than just the beach. As the sun dipped below the horizon, the pace of the island slowed. The golden light softened, and the air cooled, bringing with it a sense of calm. Chiaia Beach, my beloved beach, transformed into something magical. The chatter of the fishermen died down, and families and friends gathered together in the fading light, shedding the day's work in favor of a shared evening. The aroma of fish sizzling on the grill mixed with the salty tang of the sea, wrapped the island in a feeling of warmth and togetherness.

I can still hear the clinking of glasses, the sounds of laughter rising into the air, and the soft strum of guitars.

And then there was the music. The island's heartbeat. Guitars, tambourines, and the songs of the older men and women filled the air, their voices rising in unison in the warm night. The flickering light of the fire danced on their faces, casting shadows that seemed to hold the history of Procida itself. The rhythm of the tambourine, the strum of the guitar, the crackling of the fire, and the waves breaking gently on the shore—together, they created a harmony that felt timeless.

On some nights, the tarantella would start—a lively, spirited dance that everyone joined in, no matter their age. The sand would fly beneath our feet as we moved together, caught up in the music, in the joy, in the celebration of life. There was no place for worries or fears at that moment; there was only laughter and only dancing. In those moments, we were all connected—not just to each other, but to the island itself, to the rhythm of the sea, to the warmth of the fire.

Now, as I stand at the water's edge once more, I feel that stillness. That calmness of the sea. And yet, I know deep down that the sea isn't always calm. It has its storms, its hidden dangers, its moods that can change in an instant. But even with all of that, the sea always calls to me. It always has. It's as much a part of me as Procida itself, a place I'll always carry with me, wherever life takes me. And I'll always remember those days—the sound of the waves, the music in the air, the taste of fresh fish, the warmth of the fire—because that was home.

There are places in the world that shape you without your realizing it, and then there are places that carve their mark so deeply into your soul that you carry them with you forever. Procida is one of those places. To many, it might appear as just another small island off the coast of Naples, surrounded by the endless expanse of the Mediterranean. But to me, Procida is far more than just a dot on the map—it's the very heart of who I am.

As a child, I never thought much about how special this island really was. To me, it was simply home. But now, as I look back with the wisdom of time, I realize that Procida has shaped me in ways I couldn't have understood then. The island and I share a deep connection—one that's entwined with the fabric of my spirit. The ocean, the fishing boats, the hum of life around the docks—everything about Procida taught me something, and that something stays with me still.

Procida, though small, is one of the most historic and culturally rich islands in the Bay of Naples. The island's very existence is intertwined with the sea. From ancient times, it has been a haven for sailors, fishermen, and shipbuilders. It was here that the Greeks first settled, leaving behind their stories and traditions, shaping the land and its people. I grew up listening to those tales—the echoes of Procida's maritime past still alive in the streets and in the hearts of its people. It was this history that surrounded me from the moment I was born.

The island itself is a world of colors, textures, and smells. The houses rise up from the rocky coastline, their walls painted in vibrant shades of yellow, orange, and pink. This stark contrast to the bright blue of the sea and the sky makes Procida feel alive, as if it is a painting constantly shifting and evolving. The scent of saltwater is always in the air, carried by the wind that sweeps in from the Mediterranean, mixing with the smells of fresh fish from the docks. The constant ebb and flow of the tides, the gentle rocking of boats in the harbors, and the rhythmic sound of waves breaking against the shore became the soundtrack of my childhood.

But it wasn't just the scenery that shaped me—it was the people and their daily lives. The men and women who lived on Procida were a living witness to the island's connection to the sea. Their livelihoods, their families, their very existence revolved around the water. I would wake up to the sounds of fishermen shouting as they hauled their boats out of the water, their faces weathered by years of exposure to the harsh sun and salty air. The shipbuilders would be hard at work in the yards, shaping wood into boats that would soon sail off to distant shores. Every day, I would watch them, fascinated by the way they worked with such precision and care. For them, building a ship was as much an art as it was a skill.

I remember the dockside community, a close-knit group of men and women who worked hard and lived hard. They were my extended family, each person playing a unique role in the life of the island. The dockyards were always bustling, but there was an unspoken rhythm to it all. The tides dictated the pace of life, and the ships seemed to move in harmony with the world around them. The fishermen's boats would leave early in the morning, and by the time the sun was setting, they would return with their catch, their boats loaded down with fish that would be sold in the markets or shipped off to other parts of Italy.

I would watch them, fascinated by how they worked together in harmony, how each person had a role to play. The men who sailed the boats, the women who sold the fish, the shipbuilders who ensured that the fleet would remain strong—all were tied to the sea in ways I couldn't fully understand at the time, but which would come to define my own path in life.

The older fishermen, their faces etched with the maps of a thousand voyages, were repositories of stories as deep and mysterious as the sea itself. Their skin, tanned to the color of weathered leather, had absorbed decades of sun, salt, and wind. Every wrinkle, every line on their faces, told a tale of battles fought against the relentless sea. And it was in the dimly lit taverns that clung to the cliffs of Procida, where the low hum of the waves crashing against the rocks reminded them of the island's close relationship with the ocean, that these men shared their epic stories.

The first man whose stories I remember clearly was Nonno Antonio. He was a man whose very presence seemed to embody the island's history. One of his eyes was lost to time, but the other, still sharp, gleamed with a mischievous twinkle whenever he spoke of the old days. His voice was rough, like a sailor's, tinged with the stories of battles fought not with men, but with creatures of the deep. Nonno Antonio was the kind of man who could make even the most mundane occurrence sound like the beginning of an epic saga. The way he described the tuna he had once fought in the open sea was a tale that, if not for its sheer improbability, might have been a legend.

"I tell you," he would say, leaning in close as if revealing the secret of a lost treasure, "the tuna was as big as a boat. I threw my harpoon with all the strength I had, and when the line went taut, it was as if the sea itself had decided to challenge me. We were locked in battle, me and that fish, for hours under the hot sun. It was a fight between man and nature, a test of endurance. And, let me tell you, there were moments when I thought I would be swallowed whole by the ocean."

As he recounted the story, he mimed the motion of casting the harpoon, then tightened his grip as if feeling the weight of the fish pulling against the line once again. His face would light up with the joy of reliving the glory of that struggle. There was always a thread of superstition woven into his stories, a deep respect for the unknown forces of nature that governed his life.

"Ah, and the malocchio," he would mutter, lowering his voice, "you never know when it might strike. A fisherman's luck is fickle, my friend. But we have our ways, our charms. I wore a small silver amulet every time I went out to sea, and I never left without a blessing from the old priest. You never know when the sea might decide to turn on you."

Then, there was Giovanni, another of the older fishermen, whose voice was as creaky as the mast of an ancient ship. Giovanni's stories were less about grand battles with giant fish and more about the quiet, intimate observations of a man who had spent his life in harmony with the rhythms of the sea.

"Did you see the sky yesterday?" he would ask, his voice low, with a kind of reverence in it. "The color of the water changed, from blue to grey. That's a sign. A storm's coming."

He would pause, taking a slow sip of his wine, and then continue.

"The birds are more agitated today. They fly in circles when they're searching for fish. You see the seagulls, they dive in a different way when a storm is near. The sea speaks to you, if you know how to listen."

Giovanni's stories were quiet, filled with observations that seemed to hold the essence of a life spent in constant dialogue with nature.

But as the years passed, the stories of the older fishermen began to change. The island was evolving, and with it, the world of the fishermen. Among the younger generation, there was Peppino — barely old enough to grow a full beard, but already a man who had witnessed the changing tides of the fishing industry. His tales were neither of heroic struggles nor intimate observations, but of the challenges that came with the modern world.

"The boats are bigger now," Peppino would say, his face serious as he leaned forward. "They've got sonar and GPS, so you don't have to know the sea as well. The fish stocks are dwindling, and the big commercial boats are out there, taking what little is left."

"We've got to think about sustainability," he would say, his voice carrying the urgency of someone who knew that the world he loved was slowly slipping away. "If we don't change the way we fish, there won't be anything left for the next generation. We need to respect the sea and all that it gives us. The balance is delicate, and if we don't take care of it, it will be gone."

Despite his youth, Peppino's perspective carried a deep understanding of the interconnectedness between man and nature.

These fishermen, each with their unique perspectives, painted a vivid portrait of life on Procida. Their stories weren't just about fishing; they were about the essence of the island itself — its history, its culture, its connection to the sea.

I would sit and listen to their stories, mesmerized, absorbing not only the narrative but the very essence of their lives. The cadence of their voices, the gestures of their hands, the expressions on their faces — all of it added to the authenticity and depth of the stories they told. It wasn't just about the events they recounted; it was about the way they experienced the world, a world shaped by the sea, by time, and by the ever-present cycle of life and death.

It was in Procida, among these men and women, that my passion for the sea took root. The dockyards, the harbors, the bustling markets—all of it became a part of me. But it was the people who lived this life every day—those whose lives were shaped by the rhythms of the tide—that truly defined my connection to the sea.

Growing up in Procida, I was blessed with two extraordinary parents, whose love and resilience shaped the very core of who I would become. Each of them brought their own unique strength to our family, their contrasting personalities and life stories coming together to create a powerful foundation of love, discipline, and support.

At the heart of my story lies my father.

The war forged my father's character. Andrea's most extraordinary experience came after he was captured by the British Army during the battle. They took him as a prisoner of war and, for many, that would have been the end of the story. But Andrea was no ordinary soldier. His determination and cunning allowed him to escape, disappearing into the desert sands, returning to the fight with a quiet but fierce resolve. He became a legend among his comrades. Yet, fate had other plans. He was recaptured, this time by the U.S. Army, and sent to a prisoner-of-war camp in the United States. It would have been easy to give up then, but Andrea's spirit was unbreakable. He endured those years with a sense of quiet defiance. The conditions were brutal, but he never wavered.

In his mind, survival wasn't just about existing. It was about holding on to the values that defined him—honor, duty, and courage. These were the qualities that kept him going through those years of captivity. The medals he earned, which I now keep in a small wooden box on my shelf, stand as a silent testament to his heroism. But for me, it wasn't the medals that mattered most; it was the man who wore them. It was the lessons he passed on to me, lessons about resilience, about never giving up, about maintaining your sense of integrity even when the world seems to be against you.

Though I never asked him about his time as a soldier—he rarely spoke of the war—I didn't need to. It was in the way he lived his life that I saw the depth of his resilience. Every challenge, every setback, was met with a steady resolve. And that was the legacy Andrea left for me: a legacy of quiet strength, of perseverance, and of unyielding courage in the face of life's harshest tests.

While my father was the quiet force that instilled in me strength and discipline, my mother, Melita, was the heart of our home. Where Andrea was a pillar of strength and resilience, Melita was the warmth that held us all together. Her love was the foundation upon which our family was built, and her wisdom was the balm that soothed us when life became too overwhelming. If my father's influence taught me how to fight, my mother's taught me how to love, how to endure, and how to remain compassionate in the face of hardship.

Melita's story, like my father's, was one of incredible perseverance. Born in Sicily, she was orphaned at just six years old when both of her parents passed away, leaving her to fend for herself in a world that was cold and indifferent. But Melita wasn't one to be broken by tragedy. She carried the pain of her childhood deep within her, but it never stopped her from dreaming of a better future. Despite the hardships she endured, she was determined to make something of herself. She became an eye nurse, dedicating her life to helping those in need, using the skills she had learned to restore sight to those who had lost it.

Her Sicilian heritage was something she carried with immense pride. Sicily, with its rugged mountains, its fierce independence, and its deep cultural roots, shaped my mother into the woman she was. From her, I learned the importance of family, the unbreakable bond that holds us together even when the world tries to pull us apart. She taught me that true strength lies not just in surviving, but in caring for those around you, in being there for your loved ones when they need you most.

Melita's resilience, her ability to keep moving forward despite the challenges she faced, was something I witnessed every day. When I was growing up, I didn't fully understand the sacrifices she had made. It wasn't until I was older that I realized how much she had given up to ensure that my siblings and I had a better life. She chose to leave her career in nursing to stay home and raise us, providing the warmth and stability that we needed. She taught me that sometimes, the greatest acts of love are the quiet, everyday sacrifices we make for others.

Together, my parents created a home filled with both strength and warmth. While Andrea taught me how to stand tall and face the world with quiet determination, Melita taught me how to love deeply and nurture the bonds that connect us all. They balanced each other perfectly, with Andrea's stoic strength and Melita's nurturing spirit providing the foundation for everything I would become.

Those early days in Procida were like a foundation, firm and unshakable, setting me up for what was to come. The love and strength I absorbed from the island and my parents would follow me wherever I went. But little did I know, the world ahead was bigger than anything I had imagined. There would be moments when I'd feel lost, when the storm seemed too strong. But deep down, I would always have the island's pulse in my heart, the courage of my father, and the warmth of my mother's love to pull me through. And that was enough to keep me going.

What would come next? I didn't know—but I knew I was ready to face it.

10. Procida - Marina Corricella

Chapter 2: A Family of Resilience and Legacy

There are moments in life when you can feel your family's history in your bones, and it hits you how much the path you walk now has been influenced by the people who came before you. You start to realize that everything you are today—your strength, your values, the way you see the world—was transformed by their sacrifices and choices. For me, the heart of it all is my maternal grandmother. Her life, her courage, and the way she held everything together laid the foundation for everything that came after. She was the rock, the steady force that kept our family grounded and gave us a sense of purpose.

My grandmother, from my mother's side, is a name often spoken with reverence in our family. Born at the end of the 1800s, at a time when Sicily was still gripped by the shadows of tradition and male-dominated industries, she carved out her own path with an unyielding resolve. A woman of vision and ambition, she became a pioneering Sicilian entrepreneur, starting a food and supplies company that served the Italian Navy at the Port of Augusta. I never met her because she died when my mother was a six-year-old child, but her legacy stays in the family forever.

The Port of Augusta, with its bustling trade and ships coming in and out, was crucial to the Italian Navy's operations. Yet, at the turn of the century, it was a world dominated by men, where the role of women was often confined to the home. My grandmother's daring choice to establish a company catering to such an important industry was groundbreaking. She was not simply another businesswoman; she was a force, challenging the norms of her time. She didn't let the societal limitations of the era deter her from what she believed was possible.

With limited resources but a sharp mind, she built her company from the ground up. The business began small, with her delivering essential food supplies for sailors embarking on long journeys. She sourced high-quality ingredients, ensuring the sailors were nourished not just physically but also with the taste of home, a touch of comfort in the vast expanse of the sea. The navy was impressed with her attention to detail and dedication to quality, making her company indispensable for their daily operations.

Running a business while raising a family was no easy task, but my grandmother managed it with grace. The stories told by my mother of how she would juggle meetings with the navy officials while simultaneously organizing her children's schedules are nothing short of awe-inspiring. She was a mother, a businesswoman, and a leader all at once. Sadly, she died young, at the age of 33, when my mother was just six years old. Even though she wasn't there, I always felt her presence through the stories passed down in the family. Her resilience, resourcefulness, and vision were traits I deeply admired. And as I grew older, her influence seeped into the very way I approached the challenges of my own life—professionally and personally.

I often find myself standing on the edge of difficult decisions, wondering what my grandmother would have done. Her ability to embrace change and push forward when it seemed impossible has been a guiding star for me. She faced adversity with an open heart, never allowing the tides of societal expectations to define her course. Her legacy continues to echo through our family, a reminder that with perseverance and belief in one's abilities, even the greatest obstacles can be overcome.

Carmine Giuseppe Biancardi, my paternal grandfather who shared my exact name and last name, was another remarkable figure whose entrepreneurial spirit and dedication to craftsmanship left a lasting legacy in our family. Born in the heart of Italy, he possessed a keen eye for quality and a deep respect for traditional artisanship. In the early 1900s, driven by ambition and a desire to create something meaningful, he founded a furniture factory nestled in the Apennines around Benevento. What began as a modest workshop soon blossomed into a thriving enterprise known for producing finely crafted furniture that found its way into homes and furniture stores across Italy. His pieces weren't just functional—they reflected a sense of artistry and care, combining beauty with durability, which made them highly sought after.

What truly set Carmine Giuseppe apart was his foresight and willingness to innovate. At a time when most local furniture makers relied solely on regional materials, he took the bold step of importing high-quality wood directly from Venezuela to supply his factory. This decision wasn't simply a business move—it was a reflection of his relentless commitment to excellence. Recognizing the superior qualities of Venezuelan hardwoods, such as their strength, durability, and rich grains, he sought to enhance the quality and uniqueness of his furniture. Managing such an international supply chain in the early 20th century was no small feat. It required not only sharp business acumen but also a pioneering spirit as he navigated complex logistics and built connections across continents to ensure a steady flow of premium wood to his factory.

This dedication to sourcing the finest materials allowed Carmine Giuseppe's workshop to stand out in a competitive market. The imported Venezuelan wood became the foundation of the factory's reputation for producing durable, elegant furniture that combined Italian craftsmanship with superior raw materials. Under his leadership, the company thrived, growing steadily and gaining a strong reputation throughout Italy. His factory not only produced beautiful pieces but also provided stable employment to local craftsmen, helping to boost the community's economy.

Carmine Giuseppe was more than just a successful entrepreneur; he was a respected figure in his community, known for his fairness, generosity, and unwavering commitment to his craft. Yet, despite his achievements, life dealt him a cruel hand. He died young, leaving behind not only a flourishing business but also a family unprepared for the sudden loss. My father, Andrea, was still too young and inexperienced to take over the complex operations of the factory, especially with the growing instability leading up to World War II. Without his father's guiding hand, the business struggled to sustain itself. By the time

Andrea returned from the war, the opportunity to revive the factory had slipped away, and the family was forced to sell off its remaining assets.

Though the physical remnants of Carmine Giuseppe's work disappeared, his legacy endured. His entrepreneurial vision, his bold decision to import wood from Venezuela to elevate the quality of his craft, and his dedication to excellence became part of the family's story— a lasting testament to ambition, resilience, and the pursuit of something greater.

Beyond my maternal grandmother and paternal grandfather, it was my parents and siblings who provided the foundational support for me during my formative years. I am fortunate to have grown up with three incredible siblings and the greatest parents, each of whom played a unique role in shaping my character. They were my teachers, my guides, and, most importantly, my companions on this journey called life.

The things I've learned from them, the moments we've shared, the way we've supported each other, all of it has helped me grow. Together, they've made me who I am—stronger, kinder, more aware of the importance of love and resilience. They've taught me that family is more than just blood; it's about the connections we nurture, the lessons we pass on, and the love we give without question. It's that love, that support, that continues to guide me every day.

One of the pillars of that legacy is my mother, Melita—a woman whose spirit was as vast and deep as the Sicilian sea that surrounded the village where she grew up. She wasn't a large woman, but when she walked into a room, it felt like the sun had just come up. Her presence was that strong. Her eyes, dark as the night sky, were full of a quiet strength. If you looked into them, you could see a kindness that seemed endless but also a sharpness, like the sharp edge of a stone you find by the shore. That sharpness was the willpower that carried her through life.

In the last chapter, I shared a glimpse of what made my mother such an extraordinary person. Now, I want to tell you more, to show you just how amazing she truly was. My mother was not just a person who gave life to me, but a woman who lived her life with purpose and grace. She had the rare ability to make everyone feel like they mattered. She could make you laugh even on the toughest days, and when things felt impossible.

Since she worked as a nurse for most of her life, the way she cared for people always left a mark on everyone she met. I can still picture her hands, worn and weathered from years of work, but they always had the gentlest touch. Her hands healed people. She had the kind of magic in her touch that made you feel safe, no matter how sick or scared you were. Whether it was cradling a newborn baby, comforting someone in pain, or wiping away tears from someone grieving, she always knew how to ease the hurt without saying a word. People trusted her. I think it was because she had this gift to connect with people at a level that felt so deep, so personal. It wasn't just her training as a nurse; it was something that was just part of who she was.

Growing up, I watched her love my father with a quiet kind of devotion. It wasn't loud or flashy, but it was constant like the tide coming in and out every day. Even when life was tough, when things weren't going right, you could feel the strength of that love. She had this way of holding everything together, keeping us anchored even when the world felt like it was falling apart.

Her family was everything to her. She taught us that family was more than just blood—it was the thread that held everything together. Family meant showing up, even when it was hard. It meant the late-night talks, the meals shared around the table, and the way we always looked out for each other, no matter what. Sundays at our house were something special. They weren't just about eating. They were about being together.

She was also a deeply spiritual woman, but it was the quiet, humble kind of faith. She didn't need to wear it on her sleeve for everyone to see. Her faith was something she carried inside her, like a quiet fire that kept her going when life felt heavy. She never preached to us, but she lived her faith every day. It was in the way she gave, the way she forgave, and the way she made sure we understood that in the hardest times, we weren't alone.

Even with everything on her plate, she always found time for us. She was the one who made sure we had everything we needed, whether it was a home-cooked meal or someone to talk to when we had a bad day. She never seemed tired, even when I knew she must've been. She didn't ask for help, and if we needed something, we didn't even have to ask— she was already on it. She showed us how to live with dignity and grace, even in the face of struggle. Her strength wasn't loud or obvious; it was quiet, steady, and always present.

She was the kind of mother who didn't hover over us, but she was always there when we needed her. She let us make our own choices, even if they weren't always the right ones. She knew that mistakes were part of life, part of growing up, and she was okay with that. But when we needed guidance, she gave it, and she gave it without judgment. She believed in us, sometimes more than we believed in ourselves. And I think that belief in us is what helped shape us into who we are today.

I'll never forget the little things she did that showed just how big her heart was. Like when she helped an elderly neighbor with her groceries on a rainy day or when she stayed up all night with a sick child, making sure we were comfortable, holding our hands, and whispering reassuring words. She didn't do these things for applause. She did them because that's who she was—someone who believed in giving without expecting anything in return.

Her legacy isn't something you can measure in awards or trophies. It's in the lives she touched, the hearts she healed, and the family she helped raise. What she taught me wasn't about how to be the strongest person in the room but how to be strong when you don't have to shout about it. She showed us that true strength comes from love—love for your family, love for others, and love for yourself.

She was a woman whose spirit burned quietly, but brightly. And even now, I feel her light guiding me, reminding me to live with compassion, to love with all my heart, and to always be there for the people who need me most. That's the gift she gave me, and it's the gift I carry with me every day.

In times of struggle, Melita would often turn inward, relying on her faith and the lessons from her own upbringing. But when things became too overwhelming, she would lean on my father, Andrea, her steadfast partner in life. He was the other half of their partnership, and together, they formed a union that held us all together. It was from them both that I learned the importance of working hard, staying committed, and believing in the power of love and family.

My father was not born to the sea. For him, however, the sea came in a way that was shaped by duty, responsibility, and family legacy.

He didn't choose the Navy because he was drawn to the allure of the ocean, the freedom of the wide-open sea, or the adventure of far-flung ports—though I'm sure some part of him was captivated by those ideas. Instead, his connection to the sea was forged in the crucible of discipline, tradition, and the understanding that service to one's country was an obligation, not a choice.

Andrea joined the Regia Marina, the Royal Italian Navy, not out of romantic longing but as a sense of civic duty. It was part of his heritage— his older brother had already walked that path, carving out a life in the Navy that was marked by stories of daring exploits, far-off places, and encounters with people and cultures that Andrea had only read about. He joined the famous Battaglione San Andrea, Italy's elite marine infantry unit, often compared to the U.S. Marine Corps. Known for its rigorous training, exceptional combat skills, and amphibious warfare expertise, the Battaglione San Andrea has a storied history dating back to the early 20th century. It played a significant role during World War II, where my father served with distinction, and it continues to operate today as Italy's premier naval infantry force, participating in peacekeeping missions and military operations worldwide.

A good friend of his, a charismatic and adventurous figure, had already sailed the Mediterranean and returned with tales of naval life: the chase of smugglers in the waters off Sicily, the tense standoffs with the British fleet, and the heart-pounding excitement of maneuvering a torpedo boat through the waves.

At the age of seventeen, Andrea entered a marine-style training camp before embarking for World War II. It wasn't a formal naval academy but a rigorous program designed to prepare him for the challenges ahead. The camp was intense, and the lessons learned there would prove vital as war loomed over Europe. Andrea often spoke of the harsh training, the discipline it instilled in him, and the sense of camaraderie that developed between the men.

During the war, Andrea became part of the naval forces fighting in the Mediterranean. He fought in the famous Battle of Tobruk, a pivotal moment in World War II, where the Allies battled Axis forces in North Africa. His experiences there, in the heat of battle, shaped much of who he became.

But it was after his capture that his true test began. Andrea was made prisoner by the French and then escaped, only to be captured again, this time by the U.S. Army. He was sent to a World War II prison camp in the USA, where he would spend several years. His resilience during this time was extraordinary, and it became clear that the hardships he endured only strengthened his resolve. Training at the academy was grueling. It tested both physical and mental endurance, forcing young men to transform into disciplined officers who were ready to command. I've seen photographs of him from those days—young, lean, and intensely focused. His eyes were a mirror of the steely determination that it took to succeed in such a demanding environment. In the photos, he wore his uniform with precision: the sharp, crisp lines of the coat, the immaculate posture, the firm gaze. They captured a man who was becoming something new, a young man stepping into the weight of a marine's responsibilities.

But the man I knew, the one who was my father, was nothing like the one in those old photographs. When I came into the picture, Andrea was weathered by time, shaped by war, and marked by years of service. His laughter, which he shared so freely, often held a quiet sadness behind it—a sadness that no amount of smiling could quite hide. But there were still moments, rare and precious, when that earlier version of himself would surface and talk about the days before everything changed.

Those years before the war were a blur of endless training exercises, long deployments to various Mediterranean ports, and the camaraderie of men who had been confined together on a ship. Andrea didn't speak much of those years, but when he did, the stories came in fragments—pieces of a larger puzzle I would never fully understand. He'd tell them during quiet moments over espresso, his voice low as memories resurfaced amidst the rich aroma of coffee and the clatter of teaspoons against porcelain. He'd talk about chasing smugglers off the coast of Sicily, about the nervous tension during naval exercises with the British fleet, and about the rush of piloting a torpedo boat through the choppy waters of the Tyrrhenian Sea.

He spoke of battleships cutting through the waves with such power, the rhythmic creak of the hull beneath his feet, and the star-filled skies above him as he stood on deck, feeling the hum of the ocean beneath him. It was a world of breathtaking beauty and intense responsibility, one that Andrea never fully let go of even after so many years.

But beneath the surface of those anecdotes—those stories of excitement and adventure—there was something else. There was a deeper undercurrent of tension, of anticipation. He spoke of a subtle but undeniable feeling of unease as the winds of war began to shift in Europe. The carefree days spent in foreign ports, the exhilarating moments of naval exercises, and the spontaneous moments of camaraderie aboard his ship were starting to feel more like a memory, fading slowly under the shadow of what was to come.

Andrea's descriptions of life aboard a ship were some of the most vivid memories he shared with me. He'd talk about the engine room, how the rhythmic clang of machinery reverberated through the air, how the salt of the sea would linger on everything—the metal surfaces, the air they breathed, even the food they ate. The smell of the sea was always in the air, a reminder of where they were, of the vastness and the danger that loomed just beyond the horizon. He'd talk about the structure of life aboard the ship—the rigid hierarchies, the military precision of every task, and the way each member of the crew relied on the other. There was no room for error; everyone depended on everyone else.

But there were also moments of lighter, more human connection. Andrea would recall the laughter shared during long, sleepless watches, when they'd tell stories to pass the time. Sometimes, someone would pull out a harmonica and serenade the crew with a tune, lightening the atmosphere and offering a brief respite from the seriousness of their work. He even spoke of impromptu card games that lasted late into the night, the way the crew came together for a shared meal, and how they'd trade stories about their families or their homes.

He spoke with nostalgia about those moments of human connection, saying they were the things that kept morale high, that kept them going in times of stress and fatigue. It wasn't always easy, of course. There was always the pressure of duty, of knowing that every action had consequences. But still, there were moments of joy, moments that made the long stretches of time at sea more bearable.

The ports they visited were full of life and color, offering brief, welcome distractions from the rigor of naval life. The Mediterranean was a patchwork of cultures, and Andrea loved exploring these ports when he could, soaking in the sights, sounds, and smells of new places.

But he also remembered the ancient ruins of Carthage. That one, in particular, stayed with him for years. He described it with such awe that it seemed like he could still feel the weight of history pressing down on him, still see the crumbled columns and the remnants of a civilization that had long since passed. For Andrea, these moments of personal discovery—these breaks in routine—were as valuable as anything else in his life. They allowed him to escape the strict confines of the Navy and experience the world through a different lens, one that was as much about curiosity and wonder as it was about duty.

Andrea was a man of few words. His love was not expressed in grand declarations or dramatic gestures. No, his love was more like a quiet, persistent current running through the very essence of our lives. It was in the small things—the careful way he would mend a torn fishing net, or the precise way he repaired a broken toy. When I think of him, I can still see the quiet strength in his eyes as he watched us, steady and watchful, as we navigated the unpredictable tides of childhood. His love was conveyed into every action, every quiet moment. It wasn't showy, but it was constant.

My father didn't need to speak much to teach us the values that mattered—he embodied them. His honesty and his integrity of a better life for us—these were lessons that didn't require words. He was also a respected member of the Procida community. He was known for his integrity and kindness, qualities that extended beyond the walls of our home and into the lives of others. He fostered a sense of belonging among the fishermen and families on the island, always making sure no one was left behind, always extending a hand when needed. His respect for others was evident in every interaction—he valued understanding over conflict, always prioritizing peace and harmony. This attitude was not just something he shared with the outside world; it radiated throughout our home, shaping the way we treated each other and the way we viewed the world.

Both of my parents created a home that was both warm and stable, where love wasn't just an abstract idea but a lived reality. My mother's nurturing balanced out my father's stoic presence, creating an environment where we could thrive, emotionally and physically. Their partnership was the foundation of our family, a union of love and respect that never faltered, even in the face of hardship.

Of course, their relationship was not without challenges. The scars of war lingered in my father's soul, creating moments of quiet reflection or brief flashes of frustration. It was my mother's patience and understanding that helped absorb those moments, transforming them into opportunities for healing and growth. They communicated not just through words, but through actions—through a shared glance across the dinner table, a quiet touch in the morning, those small, unspoken gestures that spoke volumes of their deep affection for one another.

Their love story was the cornerstone of our family. It wasn't just a love born out of happiness and ease; it was a love that had endured the hardest of times—marked by the harsh realities of war and the delicate balance of island life. It was a love that had survived trials, shaped by both joy and suffering, and had become the bedrock of everything we knew.

Their partnership was the model of what love should be—a love that doesn't seek recognition but endures through both good and bad times. A love that isn't loud or flashy but that sustains, supports, and uplifts. It was in their love that I found the strength to overcome my own obstacles and to keep pushing forward even when life felt overwhelming.

As I look back on those days, I realize how fortunate I was to grow up in a family like ours—a family defined by resilience, love, and firm support.

As much as my parents' love and resilience shaped me, I would be remiss not to mention the role my siblings played in this journey. Together, we formed a team—a unit that reinforced the values of strength, unity, and unconditional love. Each of my siblings brought their own unique traits to the table, offering guidance, support, and, in many ways, lessons that were just as impactful as those I learned from our parents.

Nuccy, my eldest sister, was the one who always seemed to know the right thing to do. She was the calm in the storm, the steady hand when chaos would encircle us. I remember many nights when my parents were overwhelmed by the weight of their responsibilities, and Nuccy, despite her young age, would step in, offering advice and helping with the daily chores. Her ability to remain composed under pressure taught me the importance of patience and understanding.

But what I admired most about Nuccy was her firm sense of responsibility. She had an innate ability to manage difficult situations, and her guidance was often the anchor I needed in moments of uncertainty. When I was unsure of my own decisions, Nuccy would always take the time to listen to my concerns, offering a perspective that made me feel heard and understood.

Her nurturing nature, her willingness to put others before herself, and her innate leadership qualities left an indelible mark on me. I learned from her that true strength lies not in dominance or loud proclamations but in the ability to remain grounded and calm when faced with life's inevitable challenges. Nuccy was not just my sister; she was my role model.

Maria, my second sister, was the spirit of adventure in our family. Her energy was contagious, and her curiosity knew no bounds. While Nuccy was practical and composed, Maria was the free spirit, always seeking new experiences and challenges. It was Maria who encouraged me to break free from my comfort zone, to chase the things that frightened me, and to never settle for mediocrity.

She had a way of viewing the world that was unlike anyone I had ever met—filled with wonder and possibilities. She could make even the simplest of moments feel magical. It was through Maria that I learned the importance of independence. She taught me that life isn't just about meeting expectations or following a path laid out for you; it's about carving your own way, embracing the unknown, and finding joy in the journey.

Maria was always the first one to embark on an adventure, whether it was a spontaneous trip to a new city or a new project she had set her sights on. Her courage to embrace the unknown inspired me to chase my own dreams, no matter how improbable they seemed. She was a beacon of what it meant to be free, unburdened by the fear of failure.

In our family, Nuccy was the eldest, followed by Maria, then Sergio and finally me, the youngest. Sergio, my older brother, the last before me, was the most practical of us all, grounded and wise beyond his years Where Nuccy offered wisdom, and Maria provided inspiration, Sergio grounded us all. Sergio was the person who could fix anything. A broken chair? He could repair it. A faulty engine? Sergio would have it running in no time. His ability to see things from a logical perspective made him the problem-solver of our family.

But Sergio was more than just practical—he was also deeply compassionate. He would always take the time to help anyone who needed it, whether it was a neighbor, a friend, or one of us. His resourcefulness and determination to make things work taught me that problems are not obstacles but challenges to be tackled. Sergio's approach to life was straightforward: if something broke, you fix it; if something was difficult, you persevere.

His hands-on way of approaching life influenced me greatly. I learned from him that success is not just about grand gestures or lofty goals, but about taking the small steps, solving problems as they arise, and making sure you always have the tools necessary to face the next challenge. Sergio's steadfastness and dependability made him someone

I could always rely on, and I took comfort in knowing that no matter what life threw at us, he would be there to help me find a solution.

As I look back on the lessons imparted by my grandmother and my siblings, I cannot help but think of the place where it all began.

Every part of the island felt like a reflection of the people who lived there—resilient, hardworking, and filled with stories of perseverance. Procida was not just a place; it was a way of life. The legacy of my family, intertwined with the island's enduring spirit, is something I carry with me every day. It was there that my grandmother's entrepreneurial journey began, and it was there that I first learned the importance of community, of family, and of living with purpose.

I often think of the ships that would sail into the port, their sails billowing in the wind, and I am reminded that life is like the sea—unpredictable, but with enough courage and determination, we can navigate any storm. My grandmother's business, my siblings' influence, and the legacy of Procida have been the wind in my sails. They have guided me, transformed me, and prepared me for the uncharted waters of life. And just as the island continues to stand tall against the tides, so too does my family's legacy stand firm in my heart, guiding me through every challenge.

Chapter 3: The Call of the Sea – Early Fascination and Learning

Life has a way of testing us, pushing us to the edge, and sometimes, even leaving us feeling like we're stuck in one place. It's easy to look back on moments that hurt us, on things we lost, or on mistakes we made. We replay these things in our minds and allow them to shape who we are and how we see the world. But if we stay there, in the past, we miss out on the most important part: the future.

Life, as it turns out, isn't about staying in the same place. It's about moving forward, no matter how hard it may seem. Whether you've experienced failure, loss, or even just disappointment, every day is a new chance to take a step forward.

Think of it like this: imagine you're carrying a backpack, heavy with stones. Each stone represents a regret, a failure, a hurt, or something that's been weighing you down. Every time you look back, it feels like the weight gets heavier. But the thing is, you don't have to carry that backpack forever. The moment you realize that it's okay to put it down and walk on without it, everything begins to change. Moving forward doesn't mean forgetting the past; it just means acknowledging that it no longer controls your present.

Moving forward means accepting that you can't change what has already happened, but you can shape what's coming next. It means releasing the grip that the past has on you and choosing to step into a new chapter, no matter how uncertain it may seem.

One of the biggest misconceptions about moving forward is that it requires huge, dramatic changes. The truth is, the smallest step can often be the most powerful. It's not about having all the answers or knowing exactly where you're going—it's about making progress, even if it's just a little bit at a time.

Imagine you're standing at the base of a mountain, and the summit seems so far away. You might feel overwhelmed at the thought of climbing it. But if you take one step, then another, and another, you'll eventually get to the top. The key is to keep moving, even when it feels like progress is slow. Every step, no matter how small, brings you closer to where you want to be.

Sometimes, moving forward means facing the things that scare us. It means stepping outside of our comfort zones and trying things we never thought possible. It's easy to let fear stop us, to get stuck in a place of indecision, because taking that first step can be daunting. But here's something worth remembering: courage isn't the absence of fear. It's the willingness to act despite it.

This is where the comfort zone comes into play. Our comfort zone is that safe space where we feel in control, where we know what to expect, and can avoid the unknown. But staying in that space, while it may feel reassuring, can keep us from reaching our full potential. Growth happens when we push beyond those familiar boundaries, when we step into discomfort, and when we take on challenges that seem intimidating. It's only when we leave our comfort zone that we start discovering new strengths, new skills, and new possibilities we never thought we were capable of.

It takes courage to believe in your future, even when your past is trying to hold you back. It takes courage to trust that you are capable of moving beyond where you are right now and that better things are on the way. When you embrace that courage, when you refuse to let fear dictate your actions, you begin to realize how strong you truly are. Each time you move forward, no matter how difficult it seems, you build your resilience and create new possibilities for yourself.

From the earliest days of my childhood, the sea was a constant companion, a presence that both fascinated and shaped me. It wasn't just the sight of the waves crashing against the rocky shores of Procida, nor the feel of the salt air on my skin, but a deep, inexplicable bond that formed in those early years. The rhythm of the ocean, the pulse of the tides, it all seemed to call to me, drawing me in like a sailor to the horizon.

Before I could even walk, my father—weathered by both the sea and war—would carry me down to the Marina Grande. I can still hear the creak of the boats as they rocked gently in the harbor, the cries of fishermen shouting back and forth as they prepared their nets for the day. The scent of tar and fish would fill the air, a pungent reminder that this was a world where every day was a fresh start, but also a struggle against nature's unpredictable forces. I would grasp at the rough wood of the fishing boats, as if instinctively understanding that this was where my life would always be anchored, a life shaped by the sea.

I was too young to fully grasp the significance of those moments, but even then, I knew the ocean was more than just water. It was a way of life. Every fisherman in Procida had a relationship with the sea that went far beyond their work; it was a bond of respect, a mutual understanding. The sea could give, but it could also take away. It was a teacher and a test all in one.

My youngest sister, though older than me and not particularly strong, became my unexpected swimming instructor. She wasn't the gentle type, the kind to hold my hand and ease me into the water. Instead, she did what she had to—whether out of confidence or necessity—pushing me beyond my limits. I even risked drowning once, but she saved me, her determination outweighing any lack of physical strength.

"Learn quick, or the water will swallow you," she'd say, her tone as tough as the sea she knew so well. It was rough, it was real, and it was necessary. There was no room for fear in her world. The sea didn't care about your hesitation; it only cared about how you reacted.

Those early lessons in the water were tough. I'd choke on seawater, swallow too much, and fear I might not come back up for air. But in the midst of it all, something clicked. I learned to respect the ocean, to read its movements, and to understand its rhythms. The sea, just like life, wasn't always gentle, but it was always honest.

The sea, though a constant source of fascination, also offered a much-needed sense of calm. As I lay on the beach at night, staring up at the endless stretch of stars above me, I felt the vastness of the world in a way that made me feel both small and incredibly connected. The sea and the sky seemed to meet at the horizon, a reminder that the mysteries of life were endless. The rhythmic crashing of the waves against the shore became a lullaby, reminding me that life, like the tides, was cyclical—there were moments of peace, moments of turmoil, and moments of calm in between.

And then there were the sunsets—those unforgettable moments when the sky would explode in shades of orange, pink, and purple, the reflection of the sun on the water creating a magical glow. I would sit there, lost in the beauty of it all, feeling as though I were witnessing something sacred. Those sunsets weren't just beautiful; they were a reminder that life, too, is beautiful in its fleeting moments. They gave me a sense of purpose and inspired me to chase after those moments of beauty, even when life seemed to be pulling me in different directions.

The bond I have with the sea is as old as my first breath, as deep as the waters surrounding Procida. And as I look back, I realize that the lessons the sea taught me, from the thrill of its storms to the calm of its sunsets, have stayed with me, shaping my journey in ways I never expected. It is a constant companion, always there, always teaching, always guiding. And just as the waves crash against the shore, so too does the sea continue to shape me, reminding me that life, like the tides, will always return, bringing new lessons, new challenges, and new horizons to explore.

At the age of 6, our whole family moved to Portici, a wonderful town in Naples known for its Vesuvian Historical Villas. I left behind the small island of Procida, awash with its familiar shores, the constant rhythm of the waves, and the salty air that had been my lifelong companion.

At the age of 14, I stepped into a new world, one that would shape me for the rest of my life—the *Nautical Institute of Torre del Greco*. This school was a place of intense learning, discipline, and rigorous training, and for the next five years, it would become my home, my challenge, and my greatest teacher.

I remember my first day there like it was yesterday. The building itself had a quiet, serious presence, perched near the shore as if it had always belonged to the sea. The scent of the Mediterranean saltwater mixed with the smell of freshly polished wood and leather-bound books. The heavy wooden doors of the institute felt imposing as I stepped through them, nervous and excited in equal measure. I was far from home, surrounded by new faces, each with their own stories, their own paths. It was as if I had stepped into a new chapter of my life, one I wasn't sure I was ready for, but one that I was about to dive into headfirst.

The first thing that hit me was the discipline. At Torre del Greco, we were expected to be early to rise and quick to learn. The school's schedule was intense. Every day began at dawn, the sun barely peeking over the horizon. We began with physical training before breakfast—a rigorous routine designed to build strength, endurance, and mental toughness. After that, we'd head into classrooms that felt more like laboratories for the mind. The curriculum was a demanding blend of theory and practice, combining ancient seafaring skills with the latest advancements in maritime technology. We weren't just learning how to sail; we were learning to master the sea in every way possible.

One of the first subjects that grabbed my attention was celestial navigation. The idea of using the stars to find your way across the vast ocean had always fascinated me. There was something magical about it—the thought that sailors had been doing it for centuries, relying on the stars to guide them through the unknown.

The sextant, that seemingly simple tool, became my constant companion. I spent countless hours in the school's dark room, measuring angles, calculating coordinates, and aligning stars with mathematical precision. It wasn't easy at first. There were nights when the numbers seemed to blur together, and I felt frustrated by the complexity of it all. But slowly, over time, I began to understand the beauty of the method. I could feel the connection to sailors of the past, those brave men who had crossed oceans guided only by the stars. Every calculation I made, every reading of the sextant, felt like a small step toward becoming part of that tradition.

In between celestial navigation and countless other subjects, I was also immersed in naval and **marine engineering**, the study of the ships themselves—their engines, propulsion systems, and how everything worked together to keep a ship running. Being in my classes for Master Mariner, I spent hours every week studying and practicing navigation, ship handling, and maritime operations—experiences that truly shaped my understanding of the sea.

One of the first lessons I learned was just how fragile a ship could be. From the outside, it seemed strong and indestructible, but beneath the surface lay intricate systems and mechanisms that could fail at any moment. I spent long hours pushing myself to the limit—exhausted but fulfilled—driven by a deep sense of accomplishment. Through this, I gained a profound respect for the entire crew, from engineers to deck officers and technicians, each playing a crucial role in keeping everything running smoothly. These weren't just machines; they were the ship's beating heart, and if I was ever going to command one, I had to understand every moving part and the people who made it all work.

Then, there was meteorology—the study of weather. I had always known that weather could affect a sailor's journey, but I didn't truly appreciate how much until I began to study it. Winds, storms, barometric pressures—all these factors could make or break a voyage. Learning how to read the sky, understand the clouds, and predict changes in the weather became second nature to me. I learned to read the signs: a sudden drop in pressure could mean a storm was on the horizon, while certain wind patterns could signal a shift in the tides. Knowing how to predict the weather wasn't just a useful skill; it was essential for survival. The sea is unpredictable, and you have to know how to react when the storm hits.

Another area that I found particularly interesting was ship stability and cargo management. This subject taught us how to ensure that a ship stayed balanced and stable, no matter what the weather threw at it. Every ship has its limits, and it's crucial to understand how to distribute weight and cargo properly to avoid disaster. I learned about the principles of buoyancy, weight distribution, and how to load a ship in a way that kept it safe and efficient. It was more than just theoretical knowledge. We spent hours in the school's simulation room, running tests and loading cargo onto models of ships to see how they responded to different conditions. Sometimes, the ships would tip, and we'd have to figure out why. Other times, we'd successfully navigate the challenges, and that sense of accomplishment was rewarding.

In addition to these technical subjects, I also studied navigation—both traditional and modern. I learned how to chart a course using paper maps, compasses, and even the stars. But I also learned about the modern navigational systems used on ships today. There was a blend of old and new, and that combination fascinated me. I felt like I was living in two worlds at once, learning methods that had been used for centuries, while also understanding the cutting-edge technology that was changing the face of maritime travel.

Naval architecture and maneuverability were also key parts of the curriculum. These subjects focused on the design of ships and how they perform in the water. I learned about hydrodynamics—the science of how a ship moves through the water, how its shape affects its speed and stability. This was especially important when it came to maneuvering large vessels in tight spaces, like ports and harbors. I spent a lot of time studying how different hull designs could impact performance, and I quickly understood the importance of a well-designed ship when it came to both efficiency and safety.

As if all this academic work wasn't enough, we also had to prepare for life at sea. I took courses in medicine and mariner arts, learning how to handle onboard emergencies and take care of my crew in the event of injury or illness. I learned basic first aid, how to handle burns, fractures, and even more serious conditions like hypothermia. There was also a cultural aspect to this training. Being a mariner wasn't just about the physical demands of the job; it was about understanding the lifestyle, the discipline, and the honor that came with it.

In addition to everything I was learning, I also had to grapple with international maritime law, the set of rules that governed how ships operated in different parts of the world. This was a subject that opened my eyes to the complexity of global trade, shipping regulations, and territorial waters. I learned about the conventions that governed everything from piracy to pollution, and I began to understand how interconnected the world really was when it came to the sea.

Through all of this, I found my footing. I excelled academically, of course, but it was more than that. I developed a sense of purpose and a growing confidence in my abilities. I wasn't just another student; I was a leader, a problem solver, and someone who had a vision for the future. I took on leadership roles in group projects, helping my classmates when they struggled with difficult concepts. I often found myself explaining complex subjects in simple terms, a skill that made me respected by my peers. They knew that if they needed help, I was the one they could turn to.

At the same time, I had a rebellious streak. I wasn't afraid to question the status quo, to challenge the traditions and practices that seemed outdated. I didn't always agree with the way things were done, and sometimes, I clashed with my instructors. I believed that the maritime world needed to evolve, and I wasn't afraid to speak up about it. Some of the teachers appreciated my enthusiasm and my drive to modernize the field, but others didn't take kindly to my questioning attitude. I was labeled a "revolutionary" by some, a title I wore proudly. I wasn't trying to be difficult; I just wanted to make sure we were preparing for the future, not just the past.

As the years went by, I became more and more entrenched in the world of Torre del Greco. I mastered the skills I was taught, developed a deep understanding of the sea, and grew into a confident young man with a clear vision for his future. By the time I graduated, I had earned the respect of both my peers and my instructors. I was one of the top students in my class, but more importantly, I had found my calling. The sea had always been a part of me, but now, I was ready to truly understand it, to command it, and to shape my own path in the world of maritime adventure.

Looking back, the five years I spent at Torre del Greco were transformative. They gave me the knowledge, the discipline, and the leadership skills I needed to face the challenges ahead. I left that school a different person than when I entered, prepared not just to sail the seas, but to navigate the twists and turns of life itself. And I knew, as I walked out of those doors for the last time, that my journey had only just begun. The sea was still calling, and I was ready to answer.

Chapter 4: The Nautical Institute and My First Voyage as a Cadet

Life moves fast, and we tend to get caught up in the routine — the daily grind that makes us forget to stop and really notice what's happening around us. We live our days without realizing how much of our world is shaped by moments we don't pay attention to. But one of those moments arrives, uninvited, and suddenly everything feels different. It's like a light turning on in a dark room, illuminating things you never noticed before.

In that moment, you may not know exactly what it means, but something inside you shifts. It's the spark that ignites a new way of thinking or feeling. And from there, everything changes. The ripples begin. It could be something as simple as a decision you make — a choice you wouldn't have considered before, or maybe even an emotion you never let yourself feel. The shift is small, but it's real. It doesn't demand attention, but you can't ignore it anymore. It's a subtle nudge, a new direction, and it's one that comes with questions you hadn't thought of before.

We've all experienced this, though we might not have recognized it for what it was. You look back on moments in your life — those small, seemingly insignificant decisions, conversations, or realizations — and see how they changed everything. You see how they set you on a path you couldn't have predicted, or how they led you to become the person you are today. Those moments don't seem important in the moment, but when you look back, you realize they were the turning points. They were the pebble, and they sent ripples through the entire course of your life.

Sometimes, the moments are like a quiet thought that comes to you out of nowhere. It could be a fleeting idea, one that passes through your mind without you even fully understanding its weight. Yet, there's something about it that sticks. It's a feeling, a thought, an impulse — something that lingers. And suddenly, you start to think differently. You start to question things you've always taken for granted. "What if there's more to life than this?"

It's a simple question, but it opens doors you didn't even know existed. It makes you wonder about your choices, your desires, your dreams. You may not even know where to begin, but you know you can't go back to the way things were. The question, no matter how small, has already begun to change you.

And that's the power of those moments — they don't need to be big or loud to have an impact. They don't need to come with a guarantee of success or a clear path forward. They only need to make you realize that life is bigger than what you've been living. It's about seeing things in a new light, understanding that what once felt familiar is no longer enough. And from that point on, things begin to shift.

The beauty of life is that these moments can happen at any time. They don't follow a predictable pattern. They don't care about your plans, your expectations, or your timeline. They come when they're meant to come, and when they do, they change everything.

Let me take you to one such moment in my life.

In the 1970s, the curriculum at an Italian Nautical Institute was a demanding and meticulously structured five-year program, designed to shape students into highly skilled professionals capable of meeting the rigorous demands of the maritime industry.

The first two years were foundational, with all students—whether aspiring to become Master Mariners, Chief Engineers, or Ship Builders—studying a common core of subjects. These included mathematics, physics, technical drawing, navigation basics, maritime law, and introductory OCEAN-NAVanship. Practical training began early, with hands-on experience in simulators and the use of the *planetarium*, a sophisticated tool for teaching astronomical navigation. Under its dome, we learned to identify constellations, plot courses using celestial bodies, and calculate our position at sea as generations of mariners had done before us. This blend of traditional techniques and modern technology was essential to our education, bridging the gap between age-old practices and contemporary navigation methods.

After the initial two years, students chose one of three specialized tracks: *Deck* for Master Mariners, *Engine* for Chief Engineers, or *Construction* for Ship Building. I chose the Master Mariners track, which deepened my expertise in advanced navigation, meteorology, oceanography, ship handling, and leadership. The program also emphasized practical training, with time spent on training vessels and, for the most exceptional students, the opportunity to complete internships aboard leading Italian commercial liners.

These prestigious placements were a mark of distinction, offering firsthand experience in the heart of the maritime industry under the guidance of seasoned professionals. Alongside academic and technical training, the institute placed a strong emphasis on physical fitness and OCEAN-NAVanship skills, ensuring we were prepared for the physical and mental challenges of life at sea. By the end of the five years, graduates emerged not only with a diploma but with a profound sense of accomplishment, ready to navigate the vast and unpredictable world of the maritime industry with skill, discipline, and ambition.

From the moment I first stepped into the classroom of the Nautical Institute, I was aware of one irrefutable truth: the sea was where I was meant to be. But as much as the lessons on land gave me a solid foundation, they could not compare to the raw, real-world lessons that awaited me aboard a ship. My cadetship marked the true beginning of my journey—a journey that would shape not only my skills but my understanding of the vast and interconnected world beyond the classroom.

The first few days on board were a blur of routine and discovery. The crew, seasoned seafarers who had sailed across the Mediterranean countless times, was a mix of personalities. Some were welcoming, eager to share their knowledge, while others were more reserved, keeping to themselves or speaking in clipped sentences, as if their words were too precious to waste. I quickly learned to observe, listen, and adapt. The sea doesn't tolerate arrogance, and on the *San Giorgio*, respect was earned, not given.

The crew taught me quickly how to read the ship, from its engines to its sails. I spent hours in the engine room, learning the intricate systems that kept the ship moving, understanding the importance of maintaining balance and efficiency. I wasn't yet a part of the team in the way they were, but each day I grew more capable, more confident, and more integrated into their world.

Despite the initial feeling of being overwhelmed, the camaraderie of the crew began to show through. When we weren't working, there were moments of relaxation, where stories of past voyages were swapped over meals, or during quiet nights under the stars. I learned to appreciate the deep bonds between sailors, forged not just by shared work but by the challenges of life at sea. These men had seen storms that could tear ships apart, navigated through waters where the horizon never seemed to end, and experienced the isolation of being at sea for months at a time. And yet, they returned to port, time and again, ready to do it all over again.

After a week in Trieste, the *San Giorgio* set sail, its destination: the port cities of Egypt and Jordan. The idea of crossing the Suez Canal—an engineering marvel that linked the Mediterranean to the Red Sea—was a surreal thought. It was one of the most iconic routes in the maritime world, and I was about to experience it firsthand. As we neared the canal, I stood on the deck, mesmerized by the sight of the narrow waterway stretching ahead, flanked by barren desert on either side. It was a stark contrast to the vibrant life of the Mediterranean, but somehow, it felt like a bridge between two worlds—the ancient world of Egypt and the modern world I was navigating.

The passage through the Suez was an awe-inspiring experience. The narrowness of the canal made the ship feel enormous, its hull cutting through the water like a giant. On either side, the desert stretched out, empty and vast, as though we were sailing through the heart of an ancient land. I stood at the bow of the ship, watching the barren landscape unfold, feeling a sense of awe that connected me to centuries of sailors and explorers who had passed through these same waters.

Once through the canal, we entered the Red Sea, and it was as if the world changed entirely. The deep blue waters contrasted sharply with the golden sands of the desert coastlines, and the air was thick with the scents of distant lands. Our first port of call was Aqaba, a bustling port city in Jordan, where the mountains met the sea in an explosion of color and texture. The sight of the vibrant markets, the sounds of merchants haggling over spices and textiles, and the aroma of grilled meats and fragrant herbs filled the air. I had never seen anything like it—an entirely new world, brimming with life and history.

Aqaba itself was a city caught between past and present, a place where the ancient world of the Bedouins met the modernity of global trade. The city's location at the crossroads of Asia, Africa, and Europe made it a vital point in the network of maritime commerce. I wandered the narrow streets, taking in the mix of Arabic and international languages, the rich colors of the buildings, and the incredible warmth of the people. The markets were a maze of fabrics, spices, and ancient artifacts, a sensory overload that made me realize just how small and interconnected the world was.

The city, however, wasn't just a tourist destination—it was a working port, a place of commerce, and a gateway to the broader Middle East. I found myself marveling at the ancient fortresses and the nearby coral reefs, where the waters teemed with life. This was the world of seafaring—a world where the horizon is never quite in reach, where the tides change, and where every journey takes you into the unknown.

As my time aboard the *San Giorgio* continued, I began to understand something deeper about the sea. It wasn't just a vast, unpredictable expanse that sailors had to master—it was a world unto itself, with its own rhythms and temperaments, and it shaped the lives of those who made it their home. From the crew aboard the ship to the fishermen in Aqaba, the sea was a constant companion, a force that demanded respect and understanding.

What struck me most during my time in Aqaba was the relationship between the locals and the water. The sea was more than just a means of transportation; it was a livelihood, a way of life. I spent hours with local fishermen, learning about their ancient methods of catching fish and how they navigated the waters. There was a deep reverence for the sea that mirrored my own growing respect. It wasn't just about survival—it was about harmony. The sea gave, and the people, in return, cared for it and revered it as an equal.

Waves and Wonders: Steering Through Storms and Stars

Life aboard the ship was both challenging and rewarding. As a cadet, my responsibilities were varied and demanding, spanning from assisting the officers in navigation to performing maintenance on the ship's machinery. The long hours, physical labor, and the relentless pace of the work left me exhausted at times, but they also taught me invaluable lessons in perseverance, attention to detail, and discipline.

The feeling of being aboard a ship, of being part of something vast and interconnected, was awe-inspiring. Every day at sea brought new lessons—both practical and philosophical. The work itself was demanding; there was always something to do. I learned to climb the rigging, scrub the decks until they shone, and keep everything in perfect working order. Whether I was helping to repair the engine, oiling the gears of the winch, or inspecting the sails, it all reinforced the importance of every tiny task. No job was too small or insignificant. Out in the sea, every action mattered.

However, the most memorable part of my cadetship was undoubtedly the night watches. It was during these quiet, solitary hours that I felt most connected to the history of the sea and its vast, endless mysteries. Standing on the bridge, beneath a canopy of stars, I often felt a profound sense of awe and humility. The constellations above, once the sole guides for sailors centuries before me, now served as the reference point for my own learning. With a sextant in hand, I would carefully calculate our position, aligning the celestial bodies with precision and focus. Each reading, each calculation, felt like a small link in a long chain of maritime tradition, a tradition that stretched back across the centuries.

The task wasn't easy. On calm nights, the sky seemed endless and peaceful, but on others, the horizon could feel impossibly distant, and the vastness of the ocean seemed to swallow us whole. But I never wavered. Each night, I grew more confident in my skills, in my ability to read the stars, and to trust the techniques that had guided sailors for generations. It was a humbling experience—one that instilled in me a deep respect for the tradition of celestial navigation, and for the sailors of old who braved the unknown armed with little more than the stars themselves.

Of course, I was not alone in this journey. The camaraderie aboard the ship was one of the defining aspects of the experience. The crew, a diverse group of men and women hailing from all corners of the world, formed an unexpected family. Each person brought their own unique skills, stories, and perspectives. The kitchen staff, the engineers, the deckhands—they all had something to contribute, something that made the ship run smoothly. We came together as a team, and over time, we learned to respect one another, understanding that everyone played an essential role in the success of the ship's journey.

I quickly realized that a ship, like life, was more than just a place to work—it was a delicate balance of personalities, cultures, and skills. Each person, from the officers to the cooks, had a purpose, and the success of the journey depended on how well we worked together. I learned to navigate not just the seas but the complexities of human relationships. It wasn't just about getting the job done—it was about getting it done with respect for each other's contributions.

There were also moments when the challenges of the sea were both physical and mental. One of the greatest challenges we faced during my cadetship occurred one night in the eastern Mediterranean. We had been sailing in relatively calm waters when a sudden squall hit us from nowhere. The ship pitched and rolled violently as the waves, towering and angry, slammed against the hull. The wind howled, the rain lashed down, and the crew scrambled to secure the cargo and maintain control of the vessel.

In the chaos, I was assigned to help in the engine room. The crew worked together like a well-rehearsed dance, each person knowing their role and performing it without hesitation. The officers stood at the helm, commanding the ship with calm authority, while the rest of the crew moved with precision, securing ropes, adjusting sails, and ensuring that the ship stayed on course. In moments like these, I saw the true spirit of seafaring—a blend of courage, expertise, and unwavering commitment to safety. Despite the fury of the storm, the officers and crew handled everything with an ease that only came from years of experience.

For me, it was a lesson in composure, teamwork, and preparation. A storm at sea doesn't care about your plans—it doesn't care about your comfort or your schedule. It simply is. The key, I learned that night, wasn't in hoping the storm would pass quickly—it was in preparing yourself for it, and facing it head-on with calm and determination. It was about having the skill to know exactly what to do, when to do it, and how to work with those around you to ensure the ship remained intact.

In addition to the physical challenges, my cadetship introduced me to the evolving world of navigation technology. While celestial navigation remained a cornerstone of our training, I was also introduced to the early electronic systems of the time, such as LORAN-C and Decca. These technologies were rudimentary compared to today's GPS systems, but they represented a significant leap forward for maritime navigation. They allowed us to determine our position with greater accuracy, even when the stars weren't visible.

It was fascinating to see how the world of navigation was evolving. These technologies were the future of the industry, but they didn't replace traditional methods—instead, they enhanced them. I quickly came to appreciate how the old and the new could coexist, each complementing the other. The stars, still shining above us every night, were timeless guides. Yet, the technologies of the future were now helping us navigate more efficiently, and I had the privilege of learning both sides of this evolving story. This balance between ancient tradition and modern innovation would later shape my approach to life and work—blending respect for the past with a drive to embrace the future.

But no matter how much technology advanced, there was one truth that remained constant: the sea was unpredictable. Whether you were using a sextant or the latest electronic system, you were at the mercy of the ocean. It would give you calm days and stormy nights, quiet horizons and turbulent waters. And in the end, the true test of a sailor wasn't just their knowledge of the stars or the systems of navigation—it was their ability to adapt, to respond, and to face the ever-changing challenges that life at sea would throw their way.

The Victory Lap: A Graduation to Remember

When the day finally came to graduate from the Nautical Institute of Torre del Greco, it felt like a culmination of years of hard work, sacrifice, and perseverance. The air was filled with a mixture of excitement and pride as my fellow cadets and I stood at the precipice of a new chapter in our lives. I had completed one of the most rigorous and demanding programs of my life, and I had done so with distinction. It was an achievement that carried with it not only personal satisfaction but also the promise of a future in the maritime world that had long been my dream.

Looking back on my time at the institute, I realized how much I had changed. The young cadet who had walked through the doors of the school was no longer the same person who stood there on graduation day. I had come to Torre del Greco with a hunger for knowledge, but it was the experiences I had lived through—both the academic and the practical—that had truly shaped me. I had learned to think critically, to solve complex problems, and to always question the status quo. In fact, it was my curious nature that had often set me apart from my peers.

At first, my tendency to challenge assumptions and explore alternative solutions was viewed as something of a hindrance. My instructors, who had spent years in the field, were initially wary of my desire to understand not just *how* things worked, but *why* they worked that way. They were accustomed to cadets who followed instructions without question, who executed their tasks with precision but little curiosity beyond the basics. But I was different. I wanted to know the rationale behind every maneuver, every decision, and every piece of equipment. It was this drive to understand that had earned me a reputation—somewhat controversial at first—among my instructors.

Over time, however, that reputation shifted. The same instructors who had once regarded my questions with skepticism began to respect me for my determination and ingenuity. They saw that I wasn't just challenging them for the sake of it—I was striving to deepen my understanding, to become better, to excel. And as my skills improved and my results spoke for themselves, they recognized that my questions were not a weakness but an asset. My academic journey was no longer just about earning a degree—it had become about pushing boundaries, expanding horizons, and striving for excellence in every aspect of my training.

By the time my cadetship ended, I was no longer the uncertain, wide-eyed newcomer who had first boarded the ship in Trieste. The harsh winds and the stormy seas had sculpted me into someone who knew the value of hard work, discipline, and above all, perseverance. I had earned my place on the deck of that ship, and I had learned what it truly meant to be a mariner. My understanding of the sea had deepened, my respect for the craft had grown immeasurably, and I had gained a renewed sense of purpose.

Returning to the Nautical Institute for my final years of study, I felt a sense of transformation. I was no longer simply a student—I was a sailor, someone who had lived the challenges of the open sea, someone who had tasted both the triumphs and the hardships of life aboard a vessel. The knowledge I had gained through my cadetship now complemented my academic education. I was more confident, more focused, and more determined than ever to succeed. Every lesson felt more meaningful, every lecture more relevant. I approached my studies not with the naivety of a beginner but with the perspective of someone who had seen the world from the deck of a ship and understood the true weight of responsibility.

The graduation ceremony at the Nautical Institute was a lively blend of tradition and celebration—students dressed in formal attire, the hall buzzing with applause, and the warmth of handshakes and heartfelt embraces filling the air. Yet, amid the collective joy, there was a quiet, deeply personal triumph that only I could fully understand. I had done it. I had conquered the rigorous demands of the program, mastering complex technical subjects and overcoming countless challenges, both academic and personal.

As I stood there, I realized something about myself that had been quietly shaping my journey all along: I was an achiever. I never gave up, no matter how tough things got. That stubborn determination, that refusal to back down, had carried me through. I walked away not just with a diploma, but with something far more valuable—a clear sense of purpose, a vision for my future, and the practical skills to turn that vision into reality.

As I stepped forward to receive my diploma, I felt an overwhelming sense of gratitude for those who had supported me along the way—my dedicated teachers, who had pushed me to think critically and creatively; my classmates, who had become like family and shared in the late-night study sessions and the moments of doubt; and the mentors who had guided me through internships and projects, showing me what it meant to excel in the real world. But there was also an undeniable pride in what I had accomplished. I had pushed myself harder than I ever thought possible, and now, I stood at the threshold of a future I had worked so hard to build. The ceremony marked not just the end of an educational journey, but the beginning of a new chapter—one filled with possibility, confidence, and the unshakable knowledge that I could achieve anything I set my mind to. I was ready to take on the world, one challenge at a time.

Looking out at the sea, which had once seemed so distant, so mysterious, I realized that my journey was only just beginning. I had left the institute with more than just academic knowledge—I had left with the confidence to tackle whatever lay ahead. The skills I had acquired, the lessons I had learned, and the challenges I had overcome had given me a deeper understanding of both the sea and myself. I was ready to embrace the world that awaited me.

The years I spent at the Nautical Institute of Torre del Greco and my time aboard the ship with Adriatica Shipping Company were more than just stepping stones—they were rites of passage. They had molded me into someone who not only understood the technicalities of navigation and OCEAN-NAVanship but who also grasped the profound, philosophical aspects of what it meant to be a sailor. These experiences had prepared me not only for the adventures I would face in the maritime world but also for the trials and challenges of life itself.

Graduating from the Nautical Institute marked a new beginning for me. I was no longer just a student—I was a professional, ready to make my mark in the world. The sea had always been my passion, and now, with the tools I had gained, I could make it my life's work. My future was uncharted, but I knew one thing for certain: I was ready to navigate it with the same determination, resilience, and curiosity that had carried me through the challenging yet rewarding years of my training.

As I walked off that stage, diploma clutched in my hand, I felt the weight of the years that had led me here and the promise of the years to come. The horizon stretched out before me, endless and full of possibility. And in that moment, I knew one thing for certain: I was ready.

Ready to leave behind the safety of the classroom. Ready to embrace the uncertainty of the open sea. Ready to follow my dreams and forge my own path.

The journey was far from over. It had only just begun.

Chapter 5: Sports, Leadership, and Early Friendships

Friendship and leadership are not always learned through words; sometimes, they are forged through action, struggle, and unspoken bonds. My earliest lessons in resilience and camaraderie did not come from books or formal training—they emerged on the basketball courts, in the heat of a rugby match, and through the silent understanding between teammates who pushed each other to be better. Looking back, I realize that these moments were more than childhood play; they were the foundations of the discipline and leadership that would define my life's work.

There are moments that don't need words. They don't need explanations or grand gestures or anything flashy. They just need the simple presence of someone who, without trying, makes the world feel a little bit more bearable. During the teenage years, when everything feels uncertain and shifting, there's something so quietly beautiful about being with someone who doesn't require anything from you—except just to be there.

It's those times when you sit together, not saying anything, but the air between you feels full. It's a silence that doesn't feel heavy or awkward, but instead, it wraps around you like a warm blanket. It's knowing that you don't have to explain your thoughts, your fears, or your dreams, because somehow, they already understand. It's a connection that doesn't need to be spoken aloud—it just *is*.

And in those moments, you realize something important: you're not as alone as you sometimes feel. Just the presence of someone else can make everything feel lighter, as if the weight of the world, even for just a little while, doesn't press so hard on your chest. It's the kind of connection that reminds you that you're allowed to just exist, without needing to perform, without needing to prove anything.

You don't need to say the perfect thing, or have the right answers, or even fill every silence with sound. Just being there together, breathing in the same space, is enough. It's knowing that, no matter how messy or confusing the world might be, there's this one person who makes it feel okay to just *be*. They don't ask for your perfection; they just ask for your presence.

There's something heartbreaking and beautiful in those quiet moments. They remind you that sometimes, the most meaningful connections are the ones without words—those moments when you don't have to put on a mask or hide your true self. Because with them, you don't have to be anything other than you.

It's the simplest of things that can leave the deepest marks. That shared glance, that unspoken understanding, that comfort in knowing that, for once, you don't have to carry the weight alone. You just have to *be*, and in that quiet space, everything feels right.

When you're young, everything can feel so uncertain.

By the age of 15, life had turned into a whirlwind of new experiences and emotions. I was deep into my studies at the Nautical Institute and still dedicated to sports, but now, the evenings and weekends brought a whole new chapter into my life: the rollercoaster of early love. It was a time of discovering who I was, learning about other people, and understanding the confusing yet thrilling attractions that started shaping my teenage years.

In the quiet halls and stairwells of our building, I first saw her—*the girl next door.* There was something about her that had a magnetic pull, something that made my heart race every time I saw her. She was radiant in a way that felt almost impossible to achieve, with her laughter filling the air like music. She had a smile that seemed to light up the dullest of days. We often crossed paths in the building, exchanging nothing more than polite greetings or brief, fleeting glances. But those simple moments were enough to leave me daydreaming, wondering if she noticed me too.

Despite my growing feelings for her, I never found the courage to say anything. Every time I thought about approaching her, my nerves would take over, and I'd just walk away, unable to speak a word. It wasn't a deep love, but more of an infatuation—a feeling that burned quietly inside me, one I could never quite shake. She was untouchable in my eyes, a vision that seemed just out of reach. I didn't know how to bridge the gap between us, so I just let the infatuation simmer in the background, quietly but intensely.

In a way, it was one of those teenage experiences that didn't need words, just the feeling of *being* in the same space with someone who made your world feel just a little bit brighter.

Beyond the quiet moments in my building, my family's social connections also brought me into contact with other girls. One of these girls was the daughter of close family friends. She was nothing like the quiet, graceful girl next door. This girl was full of life, with an energy that made everything feel exciting. Her confidence, her laugh, and her mischievous spark lit up every family gathering. Unlike the girl next door, she wasn't distant or untouchable. She was there, right in front of me, and somehow that made the whole thing more confusing.

We would interact mostly during family events—birthdays, holiday dinners, and weekend visits. I always looked forward to those occasions, because being around her meant that things would never be boring. We'd joke around, tease each other, and her smile stuck with me long after we parted ways. But even though she was much more approachable, there was always that invisible line drawn by family dynamics. You didn't make moves on the daughters of family friends. At least, that's how I saw it at the time. I admired her from afar, but I never crossed that line. It was a quiet frustration, wondering how much deeper our connection could go if we didn't have all these unspoken rules hanging over us.

As much as family gatherings influenced my experiences, there was another world outside of that—a world full of excitement, movement, and discovery. In Portici, like in many towns in Italy, the evening hours came alive with dance halls and social gatherings. These were the places where young people like me would go to meet, laugh, and enjoy the pulse of the latest music. It was here that I first experienced the full rush of teenage social life.

The dance spots were full of life. Girls from other neighborhoods and schools would show up, each one with their own unique charm. Some were quiet, some bold, but they all had that infectious energy that made the night feel special. I remember the first time I asked a girl to dance. My heart was racing in my chest as I approached her. Would she say yes? Would I look foolish? The moment she agreed to dance was like a small victory, and as we moved to the rhythm of the music, I felt an instant connection, like we were in sync with each other. The world around us disappeared for a while, and it was just the two of us in that shared moment.

Every time I danced with someone, I felt like I was getting a little bit better at it, learning how to connect with others in new ways.

At the same time, there were also girls within my own group of friends. We would spend time together, joking around, hanging out in town, and just being teenagers. Our bonds were a mix of friendship and something else—something unspoken but palpable. The lines between friendship and romantic interest were often blurry, but that was part of the thrill of it. We didn't need to label everything, because just being together was enough.

These girls were part of my teenage years, adding color and depth to my life. Some of them were just friends, but with others, there was a certain tension, a feeling that something more could have blossomed if only the timing had been right. But then again, maybe it was enough to just enjoy the friendship, to let things develop at their own pace. Teenage years were confusing that way—full of emotions that you didn't always know how to deal with, but you just went along with it, letting the moments guide you.

When I first fell for someone, it wasn't like I expected. It wasn't this perfect, smooth feeling of knowing exactly what I wanted or how to go about it. Instead, it was a messy, complicated experience. One day, I would be completely sure of my feelings, and the next, I'd be unsure, doubting everything. But through it all, I learned something important: first love wasn't about having everything figured out. It was about the messiness, the confusion, and the thrill of it all. It was a time of self-discovery, of figuring out what you liked, what you didn't like, and how to navigate the challenges of relationships.

In a way, I think everyone has to go through this. You learn by making mistakes, by taking risks, and by experiencing the highs and lows that come with putting your heart out there. Sometimes it works out, and sometimes it doesn't, but either way, it shapes who you are. For me, those early experiences taught me a lot about vulnerability and trust. I learned that love wasn't always perfect or easy, but it was worth the risk.

The emotions I felt—though intense—were raw and unrefined. They lacked the depth and permanence that true love would bring years later. But that didn't make them any less real. I was learning about myself, about what attracted me to others, and about the complex dynamics of human relationships. Each encounter, whether it was a flirtation in the stairwell, a moment shared at a family gathering, or a fleeting interaction at a dance hall, taught me something about love and connection.

I learned about the excitement of a new attraction—the flutter in your stomach when you first meet someone who catches your eye. I learned about the vulnerability of putting yourself out there, about the fear of rejection, and the thrill of being accepted. I learned about the quiet joy of simply being in the presence of someone who made you feel understood and appreciated, even if only for a short time. These experiences—sometimes sweet, sometimes awkward, often confusing— were all part of the process of discovering who I was and what I wanted in relationships.

These early loves, though not lasting, were invaluable. They taught me the beauty of variety, of exploring the different ways in which people can connect with one another. They helped me understand that love isn't one-size-fits-all, but rather a complex and ever-evolving experience. Each person I met, each connection I made, added to the mosaic of my understanding of attraction and love. In a way, I was gathering the tools I would need for the future, when love would no longer be just about the thrill of new feelings, but about something deeper, more lasting.

In those moments, I also learned about the importance of patience. Some relationships blossomed quickly, while others took time to develop. Some were brief but intense, while others were quiet and slow-burning. Each one taught me that love and connection don't happen on a fixed timeline. Sometimes, things develop when you least expect them, and other times, they require waiting, listening, and understanding.

While I was going through these complicated feelings and relationships, I also had to balance everything with my ambitions for the future. I had big dreams of pursuing a life at sea. Yet, I couldn't ignore the pull of the social world, the draw of friendships, love, and the everyday experiences that shaped my teenage years.

There were moments when I felt torn between these two worlds—one where my focus was on becoming a skilled sailor, and another where I was figuring out who I was in a much more personal sense. My time at the institute taught me discipline, perseverance, and how to deal with challenges, but my social life was where I learned about connection, emotions, and the complexities of relationships. Both worlds transformed me, but in different ways.

While I was exploring the avenues of young love, my time as a Boy Scout also played a pivotal role in shaping my character and relationships. Scouting wasn't just an extracurricular activity—it was a way of life. It taught me about discipline, teamwork, and resilience. It also offered countless opportunities to meet new people, including girls who were part of neighboring scout groups or who joined us on shared camping trips.

Scouting was a world that centered around adventure and exploration, filled with challenges that tested my limits and the strength of my friendships. Our outings took us to forests, mountains, and rivers—places where we learned to navigate with compasses, build campfires, and pitch tents. Each adventure felt like a new chapter in a book that I was excited to keep reading. These experiences helped me develop a sense of resourcefulness and independence, qualities that became just as important in my relationships as in my personal growth.

In scouting, I didn't just learn about the outdoors—I also learned about camaraderie. There was something unique about the friendships forged during these trips. We worked together, faced challenges together, and celebrated victories together. The bonds we built around campfires or on the hiking trail were strong and lasting, as we learned how to support one another and push through difficult moments.

In addition to scouting, my passion for sports continued to shape my identity. I was always on the move, whether I was playing soccer, basketball, or rugby. Sports provided me with an outlet for my energy, a way to challenge myself both physically and mentally. They also taught me about teamwork, about relying on others and being relied upon in return. The discipline I learned on the field translated into other areas of my life, including my relationships.

Through sports, I met more girls, ones who were drawn to the energy and excitement of the games. Some were spectators, cheering from the sidelines, while others were friends who joined in for casual matches. Their presence added a new layer of excitement to every event. The girls who attended our games were just as passionate as the players, and they made every match feel more important, more thrilling.

As much as I loved the competition and physical challenge of sports, it was also about the social aspect. Sports brought people together in a way that few other activities could. They created a sense of unity, of shared experience, and they brought out new sides of people—whether it was the girl who surprised everyone with her unexpected knowledge of the game or the one who cheered the loudest from the sidelines.

As my journey in sports evolved, I found myself transitioning from a player to a referee. This shift not only deepened my understanding of the game but also offered a unique lens through which to experience basketball. Refereeing was not just about blowing a whistle or enforcing rules; it was about preserving the integrity and spirit of the game while ensuring fairness for all participants. It demanded a balance of quick decision-making, leadership, and emotional intelligence, especially when dealing with the passionate personalities that filled basketball courts.

My first experience officiating was local, but soon the opportunity came to work at a higher level. I started officiating games across different regions, each offering its own distinctive flavor of competition and intensity. It was in these diverse settings that I truly began to appreciate the global nature of basketball and the subtle differences in how the sport was played and perceived.

One of my earliest experiences officiating basketball was in California, a state renowned for its high-energy, fast-paced style of play. Basketball in California was full of athleticism, flair, and a frenetic tempo that kept me on my toes as a referee. The players were quick, skilled, and aggressive, and the atmosphere in the gym was electric. The energy from the fans and the intensity of the competition made every game feel like a high-stakes event.

In California, the game seemed to reflect the laid-back yet competitive spirit of the state. The players often displayed a lot of creativity, with flashy moves and unpredictable plays. As a referee, I had to adjust quickly to the flow of the game. There was no room for hesitation. Every call had to be made swiftly and with confidence, whether it was a foul, a violation, or a boundary call. I had to be constantly alert, not only to the action on the court but also to the players' emotions and the crowd's energy. It wasn't uncommon for players to express their frustration loudly, which meant that I had to remain calm and composed under pressure, keeping control of the game without letting emotions sway my decisions.

In contrast, my experience officiating in the UK was a fascinating blend of tradition and an evolving basketball culture. The UK basketball scene had a more structured and tactical approach compared to the fast-paced California style. There was a deep sense of respect for the game's history and its roots, yet players were increasingly embracing new techniques and styles from across the globe, especially from the NBA.

The UK offered a slightly more reserved atmosphere, where the crowd wasn't as boisterous as in California, but the intensity was no less palpable. The players focused more on teamwork, strategy, and precision. Refereeing in the UK required me to be a bit more methodical, calling fouls when necessary but also allowing the game to flow without interruptions. The players' respect for the referees was something that stood out to me, and while the pace of the game wasn't as fast as California's, the competition was no less fierce. The dynamics of officiating in the UK required me to be both a facilitator and a leader, ensuring that the game maintained its rhythm while upholding the integrity of the rules.

What I loved most about refereeing in the UK was the sense of history that came with each game. The fans often had a deep knowledge of the sport, and it was clear that they held basketball in high regard. Every match felt like an extension of the broader legacy of the game, and it became increasingly important to me as a referee to honor that tradition, while also being open to the evolving aspects of the sport that were making their way to British courts.

In Italy, basketball was more than just a game—it was a passion, an emotional experience that connected fans, coaches, and players in a way I had never encountered before. The atmosphere in the gyms was electric, charged with an intensity that was palpable both on and off the court. The Italian fans brought unmatched energy, and it was not uncommon for the crowds to erupt in cheers or groans depending on the outcome of each play. In this environment, officiating felt like a true test of not just skill but also composure and leadership.

What made officiating in Italy so unique was the sheer passion and intensity of the players and the fans. Every whistle I blew had consequences, not just for the flow of the game, but for the mood of the arena. Fans were fervent, often expressing their emotions loudly.

Coaches and players would engage in animated discussions with referees, sometimes pushing the limits of respect but always demonstrating how deeply they cared about the outcome of the game.

Refereeing in such an emotionally charged environment demanded a calm demeanor and quick decision-making. There was little room for doubt. As a referee, you had to be absolutely certain of your calls because any hesitation could lead to confusion, anger, or even further conflict. At the same time, it was in this high-pressure environment that I found some of my greatest moments of leadership. Whether it was diffusing tension between players or standing firm in the face of dissenting coaches, I had to ensure that the integrity of the game was upheld—no matter how intense the atmosphere became.

Officiating basketball at both the national and international levels taught me the true global nature of the sport. Each region had its own distinct culture and style of play, but one thing that remained consistent was the universal love of the game. No matter where I was, basketball transcended language barriers, cultural differences, and geographic boundaries. The game itself became a common ground where athletes, coaches, and fans could unite in their shared passion.

From the dynamic courts of California to the historic gyms of the UK and the emotionally charged arenas of Italy, basketball brought people together. As a referee, I was part of that global community, bridging gaps between different cultures while ensuring the fairness and integrity of the game. This global perspective not only enriched my experience as an official but also deepened my appreciation for the sport itself.

While basketball officiating shaped my understanding of leadership, rugby added a whole new dimension to my athletic journey. Joining the Lions Torre del Greco, a rugby team that competed in the second national division, became a defining chapter in my life. Rugby was unlike any sport I had ever played. It was a game of grit, endurance, and tactical awareness, where every match demanded both physical strength and mental acuity.

As a second-line and third-line forward, I found myself at the heart of the action. In the second-line, my role was primarily focused on scrums, where I had to use sheer power and precision to hold my ground and push against the opposition. Scrums were brutal, physically demanding, and required perfect coordination with my teammates. It was an intense, no-holds-barred aspect of the game that tested not only my strength but my ability to work in perfect unison with others.

In the third-line, my role evolved. I became more dynamic, constantly on the move, recovering balls, defending against attacks, and supporting offensive plays. This was where I could really flex my tactical mind, reading the game, anticipating plays, and reacting quickly to whatever was thrown my way. The fluidity between the second-line and third-line required adaptability, constantly shifting between strength and strategy depending on the flow of the game.

Rugby was as much about the mind as it was about the body. The physical conditioning was grueling, pushing me to my limits with every training session. But the true test came during matches, where I had to dig deep, embracing the physical toll of the game and pushing through the fatigue. Every hit, every tackle, every try was a battle, and I learned to face adversity head-on, never backing down in the face of an opponent.

When summer rolled around, a different kind of sporting adventure took over my life—one that didn't require the same level of competition as my other sports but was equally, if not more, rewarding in its own way. Water polo in the idyllic waters around Procida, the Amalfi Coast, and the nearby islands became an annual tradition, a time when the intensity of regular sports gave way to the carefree joy of summer.

The game wasn't about winning medals or setting records; it was about enjoying the moment, celebrating friendship, and basking in the beauty of the sea. The waters of the Amalfi Coast were clear and turquoise, surrounded by towering cliffs and charming villages that seemed to have popped out of a dream. Every summer, this picturesque setting provided the perfect backdrop for these laid-back water polo games. The sun would shine brightly, casting a golden hue over everything, and the waves would gently lap at the shore, providing an easy rhythm for the game.

The teams were always makeshift, a blend of friends, locals, and visitors who all shared one thing in common: a love for the sea. There was no formal competition here, just a desire to get in the water, enjoy the game, and spend time together. The rules were flexible, and often the games morphed into a mix of water polo and a casual swimming race, with everyone laughing at the silly moments.

The next was Water polo. It was the perfect sport to fit into this relaxed yet exhilarating environment. It required strength, endurance, and strategy—skills I had developed in other sports—but it also demanded something different. Unlike basketball or rugby, where I was rooted on solid ground, water polo required me to stay afloat, constantly treading water while trying to keep my eye on the ball and make strategic plays. The challenge of balancing strength with agility was what made it so unique. It was a constant test of stamina, as I had to keep moving without sinking, all while trying to outmaneuver my opponents.

Despite the strategic elements of the game, water polo wasn't as serious as the competitive sports I was used to. There was a relaxed sense of freedom that came with playing in the open sea, where the goalposts were often just marked-out patches in the water, and the players could easily drift in and out of position. The emphasis wasn't on winning, but on maintaining a rhythm, having fun, and sharing the experience with others.

Sometimes, the game would start to drag as we became exhausted from the physical exertion, and that's when the playful banter would start. Friends would tease each other about missed shots or swimming too slowly. There were occasional splashes and pranks, turning the game into a friendly battle of wits and skill, with everyone laughing in the water.

After the game, we would often linger on the beach, enjoying the warmth of the sun and the sound of waves crashing against the shore. Some would grab cold drinks from the nearby seaside cafes, while others would just sit on the sand and chat, their salty skin glistening under the late afternoon sun. These moments, these simple pleasures of being together, talking about life, or sharing a laugh, are some of the fondest memories I carry from those summers.

The games also had a way of deepening the connections between everyone involved. What started as casual interactions with strangers quickly evolved into friendships. These were people who might have started as summer visitors or occasional beachgoers, but through water polo, we shared something special. We all became part of a larger group that shared a love for the ocean and the game, and by the end of the summer, there was always a sense of community. We were all tied together by these playful, yet meaningful, games that transcended language barriers and cultural differences.

Whether it was a weekend game or an all-day event, the experience was the same—fun, laughter, and a deep sense of belonging. The ocean itself became the most important teammate of all, always offering its unpredictable nature, its calming waves, and its cool embrace when we needed a break.

Sailing: Mastering the Winds of Leadership

Beyond the courts and the fields, another passion shaped my understanding of leadership and resilience—sailing. Unlike team sports, where one can rely on direct communication and physical coordination, sailing demands an entirely different kind of teamwork—one based on intuition, trust, and an intimate knowledge of nature's forces.

At the Circolo Nautico Torre del Greco, I trained extensively in regattas, mastering the art of reading wind shifts, calculating maneuvers, and responding to sudden changes in weather. Unlike a structured game with fixed rules, sailing was unpredictable. A strong gust could turn an advantage into a struggle, and a single miscalculation could cost a race.

Sailing was not just about competition—it was about mastering the forces of nature. I learned how to adjust my sails to capture the wind most efficiently, to read the changing patterns of the waves, and to navigate through shifting currents. The experience taught me patience, precision, and the importance of adaptability. Every race was a lesson in strategy. Do I take the direct route and risk the unpredictable gusts? Or do I tack strategically, taking a longer but more controlled path?

Regattas taught me strategic thinking in real-time—balancing risk and reward, anticipating competitors' moves, and adapting to unforeseen challenges. Every wave, every gust of wind, and every tactical decision reinforced the same principle: leadership is about adaptability, trusting your instincts, and making quick, informed decisions under pressure.

The feeling of racing through the open sea, my hands steady on the tiller as the wind filled the sails, was exhilarating. The boat responded to every small movement, and each adjustment in course required precision and intuition. There was no room for hesitation—only action, calculation, and trust in both my crew and my instincts.

Beyond competitive sailing, my love for the sea deepened through long voyages, where I learned the endurance and resilience required to navigate for days without sight of land. The sea, vast and unpredictable, demanded absolute respect. I experienced the stillness of windless days and the fury of sudden storms that tested my strength and resolve.

At the Nautical Institute of Torre del Greco, my sailing experience merged with my formal maritime training. While my classmates focused solely on navigation theories and ship operations, I had already developed a visceral connection with the water. My practical knowledge from racing gave me an edge—I instinctively understood wind patterns, wave formations, and the delicate balance of sail and rudder long before we studied them in textbooks. This hands-on experience made celestial navigation and ship maneuverability feel second nature to me, bridging the gap between sailing as a sport and navigation as a profession.

One of the most profound lessons came during a particularly grueling race where an unexpected squall threatened to capsize our vessel. The team had to act in perfect unison—adjusting the sails, redistributing weight, and trusting each other completely. In that moment, I understood the true nature of leadership: a leader does not command from above but moves in sync with the team, guiding them through uncertainty with steady hands and a clear vision.

More than anything, sailing deepened my connection with the sea—an element that would become central to my career and life. The ability to steer a vessel through shifting winds and tides paralleled my later experiences navigating professional challenges. Whether commanding a team of engineers or delivering historical lectures, I often found myself drawing on lessons learned at sea—stay calm in turbulence, adjust the sails when needed, and always keep a steady course toward the goal.

While each sport tested me in different ways, they all shaped me into the person I am today. They taught me lessons in discipline, teamwork, resilience, and the importance of both competition and recreation.

What began as a boy's love for sport evolved into a lifelong philosophy: success is not an individual pursuit. Whether navigating a ship through uncharted waters or leading a team of engineers in an innovative project, the principles remain the same—trust, strategy, resilience, and the ability to inspire those around you.

Sports and sailing taught me that leadership is not about dominance but about understanding strengths—both my own and those of the people around me. The friendships I formed in those early years shaped the way I approached teamwork in every aspect of my career. Looking back, I see that the games we played and the regattas we raced were more than fleeting moments of competition; they were training grounds for the life I would build.

As a boy, I was drawn to the rhythm of the game, the precision of movement, and the unspoken connection that formed between teammates who trusted each other implicitly. Friendship, I learned, was not just about shared laughter or common interests—it was about knowing someone so well that words became unnecessary. We communicated through a nod before a pass, a glance before a sprint, a subtle shift in position that signaled a new strategy.

But friendships, I discovered, also tested resilience. Losing a match, missing a critical shot, or facing an opponent stronger than myself taught me more than winning ever could. In those moments, I saw the qualities that defined true leadership—adaptability, perseverance, and the ability to lift others when they stumbled. These lessons did not end on the court; they carried into every leadership role I would later take, from commanding research teams to delivering lectures on maritime history.

Sports have this incredible power to bring people together, to transcend language, background, and differences, and create bonds that last a lifetime. And these experiences, both competitive and recreational, are the memories I cherish most in my life.

Chapter 6: A Fork in the Road – Choosing My Path

Have you ever stood at a crossroads, unsure of which direction to take? Maybe you've been there, looking at two or three options, wondering if you're about to make the right choice or if you're just setting yourself up for failure. It's a familiar feeling. That fear of the unknown, the pressure of making decisions, and the nagging thought that maybe you'll mess it all up. It's enough to make anyone freeze in their tracks.

But here's the thing: faith—in yourself, in your choices, and in life— can be the thing that pushes you forward, even when you're unsure of where you're headed. It's not about having all the answers. It's about trusting that, no matter what happens, you'll be okay. It's about taking that step, even when the road ahead seems unclear.

It all starts with faith in yourself. We've all had those moments when we doubt our own abilities. Maybe it's a new job, a tough decision, or a leap into something completely unfamiliar. The voice in your head questions everything: *"Am I good enough? What if I fail? What if I can't handle it?"* Those doubts are normal—they're part of being human. But what's even more important is the quiet voice that says, *"I've got this."*

Faith in yourself doesn't mean you're going to get everything right. It doesn't mean there won't be mistakes along the way. It simply means that you trust you'll figure things out as you go. You trust that, even when you stumble, you can get back up. And maybe most importantly, you trust that you're worthy of success, happiness, and growth.

Each day, we make decisions—some big, some small. And yet, often, we wrestle with them, trying to make the *perfect* choice. We second-guess ourselves, afraid of making the wrong move. But here's the thing: there's no such thing as a "perfect" decision. All we can do is make the best decision we can with the information we have at the time, and then trust ourselves to adjust if things don't go as planned.

Faith in your decisions doesn't mean you always get everything right. It means you trust that, no matter what happens, you'll learn something from it. Even if things go wrong, it's not the end. It's a chance to grow, to refine your path, and to make better choices next time. Each decision is a step forward, and with faith, we can see it as part of the bigger picture, knowing that it's all contributing to our journey.

For me, one of those defining moments came when I was 18. Life stood before me like an ocean, vast and unpredictable, filled with choices that seemed equally uncertain. It was a moment I had anticipated for years—the moment when I would step beyond the walls of the Nautical Institute of Torre del Greco, diploma in hand, ready to face whatever came next. The Nautical Institute had been my second home, the place where I had grown, not just in knowledge, but as a person. It had transformed me academically, physically, and emotionally, preparing me for the challenges that lay ahead on the unpredictable waters of life.

Yet now, I found myself standing at a crossroads. Here I was, at a moment of decision, knowing that whatever I would choose would have a lasting impact on my life. I pondered if I should continue down the familiar, comfortable path towards becoming a Master Mariner, which had always been my passion, or if I should seize the opportunity to broaden my horizons by enrolling in university to explore the deeper, more theoretical aspects of nautical sciences?

At this point, you would already know that Sailing had been a part of me for as long as I could remember. The sea had always felt like home, its rhythms like a second heartbeat, its vastness offering a world of freedom and adventure. It was more than just a career choice—it was a calling. I had spent countless hours on ships, absorbing every piece of knowledge I could from the experienced sailors around me. I had learned to navigate through storms and calm seas alike, to understand the intricate balance of machinery, weather, and crew. My dream had always been clear: to become a Master Mariner, the highest rank a sailor could achieve.

But as much as I loved the sea, a new and compelling idea began to grow in me. The pull of higher education became more intense the more I thought about it. While the practical experience of sailing was invaluable, there was an entire academic world of nautical sciences that I had barely scratched the surface of. The idea of studying the science behind maritime navigation, the history of seafaring, and the technological advances that were shaping the future of the industry— this was an exciting prospect. The sea surely had always been my life, but perhaps it was time to take a deeper dive into understanding it from a different perspective, one that was rooted in academics and research.

I spent countless sleepless nights weighing the two options. Should I continue following the well-worn path of the sea, or should I step into the unknown world of academia? The decision was not an easy one. Both options held their own allure. On one hand, I knew that a career at sea would offer me adventure, excitement, and the possibility of achieving my long-held dream of becoming a Master Mariner. On the other hand, the idea of pursuing higher education offered a chance to broaden my understanding of the maritime world and open doors to other opportunities within the industry.

In the end, the decision I made was not just about following a dream—it was about expanding it. I realized that in order to truly understand the sea and the world of maritime navigation, I needed to explore it from every angle, not just from the deck of a ship. And so, I made the decision to enroll at the Istituto Universitario Navale, specifically in the Faculty of Nautical Sciences. It was a decision that would require me to step away from the familiar world of sailing and immerse myself in the academic study of maritime sciences. It was a bold move, but I felt it was the right one for me.

The decision was bittersweet, however. The sea, which had been my life for so long, would have to take a backseat, at least for a while. By diving into the theory and research of nautical sciences, I hoped to return to the sea one day, armed with knowledge that would make me a more well-rounded sailor and perhaps even a better leader.

As the time for university drew closer, I began to prepare for the new chapter in my life. Back then, Italian universities started their academic year in November, which meant I had several months between my graduation and the beginning of classes. I had the luxury of time, but the thought of sitting idle for months didn't sit well with me. The sea called to me, louder than ever, and I couldn't ignore it. So, I decided to use this time to gain more hands-on experience before stepping into the academic world.

With my decision made, I joined a merchant ship as a Junior Officer, setting sail once again. It was a decision that filled me with excitement and anticipation. The idea of spending several months at sea, working alongside experienced sailors, seemed like the perfect way to prepare for the next stage of my journey. Not only would I be gaining valuable experience, but I would also be able to explore the world through the lens of a sailor, something I had always longed to do.

The first few days aboard the merchant ship were a whirlwind. I had sailed on smaller vessels before, but this was something different. This was a real ship—massive, imposing, and brimming with equipment and machinery that I barely understood. The ship creaked and groaned as we cut through the water, a constant reminder of the forces at play beneath the surface.

As a Junior Officer, my responsibilities were numerous and varied. There were endless tasks to learn, and it was my job to take in everything—whether it was navigation, cargo operations, or the essential safety drills that kept us all secure at sea. The days were long, often stretching well into the night, and there was always something to be done. The first few weeks flew by as I tried to adjust to the rhythms of ship life, learning from the more experienced officers and crew.

I was the youngest member of the officer ranks, and in many ways, I felt like an outsider. The senior officers had decades of experience between them, their hands steady with the confidence of years spent at sea. I was eager to prove myself, but I knew I had a long way to go before I could operate with the same level of ease.

I clearly remember my first night watch. Standing on the bridge, surrounded by the dark, endless sea, I felt a strange mix of calm and purpose. The stars above were the only lights, guiding me through the vastness. It was quiet, almost too quiet, except for the soft hum of the ship's engines beneath my feet.

In that moment, I felt like I was part of something much bigger than myself. The ship wasn't just a boat; it was a piece of a long maritime tradition, a connection to sailors who'd navigated these same waters for centuries.

I also felt a sense of responsibility. Everyone on board was depending on me. I had spent months at the Nautical Institute, learning how to navigate, and now it was my turn to use those skills. With the sextant in hand, I worked to plot our position and make sure the ship stayed on course. It was quiet, but I was focused. I knew what I had to do, and the ship and stars seemed to guide me forward, each step bringing me closer to becoming the sailor I had trained to be.

The learning curve was steep, but I approached every task with determination. Whether it was managing the cargo holds or monitoring the engines, I knew that the sooner I could become proficient, the sooner I would earn the respect of my fellow officers. I was constantly asking questions, absorbing everything I could. I was hungry for knowledge, not just to do my job but to understand the machinery and processes that made it all work. How did the engines function so smoothly over such long distances? What made the radar system so accurate in even the most remote areas of the sea? How did the weather impact our course, and what could we do to adapt?

The camaraderie on board was another element that made the experience unforgettable. In the mess hall, there was a sense of familiarity, a bond that developed between us despite the vast differences in age, background, and experience. The officers, who had been sailing for decades, often shared stories of their time at sea. Some stories were funny, others were serious, and a few were downright terrifying. They spoke of storms that turned the sky black, of ports in faraway lands, and of the ships that had become their second homes.

Sitting around the table with the crew, I realized just how much I still had to learn, but also how much I could offer. The older officers respected my enthusiasm and eagerness to learn, and in turn, they shared their knowledge with me generously. There was a kind of unspoken rule aboard the ship: no one was ever truly alone, because we were all part of something that required each of us to do our part.

Whether it was cooking a meal, checking the radar, or ensuring the cargo was secure, everyone had a role to play, and we relied on each other.

This was a pivotal moment for me—a moment of clarity. I realized that my ambition wasn't limited to being on the bridge or commanding a ship. I wanted to explore the broader world of maritime science, to understand the innovations that were shaping the future of the industry, and to become someone who could contribute to the world of sailing in a deeper, more academic way.

It wasn't that I no longer loved the sea—it was that I had come to understand that there was more to it than I had ever imagined. The world of nautical sciences, with all its depth and complexity, had begun to call to me, and I couldn't ignore it.

Time went by, and when I finally returned from my stint as a Junior Officer, I felt a sense of accomplishment, but also a deep sense of change. The sea had taught me many things, but it had also shown me how much more there was to learn. The decision that had once seemed so uncertain now felt like a clear, inevitable step. I knew it was time to return to shore, to turn my attention to something greater than the rhythms of the sea and the endless horizon.

As I reflected on my time at sea, I became increasingly convinced that my path lay in the broader field of maritime sciences, where I could deepen my understanding of the forces that governed the sea, and where I could contribute in ways that went beyond the bridge of a vessel.

In the late 1970s, the Faculty of Nautical Sciences at the Istituto Universitario Navale in Naples was a prestigious and demanding institution, shaping the next generation of maritime professionals. The curriculum was intense, blending classical navigation techniques with the first signs of technological advancements in the industry. Celestial navigation, stability calculations, meteorology, and ship maneuvering were taught with precision, alongside the fundamentals of naval architecture and marine engineering. Professors were strict, expecting excellence from their students, who spent long hours mastering complex equations and simulations. The atmosphere was highly competitive but also deeply collegial—students formed strong bonds, united by their shared challenges and an unwavering passion for the sea. The Nautical Faculty was a place where tradition met the early whispers of modernization, preparing its graduates to step into a maritime world on the brink of technological transformation.

Istituto Universitario Navale, a prestigious institution known for its rigorous approach to maritime studies, was not just any place of learning. It was a place where theory met practice, where the study of maritime science was combined with engineering principles, providing students with a well-rounded education that prepared them to take on complex challenges in the maritime world. The program offered a curriculum that was on par with top engineering faculties, a perfect blend of advanced academic theory and practical applications. In 1999, the Istituto Universitario Navale (IUN) was transformed and expanded into the University of Naples "Parthenope", broadening its academic offerings while maintaining its historical focus on maritime studies and economics.

As I walked into the grand halls of the Istituto Universitario Navale for the first time, I felt a sense of awe. The place was alive with energy, with students bustling around, professors engaging in animated discussions, and the hum of intellectual activity filling the air. I had spent years preparing for this moment, and now, with the doors of the university wide open before me, I could sense the weight of the journey ahead.

The program was demanding, but I welcomed the challenge. It was comprehensive, touching on many aspects of maritime science and engineering, and each course promised to expand my knowledge in ways that I could not have imagined.

One of the first courses I encountered was Naval Architecture—a subject that delved into the design and structure of ships. We studied the principles behind stability, hydrodynamics, and construction techniques. I had always admired the sleek, powerful shapes of the vessels I'd sailed on, but now I was learning the science that made those ships so impressive. The way hulls were designed to interact with the water, how materials were chosen for strength and durability, and how stability was ensured even in the roughest seas—all of it fascinated me. It was as if I had been given a key to understanding the hidden world of ship design, the magic that allowed such large, complex vessels to glide across the waves with apparent ease.

Alongside Naval Architecture, there was Ship Construction and Maneuverability, where we studied the construction process of ships and how they responded to different operational conditions. It was eye-opening to learn about the various materials used in shipbuilding and how each component, from the hull to the engine room, played a role in ensuring that the ship could perform at its best, whether navigating through calm seas or harsh storms.

Physics and Chemistry were also integral parts of the program. These subjects might have seemed abstract at first, but as I dove deeper into them, I realized how essential they were to understanding the forces at play in maritime operations. Physics helped explain how ships interacted with the sea, how buoyancy and propulsion worked, and how materials behaved under stress. Chemistry, on the other hand, provided insight into the composition of materials—why certain metals were chosen for construction, how fuel burned efficiently, and how we could minimize the environmental impact of ships.

Then there was Mathematical Analysis, a subject that challenged me in ways I had never anticipated. It wasn't just about solving equations—it was about understanding how to apply complex calculations to solve real-world maritime problems. From navigation to engineering, mathematical analysis played a crucial role in everything from determining the best course to understanding how forces like wind and currents impacted a ship's performance. The skills I developed in this course gave me the tools I needed to think critically and solve problems in real time.

One of my favorite courses was Advanced Navigation. It was built on everything I had learned at the Nautical Institute, but it took it much further. This course focused on modern technologies, such as GPS, radar, and satellite systems, that revolutionized how we navigate the seas. But it wasn't just about the gadgets—it was about understanding how to use those tools to their fullest potential. It taught us how to plan routes in real-time, adapt to changing conditions, and ensure the safety and efficiency of the voyage. The most exciting part was learning about new methods in digital navigation and the potential they had to shape the future of shipping.

Perhaps the most profound course I took was Oceanography. This subject was a study of marine environments, ecosystems, and ocean currents. It provided a deeper understanding of how the oceans worked, from the movements of water to the effects of climate change on the sea. We learned about the global interconnectedness of the oceans, how one part of the world could affect another in unexpected ways. Oceanography gave me a sense of humility—a recognition that the sea is not just a resource to be used but a living, breathing entity that demands respect. The knowledge I gained in this course made me more aware of the environmental challenges facing the maritime industry and instilled a desire to be part of the solution.

As I progressed through the program, I realized that I had made the right choice. The academic rigor was intense, but the rewards were immeasurable. I was gaining a deeper understanding of the world I had spent so much time in, but now I was seeing it through a new lens. I was no longer just a sailor on a ship; I was becoming part of a larger community of thinkers, scientists, and engineers who were shaping the future of the maritime world.

Looking back on it now, the decision to go to university instead of continuing directly on the path to becoming a Master Mariner was one of the most significant and transformative choices of my life. It wasn't an easy decision—I loved the sea, and I loved being a sailor. But I realized that my passion for the maritime world was not limited to the everyday workings of life on board a ship.

I didn't have to choose between the sea and academia. I could bring them together. I was still that sailor, but now I was adding more layers to who I was. In a way, the decision I'd made wasn't just about the path I was walking—it was about opening up new doors to understanding the very thing I loved.

I smiled to myself, thinking of the sea, knowing I would carry it with me no matter where I went. It wasn't goodbye. It was just the next chapter.

Chapter 7: A Life in Overdrive – Balancing Academics, Sports, and Journalism

It's incredible how life can change in an instant, how everything can feel so certain one moment and so uncertain the next. One minute, you have everything figured out, and the next, you're left wondering which direction to take. Over time, I've learned that moving forward isn't always about charging ahead with confidence or setting clear, rigid goals. Sometimes, it's about stepping into the unknown, letting go of what you thought you knew, and trusting that even when you can't see the road ahead, you're still heading somewhere important. It's about faith—faith that the journey, even when unclear, will lead to something worthwhile.

In my experience, every major change or challenge in my life has been tied to the theme of change. Change is the one thing in life that is inevitable. It's something we all face, whether we want to or not. At times, we try to avoid it, fight it, or even fear it. We resist the unfamiliar, holding onto what feels comfortable, and yet, no matter how hard we fight, change comes. It's the one constant we can't escape. The real challenge, then, is not in trying to stop change, but in learning to embrace it. The ability to step into the unknown with hope, rather than dread, is what truly defines growth.

There are certain pivotal moments that mark the beginning of a new chapter in our lives, moments that we never forget. They are the moments that change us, shape us, and define who we become. The first time I had to say goodbye to something or someone familiar was one of those moments. It wasn't just a casual farewell; it felt as if I were closing a door on a part of my life, locking it behind me, and walking away without any clear idea of what would lie ahead. That feeling of uncertainty, that sense of loss, was both painful and freeing at the same time. It was the kind of goodbye that marked a turning point, signaling that life was about to shift in a way I couldn't yet understand.

The years between 1977 and 1983 were a whirlwind of change, growth, and discovery. University life was intense, but it was also a time of excitement, learning, and self-discovery. I had chosen to immerse myself in maritime studies, and every day presented new challenges. Between lectures on ship design, navigation, and oceanography, I was also balancing a busy social life and a growing passion for rugby.

Rugby became more than just a sport for me; it was a way to channel the energy and focus that the academic demands of university required. The adrenaline of the game, the camaraderie of teammates, and the satisfaction of pushing myself physically created a perfect counterbalance to the intellectual challenges I faced in the classroom. I quickly became a regular on the university rugby team, and those weekends spent on the pitch were some of the most exhilarating moments of my life. The sport helped me stay grounded, taught me discipline, and pushed me to strive for excellence in everything I did.

But life wasn't all about books and rugby. My love for the sea never faded, even as I settled into university life. There were still weekends when I would join friends on smaller sailing trips, always finding peace in the rhythm of the water. The sea was my constant, always there when I needed to escape from the noise of the world. Even as my academic focus shifted to more theoretical aspects of maritime sciences, I never lost the feeling of connection to the ocean, which had been my home for so long.

During my university years, I took the initiative to establish the Istituto Universitario Navale di Napoli (IUN) as an active participant in the prestigious Course de l'Europe —a highly competitive European university sailing championship. The competition had a unique structure: each crew had to consist of five members, including at least one woman, and the sailboats were provided locally, ensuring a level playing field where victory depended solely on the crew's skill, strategy, and teamwork.

As both skipper and navigator, I led IUN's team into some of the most intense offshore battles, competing against renowned maritime institutions like Southampton University (UK), École Navale (France), and TU Delft (Netherlands). Our team's racing skills were sharpened in the strong maritime tradition of Naples, allowing us to thrive in various conditions, whether in the rougher waters of the Atlantic or the shifting breezes of the Mediterranean. We often competed aboard Figaro Beneteau or First Class 8 keelboats, both demanding exceptional teamwork and precise navigation.

I can still vividly recall our daily training sessions, which were some of the most incredible moments of my university years. Almost every day, during our lunch breaks or after classes, we would head out onto the Bay of Naples, training tirelessly to perfect our maneuvers and teamwork. Some days, we would push ourselves even further, sailing all the way to Capri, refining our tactics while being surrounded by one of the most breathtaking seascapes in the world. Those hours on the water—feeling the wind shift, adjusting to the rhythm of the sea, and working as one cohesive unit—were instrumental in shaping us into a formidable crew, both in skill and in spirit.

One particularly thrilling edition took place in 1982 in mixed conditions off the French coast. I remember an upwind leg where our closest rivals misjudged a crucial tack, giving us a fleeting opening. Trusting my instincts and knowledge of shifting currents, I called for an immediate adjustment—just seconds before our competitors realized their mistake. That perfectly timed maneuver shaved precious seconds off our course and helped us secure a top-five finish in the race. Our relentless tactical approach earned us the nickname "i lupi del mare" (the sea wolves), a title we wore with pride.

Beyond my time with IUN, I also competed in prestigious offshore regattas aboard Excalibur, a highly successful racing yacht based in Naples and owned by a private sailor with a passion for victory. Sailing with Excalibur's seasoned crew, I gained invaluable experience in high-stakes competitions, further refining my tactical skills and ability to read the sea in unpredictable conditions. The combination of university sailing and professional-level offshore racing deepened my understanding of wind patterns, sail trim, and race strategy, all of which I carried forward into future competitions.

Throughout the years, IUN continued competing, facing some of the best university crews in Europe. We sailed in editions hosted in France (La Rochelle, Brest) as well as Mediterranean venues like Naples and Sardinia. Many of my teammates, including myself, went on to distinguish ourselves in offshore sailing, with some competing in renowned events like the Giraglia Cup and Middle Sea Race.

These competitions were not just about winning; they were about pushing limits, making split-second decisions, and learning the profound discipline of the sea. The legacy of IUN's participation in the European University Regatta, combined with my experiences aboard Excalibur and those unforgettable training days sailing to Capri, remains a testament to the determination, skill, and unwavering passion that defined our team.

Amid all of this, I was also in a long-term relationship with Lia. She was a caring, sweet woman with bright blonde hair, and for five years, we shared a relationship built on love, trust, and companionship. We found joy in the simple moments together—whether it was exploring new parts of Naples, sharing quiet evenings at home, or supporting each other through the ups and downs of life. Lia was my anchor in many ways, always there to offer her encouragement and love, especially when the pressures of university, rugby, and journalism seemed overwhelming.

Despite the busyness of those years, I learned the art of balancing priorities. It was a constant juggling act, with days that seemed to never end. Some nights, I would stay up late studying, writing articles, or preparing for a rugby match the next day. But through it all, I discovered something important about myself: I thrived on the challenge.

Just as I was learning how to manage my time effectively, an unexpected opportunity arose that allowed me to blend my passion for sports with my professional life. While living in Naples, I found myself stepping into a role I had never planned on—becoming a sports journalist.

It wasn't something I had ever seriously considered, but once I started, I realized just how much it connected me to the pulse of the city's vibrant sports culture. I started writing for local newspapers and contributing to regional radio stations, covering some of the most exciting events in Italian basketball and soccer.

One of the highlights of this job was being able to provide live commentary for basketball games. Basketball had always been a huge part of my life, so getting the chance to share the energy of the sport with listeners was something I truly cherished. Calling the game as it happened, describing the fast breaks, the dunks, and the last-second shots—there was something special about making the action come alive for those who couldn't be at the game.

Basketball in Naples during that time had a certain electricity to it. The fans were intense and passionate, and the games felt like more than just a sport—they were an event, a spectacle. I had to keep up with the tempo of the game, describe what was happening as it unfolded, and match the excitement of the crowd. The challenge of it all made it even more thrilling. Every play was an opportunity to paint a picture, to bring the listener into the moment.

But soccer in Naples? That was a whole different level. I had the chance to cover Napoli's games during the years when Diego Maradona was in his prime, and honestly, it felt like something truly special was happening. Maradona wasn't just a player—he was the heartbeat of the city, and watching him on the field was like watching magic unfold. The energy in the stadium was beyond anything I'd ever experienced. When Maradona touched the ball, you could feel the entire crowd holding its breath, waiting for what he would do next.

Being there for Napoli's games, feeling the roar of the crowd, and hearing the chants of "Forza Napoli!" echo through the stands—it was incredible. I remember vividly the way the entire city seemed to come alive when the team played. People would gather, not just in the stadium but in bars, at home, everywhere, to watch the games. It was like the city's spirit was tied directly to the team's success, and Maradona was the man who gave them hope, joy, and pride.

As a journalist, I had the honor of capturing those moments, of sharing with others the magic of watching Maradona's genius on the field. It wasn't just about the goals or the stats—it was about the feeling in the air, the connection between the team and the city. Every game felt like a story unfolding, and I had the job of telling it to everyone who couldn't be there. It was a once-in-a-lifetime experience.

More than anything, I learned that sports have a unique way of bringing people together. It's more than just a game—it's about shared experiences, emotions, and the power of a single moment to unite a crowd. And I was lucky enough to be a part of it all.

One of the most exciting and unforgettable experiences I had in Naples was when I got the chance to help organize an NBA-friendly game at the Naples Arena. It wasn't just any game—it was a rare opportunity to see some of the best basketball players in the world come to my hometown. It felt surreal to be a part of making that happen, to bring a piece of the NBA to a city that doesn't usually get that kind of spotlight.

The game was an incredible event, but the real magic was in the atmosphere. We had some true legends in attendance, and among them was the towering figure of Bob Lanier. For those who didn't know, Lanier was an eight-time NBA All-Star and a Hall of Famer, widely respected for his scoring, his dominance in the paint, and his leadership on the court. He wasn't just a force on the basketball floor, but his personality off it was just as impressive. Meeting him in person was like meeting a living legend, but the thing that really stood out about Bob Lanier was how down-to-earth he was. He had this warmth about him that made everyone feel comfortable, even though he had achieved so much in his career.

Alongside Lanier were other basketball greats, including Kevin Porter, Chris Ford, John Mengelt, and Phil Hubbard. Each one of them brought their own unique style and energy to the game. Kevin Porter, with his speed and agility, made every play look effortless. Chris Ford's calm presence on the court was something special. John Mengelt and Phil Hubbard, too, added their own charm and skill, making the whole game feel like a highlight reel from start to finish. Seeing all these incredible players together in Naples was a rare treat, one that no one in the city would ever forget.

But the event wasn't just about the game—it was about everything that happened around it. Over the course of the event, I had the privilege of attending lunches and dinners with the NBA players and teams at the Ambassador's Hotel, one of Naples' most iconic spots. Those meals were like nothing I had ever experienced. At the table, it wasn't all basketball talk. Sure, there was plenty of basketball conversation—what they thought of certain plays, how they felt about the game, and their plans for the rest of the season—but it was also about life beyond basketball. We shared stories about where we grew up, our favorite cities, and the cultures that shaped us. There was laughter, plenty of jokes, and a sense of camaraderie that you wouldn't expect from such high-profile athletes.

For me, sitting down at those tables with NBA legends felt almost surreal. It wasn't like meeting a celebrity; it was more like meeting a person who had lived a rich, full life, and had seen and done things most of us could only dream of. The conversations we had weren't just about basketball strategies or stats. They were about the human side of the game—how basketball connects people, how it transcends borders, and how it can teach life lessons. Bob Lanier, in particular, was incredibly humble, and his presence was more than just his basketball career. He had this genuine interest in other people's stories. It wasn't just about him talking; it was about him listening and engaging. I remember one night, after dinner, we ended up chatting about the power of sports to bring people together, and how we could use that energy to make a positive impact on our communities. It was one of those conversations that stays with you long after it's over.

Those dinners weren't just about the players showing up to eat—they were a chance to connect on a deeper level. There was an authenticity to these athletes that I didn't expect. Sure, they were stars, but they were also real people with real stories. And for me, those moments, those quiet conversations in between the games, were as memorable as anything that happened on the court.

Being involved in organizing this event, seeing the behind-the-scenes workings, and witnessing the interactions between these basketball legends was a truly unique experience.

During this time in my life, the balancing act between work, studies, and personal commitments felt like a constant juggling act. My days were packed with a diverse range of responsibilities, each one demanding its own level of attention and focus. Despite the whirlwind pace, I found a way to navigate it all, even if at times, it felt like I was running on pure adrenaline.

University Studies: The Demanding World of Nautical Sciences

One of the biggest challenges I faced during this period was my enrollment at the Istituto Universitario Navale, where I was diving deep into the world of nautical sciences. The Faculty of Nautical Sciences was no easy ride. Subjects like Naval Architecture, Ship Construction, and Advanced Navigation were not just theoretical; they required an immense amount of dedication and mental focus. The coursework was demanding, and the deadlines were unforgiving. Many evenings were spent hunched over textbooks, trying to absorb the complex equations and diagrams that formed the backbone of these subjects. The program left little room for distractions, and often, I found myself stretched thin, balancing lectures, assignments, and exams. It wasn't just about getting good grades—it was about developing a deep understanding of the science that governs the sea, something I had always been fascinated by.

Outside of my studies, I had also taken on a major responsibility—national-level basketball refereeing. Officiating basketball games at such a high level wasn't just about knowing the rules; it was about executing them with precision and fairness in the most intense of environments. The pressure was immense. Every call had to be spot-on, and every decision had to be made in the blink of an eye, often in front of thousands of spectators. There was no room for hesitation. I had to be calm, composed, and confident, even in the face of passionate players, coaches, and fans.

This experience pushed me to develop my leadership skills, as I was tasked with managing conflict and maintaining control of the game. It allowed me to be a figure of authority and earn the respect of everyone involved. That role sharpened my ability to think on my feet and make quick decisions under pressure, skills that would prove valuable in many other aspects of my life.

Rugby: Strength, Discipline, and Camaraderie

While basketball refereeing required mental focus and quick decision-making, playing rugby with the Lions Torre del Greco was a completely different challenge. Rugby, with its raw physicality, demanded not only strength and discipline but also a deep sense of camaraderie. Every practice and match was a test of endurance, teamwork, and resilience. The game was a way for me to push my physical limits, but it also became an emotional outlet. The camaraderie that comes with being part of a team, especially in a contact sport like rugby, was something that grounded me during some of the busiest times. The bonds I formed with my teammates were as crucial as any victory, and the shared experience of overcoming challenges together only strengthened these bonds.

Despite it all, the sea remained a constant in my life, and whenever I could carve out the time, I would escape to the water. Sailing became my refuge, offering a sense of peace and adventure that helped me recharge. There's something unique about being out on the open water—the wind in your hair, the sound of the waves, the smell of the sea—that calms the mind and puts everything into perspective. Sailing wasn't just a hobby; it was a way for me to reconnect with myself and the world around me. It was both an escape and a challenge. Whether I was navigating through rough waters or enjoying a quiet sunset on a calm sea, those moments on the water were the ones that kept me grounded amidst the chaos of my busy schedule.

I knew the importance of maintaining my social life even with the overwhelming nature of my commitments. It would have been easy to become consumed by work and studies, but I made a conscious effort to keep in touch with friends, family, and colleagues. These relationships were a vital part of my life. They offered support when things got tough, celebrated the wins with me, and reminded me that there was more to life than just the hustle. Whether it was meeting friends for coffee, attending social events, or spending time with family, those moments of connection helped me stay balanced. They provided a sense of normalcy and grounded me during the most hectic times.

In the midst of all these commitments, I learned the value of time management and prioritization. There were days when I felt like I was running on fumes, constantly shifting gears between studying, refereeing, playing rugby, and working on journalism projects. Yet, each of these activities contributed something essential to my personal growth. Whether it was the discipline of my studies, the quick thinking required for refereeing, the camaraderie of rugby, the peace I found in sailing, or the connections I kept with friends and family, they all played a role in shaping who I was during this time. It was a lot, but somehow,

I found a way to make it work, and in the process, I gained a deeper understanding of how to manage my time, my energy, and my passions.

Amid the whirlwind of my life, filled with so many responsibilities, there was one constant—Ida. She was the calm in the storm, a steady presence who made everything feel a little easier to handle. With her golden hair and warm, caring heart, Lia was my rock. She was the person who supported me through everything, both the highs and the lows, and always knew how to help me stay grounded.

We spent five years together, and in that time, we created a collection of memories that I still treasure. Not all of them were grand moments or big events. Some of the best times were the quiet ones—the evenings spent talking, the laughter shared with friends, and those rare moments of just being with each other.

Ida's calmness was the perfect balance to my fast-paced lifestyle. While I was constantly on the move, juggling my work, studies, and sports commitments, she remained my peaceful center. She was more than just supportive—she was a true partner, sharing in everything I went through. Her presence gave me the strength to keep going, to handle whatever came my way.

I'll never forget the simple things we did together—the long walks along the Naples waterfront, just the two of us, or sitting quietly, watching the sunset over the Bay of Naples. Those moments may have seemed small, but they were some of the most meaningful times of all.

They were a chance for us to step away from the craziness and just enjoy each other's company.

Ida was always there for me—whether I was working on my basketball commentary, officiating games, playing rugby, or hitting milestones at university. No matter how busy I got, she was my biggest cheerleader, always encouraging me and reminding me that, in the middle of everything, love and connection were what really mattered.

Looking back, the years between 1977 and 1983 feel like a blur—a time full of energy, growth, and challenge. It was a period where I threw myself into everything, from my work and studies to my passions. It tested me in ways I hadn't expected, but it also taught me some valuable lessons.

I learned the importance of resilience—how to keep pushing forward, even when things felt overwhelming. I learned how to manage my time better, how to balance my commitments, and how to make sure I didn't lose sight of the people who really mattered. Those years helped me understand that, while passion and drive are important, so is taking time for the things that bring you peace and joy.

The memories from that time are still so clear in my mind—the roar of the basketball crowd, the brilliance of Maradona on the soccer field, the bond I shared with my rugby teammates, the sense of freedom on the water, and the thrill of organizing an NBA-friendly game in Naples. But the moments I treasure most are the quiet ones with Lia—her presence made everything more meaningful, and she was there through it all, offering support and love.

Together, all of these memories form a picture of a life fully lived—a life filled with challenges, yes, but also with triumphs, growth, and connection. Those years may have been chaotic, but they were also some of the most rewarding of my life. They remind me of the importance of balance, of love, and of taking the time to appreciate the simple, everyday moments.

Chapter 8: Crossing Borders – My First Steps into an International Career

Life is full of changes, some big, some small. We wake up one day and everything feels normal, but the next second, something shifts. Maybe it's a change in our routine, or maybe it's something bigger—like a job loss, a breakup, or the loss of a loved one. And in these moments, we're faced with a choice: resist or adapt.

Adapting isn't easy. In fact, it can be one of the hardest things we ever do. It means letting go of what we thought was permanent, what we thought we could count on, and finding a way to move forward with what we have now. But here's the thing about adaptation: it's the key to survival, to growth, to becoming who we are meant to be.

When we adapt, we're not just changing how we react to the world around us. We're learning to see the world in a new way. Think about it for a second—each time we face a challenge and find a way to move forward, we grow stronger. We learn something new about ourselves, about the people we love, and about life itself. The art of adapting teaches us to be flexible, to be open-minded, and to trust that we can face whatever comes our way.

In nature, animals adapt to their surroundings in ways we can't always understand, yet it's what allows them to survive. We, too, have this same ability within us. When we're faced with hardship, we have the same power to adjust, to shift our thinking, and to find new ways to move forward. But it's not always a smooth transition. Sometimes it's messy. Sometimes, it feels like we're taking two steps forward and one step back. And that's okay.

The key to adapting isn't about being perfect; it's about being persistent. It's about continuing to move, even when we don't know where the road will take us. It's about accepting that we can't always control everything that happens, but we can control how we respond to it. And with each small step forward, we build a new version of ourselves—one that is stronger, more resilient, and more capable than we were before.

Adaptation is not just about overcoming obstacles; it's about finding peace in change. Sometimes, when everything around us is shifting, it's easy to feel lost or uncertain. But in those moments of uncertainty, there's an opportunity to pause and reflect. Maybe the change is leading us to something better. Maybe it's not about holding onto what we've known but letting go and trusting that something new is waiting for us, something that will help us grow.

Think about the seasons and how they change with such certainty. Spring doesn't fight with winter. It just comes. And in that quiet, natural progression, we see that adapting doesn't require force. It requires trust. It requires patience. Just like the seasons, our own journey of adaptation will unfold at its own pace.

At the age of 19, I made a decision that, at the time, felt like the beginning of an exciting new chapter in my life. It was summer, and the opportunity to spend it studying English in Oxford *through a university scholarship for the overall best students* was too alluring to resist. Oxford! A city famous for its ancient history, the birthplace of countless intellectuals, writers, and thinkers. To me, it felt like a dream come true—*an honor bestowed upon me for my academic dedication.* I imagined walking along those cobbled streets, the walls steeped in centuries of wisdom, all while learning the language of Shakespeare. The thought of immersing myself in such a storied place made my heart race with excitement.

I arrived in Oxford full of ambition, eager to dive into the intricacies of English grammar and perfect my accent. My mind was flooded with images of elegant lectures, engaging discussions, and the joy of mastering a language that had fascinated me for years. The idea was simple enough: study English in one of the world's most prestigious academic cities and return home with not only an improved language skillset but also a deeper understanding of the culture that shaped it.

However, as I soon discovered, my journey was destined to take some unexpected turns.

The first sight of Oxford struck me like a scene from a fairytale. As the bus dropped me off at the city center, I stepped out into a place that felt as if it had stepped out of history itself. Cobblestone streets stretched out before me, each one worn smooth by centuries of footsteps. The buildings—tall, imposing, and covered in ivy—seemed to whisper their secrets to the sky, and the spires of ancient Gothic structures towered over everything. The atmosphere was quiet, almost reverent, like I had entered a sacred space where time itself slowed down.

I walked through the streets, my eyes wide with wonder at the blend of old and new. Oxford had this magical ability to make you feel small and humble yet somehow significant in the face of its age-old wisdom. I wondered if the city had changed much since the days of those early scholars who had walked these very streets.

My accommodation was not far from the historic heart of Oxford. I was placed with an English host family, and their home was as quaint and charming as the city itself. The house, nestled between two other terraced homes, was warm and inviting, with its creaking wooden floorboards and fire-lit hearths. As I settled in, I began to notice that there was something timeless about this place. The shelves were lined with books that seemed to have stories of their own, and every corner was filled with memories of a life lived with great simplicity.

Despite the charm of my surroundings, I couldn't shake the feeling that I was in for more than just a language lesson. This was not going to be the easy immersion I had imagined.

The English course I had enrolled in was hosted in a building that could have easily been mistaken for a medieval castle. Its ivy-clad exterior and stone walls seemed to breathe history. But the moment I entered the classroom, the magic began to fade. Instead of the lively debates or thought-provoking discussions I was expecting, the lessons were based on rote memorization and endless grammar drills. We were drilled on tenses, sentence structures, and vocabulary, often repeating the same exercises over and over.

The teacher, while pleasant, seemed more focused on making sure we knew our conjugations than on sparking any sort of passion for the language. It felt like the approach was outdated, and I quickly found myself zoning out, counting the minutes until the class would finally end.

I had come to Oxford thinking that I would absorb knowledge effortlessly, that the city itself would infuse me with wisdom simply by being there. However, I soon realized that the classroom setting wasn't quite what I had hoped for. It was disheartening to see that language learning, at least in this setting, wasn't as magical as I had imagined.

Nonetheless, there was something undeniably valuable in the experience, even if it wasn't what I had expected. As much as I hated the drills, they did force me to pay attention to the details of the language— details that I might have overlooked if I had been allowed to glide through the lessons.

While the classroom left much to be desired, life outside it was full of excitement and unexpected lessons. The first few days in Oxford were filled with exploration. My friends and I, each from a different corner of the world, would wander through the city's winding streets, discovering new cafes, bookstores, and parks. Oxford was a city for dreamers and thinkers, but it was also a city for wanderers, those who wanted to get lost in its beauty.

One of the best ways I connected with my peers was through basketball. Despite being from different countries, we quickly found common ground in the universal language of sport. The basketball court became our shared space, a place where we could forget about our accents, our differences, and our struggles with the language. There, we were just people—laughing, running, sweating, and competing. It was a liberating experience, knowing that you didn't need to speak perfect English to communicate with someone. The game itself spoke louder than words.

Through these friendships, I learned something incredibly valuable: language isn't just about grammar rules and perfect pronunciation. It's about connecting with others, sharing experiences, and understanding each other on a deeper level. The basketball court was where I truly grasped this lesson. In that space, the divide between me and my friends dissolved, and I realized that sometimes, communication isn't about words at all.

Perhaps the most eye-opening part of my time in Oxford was living with an English host family. Their home was a place where I learned about the English way of life in a way that no classroom could ever teach me. There was simplicity in their daily routines, quiet comfort in the way they moved through the house, each person knowing their place, and each action filled with purpose.

Their kitchen, however, was a whole new world for me. I was immediately struck by the use of pig lard in their cooking. The smell, the texture, and the whole concept were so foreign to me. Back home, we would never dream of cooking with something like that, but in their kitchen, it was a staple. They explained that it was traditional, a part of their family's history, and I couldn't help but admire the way they carried on these customs with pride.

I learned to appreciate the differences between our cultures, and although I found some of their practices unusual, I came to see them as a beautiful expression of family and tradition. Their ways were rooted in history, shaped by generations before them, and there was something comforting about that consistency.

I had come to Oxford thinking I was simply going to improve my English, but in the end, I left with so much more. I learned the importance of embracing differences, of stepping out of my comfort zone, and of connecting with others on a deeper, more human level. The language itself was just a tool—a bridge that allowed me to cross into new worlds, both within myself and with others.

By the time I left Oxford, I had not only improved my English but also gained an understanding of how vast and beautiful the world is. I realized that language, much like life, is not just about the rules—it's about the connections we make, the stories we share, and the memories we create along the way.

A few years after my unforgettable experience in Oxford, my journey led me to a new chapter, this time in Buffalo, New York. It was a decision that, at first glance, seemed like a natural progression. I was seeking a deeper, more rigorous understanding of the English language, and the

University of New York at Buffalo's renowned English for Foreigners program seemed like the perfect fit. It promised a focused, intense immersion in English, designed to push students to their linguistic limits. *My studies there were partially funded by a Fulbright Junior Fellowship, a prestigious opportunity that recognized my academic potential and opened doors to this transformative experience.*

Buffalo was vastly different from Oxford in many ways. While Oxford had enchanted me with its old-world charm and history, Buffalo was a city that stood on the shoulders of industrial ambition and resilience. Its grand architecture and historic neighborhoods spoke to a past defined by labor, industry, and progress, while the city itself radiated a sense of quiet strength. The buildings, once the symbols of a booming industrial age, now stood as proud monuments to Buffalo's past—a past that had weathered economic decline yet found new meaning in the present.

The *English for Foreigners* course was a far cry from my experience in Oxford. Whereas the lessons in Oxford had been static and uninspiring, the program in Buffalo was dynamic, rigorous, and focused. The curriculum was meticulously structured, covering every aspect of the language—from grammar and conversation to writing and reading comprehension. The program didn't just teach English—it transformed it. The professors, all experts in their fields, were passionate and deeply invested in our success. They were determined to push us not just to learn the technical aspects of the language but to truly *live* it. Every class felt like an opportunity to stretch my abilities further to test my limits.

By the time I left the program, my understanding of English had transformed. My grammar, once shaky and inconsistent, had become much more fluid. My vocabulary had expanded, and my writing was more confident and nuanced. But the biggest shift was in my confidence. For the first time, I felt truly at ease with my command of the language.

Buffalo, much like the program itself, had a certain rawness to it, an energy that was impossible to ignore. The city was marked by contrasts—between its industrial past and its emerging cultural present, between the urban sprawl and the natural beauty surrounding it. Just a short drive away from the city, the mighty Niagara Falls stood as a testament to the power of nature, its thunderous roar filling the air with a sense of awe and wonder. I often visited the falls with friends, and each time, I was struck by the immense beauty of the cascading water. Standing there, watching the water rush over the edge, I felt a kind of peace that was hard to describe, as if the falls were washing away the doubts and uncertainties of my journey. The falls provided a backdrop for many of our conversations, the sound of water cascading down offering a rhythmic and calming soundtrack to our discussions. We talked about everything—our homes, our dreams, our lives—but it was in the presence of such raw, untamed beauty that I felt most connected to the world around me.

Evenings in Buffalo were a delight. The city was alive with energy, and there was always something to do—concerts, street festivals, cultural events—each one an opportunity to engage with the community. The people in Buffalo were warm and welcoming, and I quickly found myself blending with the city's vibrant life. The local coffee shops and diners became my regular haunts, and I developed deep friendships with my fellow students, many of whom had come from all over the world in pursuit of a better grasp of the English language. Buffalo, with its warmth and vitality, became a place of profound personal growth, where I was not only able to refine my English skills but also to reflect on who I was and where I was headed.

From Buffalo, my academic journey continued to the University of California, Berkeley, where I joined the Department of Naval Architecture. *This move was also partially funded by a Fulbright Junior Fellowship, which allowed me to pursue my growing passion for maritime engineering in one of the world's leading institutions.* The decision to study naval architecture was a step in a direction that had always intrigued me, but I didn't fully realize the depth of the challenge and excitement it would bring.

The moment I arrived in Berkeley, I was struck by the energy of the place. The city was vibrant, eclectic, and ever-changing, and the nearby San Francisco Bay provided the perfect backdrop to my studies. The area was a blend of natural beauty and cultural dynamism—everything from the rugged coastline to the cutting-edge technology in Silicon Valley seemed to influence the air I breathed.

Despite the beauty of the surroundings, Berkeley was not without its challenges. The political climate of the university was often tense. Protests and heated debates were a regular feature of campus life, and it was impossible to ignore the sense of unrest that permeated the air. The tensions on campus reflected the broader societal struggles of the time, and navigating these complexities required a certain level of resilience. I quickly learned that Berkeley was a place that demanded not just intellectual rigor but also a capacity to adapt and respond to the fast-paced, sometimes volatile environment.

The academic side of Berkeley was equally demanding. The Department of Naval Architecture was home to some of the brightest minds in the field. Every professor I encountered had a passion for the subject that was contagious. There was no room for complacency here. If anything, the more I learned, the more I realized how much I didn't know. The world of naval architecture was vast and intricate, and I was eager to dive deep into its complexities. From studying the theoretical aspects of ship design to observing maritime operations firsthand, I was constantly challenged to think creatively and critically.

The proximity to the Pacific Ocean was a unique advantage. Many of my classmates and I would spend weekends sailing in the bay, learning firsthand about the intricacies of navigation, boat design, and maritime safety. The experience of being out on the water, feeling the sway of the boat beneath my feet, and observing the mechanics of sailing provided a profound connection to the sea. It was during these outings that I truly began to appreciate the fusion of theory and practice in naval architecture. Being on the water made the designs we studied come to life in a way that textbooks never could.

But even beyond the academic and practical aspects, my time at Berkeley became a journey of self-discovery. The university's diverse student body and intellectual climate created a space for exploring new ideas, challenging old assumptions, and developing a worldview that was broader and more nuanced. It wasn't just about the technical aspects of naval architecture—it was about understanding how the designs we studied affected people, the environment, and the world around us. Berkeley, much like Buffalo before it, became a place where I grew not just academically, but also as a person.

The Harvard Experience – Refining the Art of Expression

After my transformative years at Buffalo and Berkeley, the next step in my academic journey took me to Harvard University. My time at Harvard was partially funded by a COLLABORATIVE DEFENSE RESEARCH GROUP Senior Fellowship, a recognition of my growing expertise and potential to contribute to international fields of study. Harvard was a world unto itself—intellectually rigorous, culturally vibrant, and home to some of the brightest minds in the world. It was here that I decided to pursue a diploma in Communication, a field that seemed to complement my technical background in naval architecture.

At Harvard, I encountered a demanding environment that pushed me to think critically and communicate even more effectively. It wasn't just about language or grammar anymore; it was about shaping how I expressed myself—how I presented my ideas, how I led discussions, and how I engaged with the world. Communication was a tool not only for speaking but also for listening. Through countless essays, seminars, and discussions, I honed the ability to articulate my thoughts clearly and persuasively. My professors, many of whom were influential figures in the field of communication, guided me in exploring the deeper aspects of storytelling, persuasion, and rhetoric. But it wasn't just about speaking well; it was about leading, thinking, and influencing others through the power of language.

I had come to Harvard expecting to simply refine my communication skills, but what I discovered was far more profound. I was taught how to be a leader—not in the conventional sense, but as someone who could inspire and motivate others with their words and ideas. Harvard's storied traditions and intellectual vibrancy encouraged me to stretch my thinking and approach challenges from different perspectives. I became not just a better communicator but a more well-rounded individual. The technical expertise I had gained at Berkeley and Buffalo began to integrate OCEAN-NAVlessly with the storytelling and leadership skills I was developing at Harvard. The result was a more holistic professional—someone who could bridge the gap between technical knowledge and human connection.

Harvard also taught me the importance of community. I forged connections with brilliant minds from all over the world, and these relationships enriched my understanding of both communication and the world itself. Through group projects, discussions, and even casual interactions, I learned that communication is as much about connecting with others as it is about conveying your own ideas. Harvard, with its rich intellectual environment, provided the perfect place for this kind of growth. I graduated with enhanced communication skills and a deeper understanding of how to lead, think, and inspire—qualities that would shape my path in ways I hadn't yet imagined.

After completing my studies at Harvard, the next chapter in my academic life took me to the United States Merchant Marine Academy at Kings Point, New York. My work there was also partially funded by a COLLABORATIVE DEFENSE RESEARCH GROUP Senior Fellowship, which supported my transition into advanced research and teaching roles. I was fortunate to be involved with Kings Point on two distinct occasions, each marking a significant milestone in my career. The first time I arrived as a Scientist at the National Maritime Research Center, where I joined a team of five tasked with developing the first Large Ship Maneuvering Simulator—an innovative project that pushed the boundaries of maritime technology and simulation. The second time, I returned as a Visiting Professor at the Academy, a role that would change the course of my career and life in profound ways.

My initial stint as a Scientist was a thrilling dive into the practical application of naval architecture. Working alongside four brilliant colleagues, we labored to create a simulator that could replicate the complex dynamics of large ship navigation—a tool that would revolutionize training and safety in the maritime industry. It was an intense, collaborative effort, blending theoretical expertise with cutting-edge technology, and I felt immense pride in contributing to such a groundbreaking advancement.

My return to Kings Point as a Visiting Professor shifted my focus from research to education, though the passion for naval architecture remained at the core of my work. Teaching cadets was a deeply rewarding experience that allowed me to share my enthusiasm for the field, guide young minds in their academic pursuits, and help them navigate the complex world of maritime engineering. I quickly realized that teaching was more than just sharing knowledge—it was about sparking curiosity, instilling a sense of discipline, and helping students develop the skills they needed to succeed in the real world.

The role of professor brought with it a great deal of responsibility. I wasn't just imparting knowledge; I was helping to shape the future of my field. My students looked to me for guidance, not just in the classroom but in their careers and lives. I took this responsibility seriously, striving to be more than just a teacher but a mentor and a guide. There was something deeply fulfilling about seeing my students grow, watching them tackle complex problems, and knowing that I had played a small part in their journey.

Living in the picturesque towns of Great Neck and Roslyn, I found myself immersed in a lifestyle that felt almost surreal. These towns, with their grand homes, tree-lined streets, and charming boutiques, felt like something straight out of The Great Gatsby. There was an elegance to life here, a sense of timeless sophistication that contrasted sharply with the demanding nature of my work at Kings Point. In the evenings, I would often attend lavish gatherings and social events, rubbing shoulders with people from all walks of life—academics, engineers, naval officers, and business leaders. The community's warmth, combined with its understated luxury, made this period of my life feel like something from a novel. It was in this world of beauty, intellectual rigor, and professional growth that I felt truly fulfilled.

It was during my time at Kings Point that I met Corinne, the woman who would become my partner for life. She was everything I had ever wanted in a companion—intelligent, vivacious, and full of life. Her smile had the kind of warmth that could light up even the darkest of days, and her presence was like a breath of fresh air. Our connection was immediate as if we had known each other for years. Over time, our bond deepened into a love that felt destined, a connection that transcended the circumstances that brought us together.

Corinne became not just my partner but my anchor. In the whirlwind of academic pursuits, professional responsibilities, and the challenges of living in a high-pressure environment, she provided the stability and joy I needed. With her by my side, I was reminded of the simple pleasures of life—the quiet moments, the shared laughter, the joy of just being together. We married soon after, and our relationship became the foundation upon which we would build a future full of shared dreams, adventures, and aspirations. Our love was a reminder that no matter how demanding life becomes, there's always room for connection, support, and mutual growth.

As I reflected on my experiences—from my early days in Oxford to my time in Buffalo and Berkeley, to the intellectual and personal growth I experienced at Harvard—meeting Corinne felt like the final piece of the puzzle. She brought balance to my life, offering a sense of peace and direction as I navigated the complexities of academia and professional life.

Each chapter of my life, from Oxford to Kings Point, has shaped me in unique ways. The lessons I had learned—whether from technical challenges in engineering, the power of effective communication, or the joy of teaching—had molded me into the person I had become. Along the way, I learned resilience, adaptability, and the importance of connections—both personal and professional. I discovered that the pursuit of knowledge was never linear. It was a winding road, full of unexpected turns and new opportunities, each of which had contributed to my growth.

What stood out most from my journey was the importance of human connection. Whether it was through friendships formed in Buffalo, the shared experiences of teaching at Kings Point, or the deep bond I had with Corinne, I realized that the greatest rewards of my academic and professional life came not from my technical achievements or accolades but from the relationships I had built along the way. It was these connections that enriched my life and made the pursuit of knowledge feel meaningful.

In the end, I came to understand that life's greatest lessons are not just about what we learn in the classroom but about how we connect with others, how we grow through those connections, and how we use that growth to contribute to the world around us

Chapter 9: Glasgow – Pursuing a PhD in Naval Architecture

"The journey is never-ending. There's always gonna be growth, improvement, adversity; you just gotta take it all in and do what's right, continue to grow, continue to live in the moment."

\- _**Antonio Brown**_

You aren't born with innate strength, like a superhero with a hidden well of bravery waiting to be unlocked. Instead, strength is something you grow into, much like learning to ride a bike. In the beginning, your legs are shaky and unsteady. You grip the handlebars so tightly that your knuckles ache, and a wave of panic washes over you at the thought of falling. Your heart races as you picture the worst-case scenario. You're afraid, uncertain, and convinced that the ground might just leap up to meet you. Yet, in the next moment, you push off, and suddenly, you're gliding, riding faster and faster down the road with the wind rushing past your face. The fear that once gripped you begins to dissipate, replaced by a sense of freedom and pride. You realize that the hardest part wasn't the bike ride itself but the act of getting on it in the first place.

It's the same with strength. The journey doesn't start with confidence; it starts with fear. Everyone, at some point, has faced that tiny voice inside saying, "Don't do it! It's too scary. You'll fail." We build walls around ourselves to protect against the unknown, terrified that taking that next step could lead to something we can't control. Fear whispers that staying where it's safe is the best option. But something extraordinary happens when we decide to take that leap despite the fear. Maybe you stand up to a bully or speak out for someone who can't. Maybe you see someone else act bravely and think, 'If they can do it, maybe I can too.' A spark ignites deep inside you, a tiny flame that flickers and grows, whispering softly, "You can do this. You are stronger than you think."

This is the moment of transformation. It's the breaking down of the walls you've carefully built to protect yourself from fear. With each act of bravery, no matter how small, you take one more step into a new territory, where strength is born from the very act of pushing through the fear. You begin to see that bravery isn't the absence of fear, but the courage to walk right through it, even when your heart is pounding in your chest. Strength isn't about always being unafraid; it's about continuing to move forward, even when every instinct tells you to stop.

Having strength doesn't mean you'll never experience fear again. In fact, the opposite is true: the more you step into the unknown, the more opportunities there are to feel fear. But here's the thing: fear isn't something to avoid. Fear is the compass that points to areas where you can grow. Strength comes not from the absence of fear, but from the courage to face it. It's the willingness to venture into uncharted territories, knowing that failure might be waiting just around the corner. But that's okay. Because each stumble, each misstep, is a part of the journey. With each challenge, you learn more about yourself, about what you're capable of, and about how to harness that fear to fuel your growth.

There will be moments, without a doubt, when you'll feel like giving up, when the weight of your fears seems too much to bear, when the path feels too long and the hurdles too high. But even in those moments, you must remember that strength isn't about pushing through without pain or fear; it's about moving forward, despite them. It's about keeping that little flame of courage alive, no matter how faint it may seem. Because with every tear shed, every moment of doubt, and every challenge faced, you become braver.

Bravery doesn't happen all at once. It's forged in the small, everyday decisions you take to keep going, to keep believing in yourself when everything feels impossible. Strength isn't something you're born with. It's something you create—through each risk, each leap of faith, and each time you choose to embrace fear as part of your story, not the end of it. You'll find that, with time, the bumps and scrapes aren't the things that hold you back; they become the very evidence of how far you've come, and how much further you're willing to go.

From the very beginning, I knew I wanted something more than what the world had set out for me. It wasn't just about following a prescribed path or hitting the usual milestones. I was always a little restless, a little eager to see what lay beyond the next horizon. It started in Naples, where I completed my marine education, a place that felt like home. The salty air, the rolling waves, the Mediterranean sun—it was everything I had ever known. But even in that paradise, I knew there was something bigger calling me. I didn't just want to be part of the sea; I wanted to shape it. I wanted to understand its mechanics, its science, its design.

So, I decided to continue my studies. I pursued an M.Sc. in Nautical Sciences and Ship Design at the Istituto Universitario Navale, now University of Naples Parthenope. It felt like the right next step. But even then, something was missing. Sure, I was learning a lot, but my mind was constantly craving more. It wasn't just about textbooks or lectures; I wanted to see things differently. I wanted to stretch my thinking, challenge my limits, and explore ideas that weren't just confined to the pages of academic journals.

That's when I made the decision that would change my life: I would go to Glasgow.

Glasgow was a far cry from the sun-drenched shores of Procida. It was colder, grayer, and the streets were perpetually shrouded in mist. But it was the perfect place for me to expand my vision. I enrolled in the PhD program in Naval Architecture and Ship and Marine Technology at the University of Strathclyde. There, I was immersed in a world where the very essence of ship design was questioned, analyzed, and reimagined. The faculty were brilliant, the resources were cutting-edge, and the challenges were constant. For the first time, I felt truly out of my depth—but in the best way possible.

In the tapestry of our lives, one of the most beautiful threads was when Corinne, my beloved wife, joined me at the University of Strathclyde. While I was immersed in my studies, she pursued her own dreams, enrolling for her second university degree with a quiet determination. She chose to teach the languages of love and culture—English, German, French, Italian, Spanish, and Dutch—an endeavor that would not only shape her future but also bring a rich layer of connection to the world. Her intellect, grace, and passion were evident from the moment she began, and she succeeded with the kind of brilliance that was as magnetic as it was humbling. Through those years, we shared the pursuit of knowledge side by side, our hearts beating in synchrony, as we built a life of love and learning. It was a time of dreams fulfilled, of quiet moments together in the university's halls, and of a shared vision for the future. The world around us seemed brighter, more connected, because she was by my side, a woman whose brilliance in language matched the depth of her heart.

It was in that unfamiliar setting that I experienced one of the most defining moments of my life. It was an evening, the kind where the campus seems quieter, more introspective. I was taking one of my usual walks through the university grounds when I stumbled upon someone who would change everything. He was a fellow student and a marine engineer with a vision that matched my own—a shared hunger for innovation, for pushing boundaries. Our conversation flowed easily, as if we had known each other for years. We spoke about everything: the future of naval architecture, propulsion systems, and sustainable ship design. It was clear that we both saw the world of maritime engineering in a way that few others did. That evening, our partnership was born.

We spent the next several years working together, developing ideas, and launching projects that seemed almost impossible. The designs we came up with were unconventional, pushing the limits of what people thought was possible in shipbuilding and propulsion technology. We weren't just building ships; we were rethinking the very concept of what ships could be. That partnership in Glasgow was the catalyst for everything that came after. It was there that I truly began to understand the power of collaboration—the way two minds, working in harmony, can create something far greater than what one person could achieve alone.

But there was so much more to my journey than just research and innovation. While I loved working in the lab and exploring new ideas, I soon realized I had another deep calling: teaching. It wasn't just about conducting experiments or creating new technologies. It was about sharing what I had learned, passing on the knowledge that had been passed to me. The mentors who had guided me throughout my education had shown me that knowledge is meant to be shared. I had been fortunate enough to learn from brilliant professors and colleagues, and I felt a strong need to give back by doing the same for others.

Teaching became my way of contributing to the world in a meaningful way. It was never just about standing in front of a classroom and giving lectures. I wanted to inspire curiosity in my students, to spark their imaginations and get them thinking. I wanted to nurture the minds of young students who were eager to learn, students who wanted to make a difference in the world, just as I had. I realized that when you teach, you don't just share facts or theories; you share experiences, you share inspiration, and you share the belief that they, too, can succeed.

Over the years, I've had the privilege of teaching in many different places: Naples, Genoa, Glasgow, New York, Tokyo, Tasmania, and later Hoboken. Each place had its own unique energy, and I learned something valuable from every experience. However, one of the moments that stood out the most was in 1999, when I was invited to give a lecture at the US Merchant Marine Academy. That day, I walked into a room filled with young cadets, all eager to learn and set out on their own journeys across the seas. Their faces were bright, full of hope and excitement, ready to embark on a life full of challenges and adventures. I could sense their energy, their desire to make a mark on the world.

During my time in Glasgow, a city that held its own charm with its blend of industrial elegance and vibrant culture, I experienced one of the most beautiful moments of my life—the birth of my first daughter. It was during those intense years of study, when I was fully immersed in the world of knowledge and exploration, that life offered me a gift beyond any academic achievement. Rebecca, with her delicate features and the softest of cries, arrived on a crisp autumn day, as if the city itself paused to witness her arrival. I remember the warmth in my heart, a sense of peace and joy unlike any other, as I held her for the first time. The feeling was so profound, so pure, that even the toughest challenges of my studies seemed insignificant in comparison. She was my little miracle, a beacon of light that reminded me that life, in all its complexities, also had moments of simple and profound beauty. Every evening, as I worked late into the night, her presence was a comforting thought, a reminder of the love and the future I was building. It was in that city, amidst the whirlwind of books and exams, that I truly discovered what it meant to be a father.

As I spoke to them about the importance of integrity, perseverance, and vision, I felt a deep connection to their journey. I wasn't just talking to them; I was reminding myself of everything I had learned on my own path. I encouraged them to stay true to their values, to push through the hard times, and to always keep sight of their goals, no matter how difficult the road might seem. I knew that the sea they would soon sail was as unpredictable as life itself. The storms they would face, both literal and metaphorical, would test their resolve. But if they remained steady and focused, they could navigate through any challenge.

After the lecture, a student came up to me. He was young, earnest, and his eyes were full of questions. "How did you get to where you are?" he asked, his voice full of respect. I smiled because I knew the answer, but I also knew it couldn't be captured in a single sentence. It wasn't a simple path, nor was it a destination I had reached. My journey was filled with twists and turns, highs and lows, and moments of doubt as well as triumphs. So, I took a breath and simply said, "It's not about the destination—it's about how you navigate the storm."

That phrase has stayed with me ever since. It's become a guiding principle for me, and I've shared it with many others since then. Life, like the sea, is full of unpredictable challenges. You can't control the winds or the waves, but you can control how you respond to them. You learn how to sail through them with strength, resilience, and a clear sense of purpose. And that, I believe, is the most important lesson I can teach. It's not about reaching some perfect endpoint; it's about growing, adapting, and finding your way through the rough waters, one step at a time.

When I first arrived at the Australian Maritime College, I never imagined it would become the final chapter of my academic journey. But it did, in the most fulfilling way possible. This place became where everything I had worked for in my career came together—where my knowledge, passion, and experiences combined to create something meaningful. It wasn't just an end; it was a new beginning. This was the place where I could finally focus fully on research, share my knowledge with eager students, and take on ambitious projects that would potentially change the marine industry forever.

One project in particular stands out as the heart of my work—the one I called "the Green Dream." It was a concept that had been brewing in my mind for years, and at the Maritime College, I finally had the chance to bring it to life. I'd always believed the shipping industry, with all its environmental challenges, had the potential to be a force for positive change. While most people saw the industry as a major polluter, I saw an opportunity to transform it, to reimagine the way ships operated so that they could navigate the seas without causing harm to the oceans.

It all started with a simple idea: a research initiative aimed at developing sustainable marine propulsion systems. However, as I began working alongside my students, their enthusiasm and sharp minds made me realize this could be much more than just another academic project. It had the potential to spark a real revolution in the way we think about marine technology. It was a chance to change the shipping industry from the inside out.

We began by brainstorming ways to reduce the environmental impact of marine vessels. Our goal was to design a propulsion system that would minimize fuel consumption, cut carbon emissions, and improve sustainability. Our team, made up of students and myself, spent countless hours testing ideas, analyzing data, and experimenting with new technologies. We explored wind-assisted propulsion, hybrid engines, and even solar power integration. The ideas were endless, and the energy in the lab was contagious. Some ideas worked better than others, and at times, it felt like we were swimming against the tide. The shipping industry is notoriously slow to embrace change, especially when it involves new technologies that could disrupt established ways of doing business. But I wasn't deterred. I had a vision, and I was committed to seeing it through.

Then came the breakthrough. We were awarded a grant from the Australian government—a recognition that what we were working on was not only feasible, but important. It was a turning point, not just for me but for my students, who began to see how their work could have a real-world impact. Those late nights we spent drafting blueprints, debating designs, and tweaking ideas started to pay off. We had proof that the Green Dream wasn't just a pipe dream. It could become a reality.

With the support of the grant, we moved forward and developed a working prototype for an eco-friendly propulsion system. This system combined renewable energy sources—wind, solar, and hybrid fuel technology—into one integrated solution. The results were incredible. We showed that it was possible to achieve a significant reduction in emissions without sacrificing the performance of the vessel. Our work demonstrated that the shipping industry could evolve to be more sustainable, and that the solutions were already out there, waiting to be implemented.

As the project grew, we became more than just a research initiative. We became a model for what sustainable marine technology could look like. The Green Dream wasn't just an academic study anymore—it was something that could change the world. And it did. Our technology caught the attention of global players in the shipping industry, and we began to see our designs being adopted by shipping companies around the world. It was a remarkable feeling to know that what we had created was having a real-world impact. More than just the technology, I was proud of the students who had worked on the project. They were the future of the industry, and seeing them step into leadership roles in the maritime world was one of the proudest moments of my career.

While my professional journey was defined by innovation and progress, my personal life was also deeply influenced by passion and love—both in the literal and figurative sense. As a young man, I had always been fascinated by the sea. I had fallen in love with it long before I ever fell in love with a person. But there was one woman who had captured my heart and my imagination like no one else. She was an Italian engineer, a brilliant mind who shared my love for the oceans and a drive to push the boundaries of marine technology. Our relationship was short but intense—marked by fiery debates about the future of marine engineering, long walks along the beaches of Naples, and late nights dreaming together about a future where ships could sail without harming the environment.

Though our paths eventually diverged, I never forgot her. She was the spark that pushed me to think bigger. She challenged me not only to dream but to take action and to bring my ideas to life. It was with her that I first envisioned a future where ships didn't pollute the oceans, where we could create technology that worked in harmony with nature. Our time together shaped my thinking and set me on a path that led to my work on the Green Dream.

Years later, as I reflected on those moments of youthful idealism and passion, I realized how much they had shaped my deeper commitment to sustainability. My belief in the power of technology to improve the world became even stronger as I worked on my projects, particularly in the maritime industry. The more I worked on projects like the Green Dream, the more I realized that the shipping industry wasn't beyond saving—it was just waiting for someone to come along and reimagine it.

As President of Futuraships, I took my passion and experience to the next level, pioneering zero-emission ferries and propulsion systems designed for both sustainability and uncompromising efficiency. Late nights in my workshop became a ritual. Surrounded by blueprints and prototypes, I refined designs that didn't just reduce emissions—they redefined the economics of maritime transport.

Then, the call came. A major shipping company, facing rising operational complexities and the mounting costs of outdated technology, saw what we'd built. Our systems delivered more than environmental benefits; they offered predictable lifetime costs, resilience against fuel market shocks, and streamlined compliance as regulations evolved. This wasn't about short-term savings—it was about long-term operational superiority.

That moment changed everything. The industry had reached a tipping point: sustainability was no longer a trade-off for performance. Our solutions lowered the total cost of ownership, reduced downtime with modular designs, and future-proofed fleets against the volatility of traditional fuels. The 'Green Dream' was now an operational imperative—a way to lead, not just comply.

Years of relentless innovation had proven something profound: responsibility and competitiveness could go hand in hand. And that was a legacy worth building.

As I look back on my journey, I can see how every experience, every relationship, and every late-night session in the workshop led me to this point. It was about pushing the boundaries of what's possible and creating a better world for future generations. And I couldn't be prouder of the work we accomplished.

Chapter 10: Finding My Voice – Entering Academia and Industry

Have you ever heard of the term *the butterfly effect*? It's a fascinating idea from something called *chaos theory*. At first glance, the name might sound a little strange or even poetic. However, the concept behind it is much deeper and more powerful than it first appears. The butterfly effect tells us that small changes in one place can lead to huge consequences somewhere else, far away, and completely unexpected.

Imagine this: A butterfly flaps its wings in one part of the world. It seems so insignificant, right? Just a small movement in the air that's barely noticeable. But what chaos theory suggests is that, over time, this tiny action could set off a chain of events that eventually leads to something much bigger—like a storm happening on the other side of the world. It sounds impossible, doesn't it? But that's the beauty of the butterfly effect. It teaches us that the world is connected in ways we might not always understand.

To better grasp the butterfly effect, think about something as simple as a row of dominoes. You line them up, each one standing tall, side by side. You push the first one, and it falls, knocking over the next one. That one falls into the next, and so on, until the entire row is toppled. This is a basic chain reaction. Each domino's fall causes the next one to fall, and the entire sequence continues, causing a bigger change than the initial push.

The butterfly effect is like that, but on a much larger scale, affecting the world, people, and events in ways that are sometimes hard to predict. Just like with the dominoes, where one piece falling leads to a bigger change, in life, one small action can start a series of events that may end up influencing something far away, something that might seem completely unrelated.

You might be wondering, how does this apply to our everyday lives? Think about this: What if you smile at someone in the morning, someone who is having a bad day? Maybe your simple act of kindness brightens their mood. They might then be kinder to someone else, which creates a ripple effect. Or maybe, your smile gives them the energy to tackle something difficult, making their day better in a way you could never have imagined. That small gesture could be the start of a chain of positive events that affect more people than you know.

On the flip side, a seemingly harmless decision could have unintended consequences. Let's say you decide to skip a meeting or arrive late to an appointment. You might think it's no big deal, but that small change could affect the people waiting for you. They might end up missing an important opportunity, or worse, it could lead to a larger problem down the road. A simple choice, like hitting snooze on your alarm one morning, could set off a chain reaction that ripples through your entire day, affecting everything you do afterward.

The butterfly effect teaches us that even the smallest actions matter, whether they're positive or negative. Everything you do has the potential to affect not only your own life but also the lives of others. These effects might not always be immediately obvious, and they might not always be in the ways you expect. But they exist, and they are powerful.

One of the most interesting things about the butterfly effect is that it reminds us of how interconnected everything is. It's easy to think that our actions are isolated or that they don't have much of an impact. But in reality, we're all part of a vast network of people and events, and what we do can create a ripple that spreads far beyond our immediate surroundings.

Imagine a situation where you're walking down the street, and you see someone drop a wallet. You pick it up, hand it back to them, and smile. You might think, "Well, that was just a small thing. It didn't mean much." But for that person, it could mean the world. Maybe they were having a rough day, feeling lost or stressed. By returning their wallet, you might have made them feel seen, cared for, and less anxious. That one action could make them more likely to help someone else, creating a series of kind acts that spread through your community. It's a small moment, but it could have a lasting impact on the people involved.

At the same time, the butterfly effect can teach us about the unpredictability of life. Just like with the butterfly flapping its wings and causing a storm somewhere far away, the consequences of our actions might not be immediately clear. Sometimes, we can't predict how one decision will lead to another. Life is full of surprises, and the butterfly effect reminds us that we never truly know what our choices might set into motion.

This is where the idea of *chaos theory* comes in. Chaos theory is the study of how small changes can lead to complex outcomes that seem random or unpredictable. It's about finding order in what seems like disorder. The butterfly effect is one example of how chaos theory works in the real world. It tells us that even in a world that feels chaotic and out of control, small actions have meaning and can create lasting changes.

Think about sailing the ocean. It seems vast and like anything could happen out there with the weather and currents. Just like in chaos theory, even small changes in the wind or the way the water moves can have a big impact on a ship's journey. You have to pay close attention to everything, even the little things, to stay safe and get where you're going.

For me, the hum of the ship's engines was a constant presence, a low, rhythmic pulse that echoed through the metallic frame of the vessel. It felt like the heartbeat of the ship, steady and unyielding, a sound I had come to know intimately over the decades I had spent working in the maritime world.

In the world of shipping, every decision matters, no matter how small it seems. A slight change in course, a minor adjustment in speed, or even a shift in the wind can all lead to drastically different outcomes. When you're out there on the open water, nothing is certain. Just like the butterfly effect, the smallest tweak in one area can cause a ripple, a chain of events that extends far beyond what you initially expected.

I had made it my mission to study the maneuverability and safety of ships, ensuring that every vessel, no matter its size or purpose, could operate with confidence in even the most dangerous conditions. What started as an academic curiosity evolved into a lifelong passion, one that has driven me to pursue research, develop new theories, and design innovative approaches to ship safety.

In 2012, after years of research and hands-on experience, I finally encapsulated my extensive work into a single, comprehensive volume: *Maneuverability and Safety of Ships*. It was more than just a book to me—it was a testament to everything I had learned throughout my career, a blueprint for the future of maritime engineering. The work wasn't just a manual on ship design and operation; it was a manifesto, a declaration of the path I believed the maritime industry should follow. It was about shifting the way people thought about safety at sea, moving beyond traditional methods, and embracing a new era of shipbuilding and operation.

From the very beginning, my goal was clear: to bridge the gap between theoretical research and practical application. As much as I had spent years delving into mathematical models and scientific papers, I knew that the real test lay in how those theories could be applied in the real world. How could we make ships safer? How could we ensure they remained maneuverable, even in the harshest conditions? I didn't want to just add to academic literature—I wanted to give shipbuilders, operators, and engineers a clear roadmap, something they could turn to when faced with difficult decisions.

In the pages of my book, I examined the very essence of what made a ship maneuverable and safe. I didn't settle for the conventional approaches that had been passed down through the generations. Instead, I took a critical look at existing methodologies, pointing out their flaws, their limitations, and their inability to fully address the challenges ships faced on the open water. I wasn't interested in merely improving existing methods; I wanted to create something new, something that would revolutionize the way we thought about ship safety and performance.

One of the key concepts I introduced was the integration of safety with maneuverability. Until then, many engineers and designers treated these two aspects as separate entities—safety measures were often seen as reactive, something to be implemented only once an issue arose, while maneuverability was prioritized for its own sake. I argued that this approach was flawed. The safety of a ship should be intertwined with its ability to maneuver from the very beginning, not something that could be addressed after the fact. By linking safety to all phases of a vessel's lifecycle—from design to construction, from testing to operation—I introduced a holistic view that reshaped how we approached the entire process of shipbuilding.

But it wasn't just about theoretical changes. I knew that for my ideas to truly resonate within the industry, they had to be grounded in real-world examples. That's why I included two case studies in my book, each serving as a practical illustration of my theories. One of the case studies focused on a dry cargo ship, a type of vessel that was commonly used in international trade. Dry cargo ships are often burdened with the challenge of balancing payload efficiency with safe navigation. The heavier the load, the harder it is for a ship to maneuver effectively, especially in tight spaces or adverse weather conditions. In this case, I showed how my approach to integrating safety and maneuverability could be applied to ensure that the ship could carry its cargo efficiently while maintaining its ability to navigate safely through any scenario.

The second case study focused on a service vessel, a type of ship often used in offshore operations, such as supporting oil rigs or carrying personnel to remote locations. Service vessels are typically required to operate in a wide range of conditions, from calm seas to stormy, unpredictable waters. In this case, I emphasized the importance of adaptability—how a vessel's design had to allow for quick, safe reactions to a variety of changing environmental conditions. The adaptability I proposed went beyond the vessel's ability to physically maneuver; it also involved the integration of advanced technologies that could make the vessel smarter, capable of responding more efficiently to changing conditions.

But my vision extended beyond just improving the designs of individual ships. I wanted to see a shift in how the industry as a whole approached shipbuilding and operation.

In the beginning of my career, I had a deep belief that technology alone couldn't solve everything—especially when it came to ship operations. The idea that a piece of machinery or a computer system could completely remove the human element was, in my view, a fallacy.

Even the most advanced technologies we used were still operated by humans, and humans are prone to emotion, stress, and fatigue. The reality of maritime operations, especially in stressful situations, is that no matter how reliable the technology, the psychological state of the people in charge could make or break a mission. I found myself particularly fascinated by how fear, anxiety, and stress could affect decision-making on the bridge of a ship. These emotions could cloud judgment, impair rational thinking, and lead to critical mistakes, sometimes with dangerous consequences.

In the early stages of my research, I came to a realization: while technical skills were crucial, they were not enough. I noticed a gap in training programs—there were plenty of courses that focused on navigation, machinery operation, and emergency procedures, but few that addressed the emotional and psychological challenges of being at sea. The maritime world, as much as it relied on technology, also relied on the human operators who had to manage stressful, high-pressure situations. For me, it became clear that without addressing the human side of ship operations, we were overlooking a fundamental part of safety.

I began to dive deeper into the psychology of fear and anxiety, particularly how these emotions played out in real-life maritime situations. Seafarers work in environments where their lives can be in constant danger, whether it's from unpredictable weather, mechanical failure, or human error. The psychological toll this takes on a person is enormous. I focused on understanding how stress—whether from being away from family for long periods, navigating dangerous waters, or facing mechanical malfunctions—could impair an operator's ability to think clearly and make quick decisions. As I studied these factors, I realized that even the most advanced technology would not eliminate human error, and that training programs had to go beyond just technical knowledge. They needed to equip operators not only with the skills to manage the vessel but also with the mental resilience to handle the stresses of the job.

My goal, then, became clear: to create training programs that would help maritime professionals develop both technical skills and psychological resilience. These programs would focus on helping seafarers recognize and manage stress, stay calm under pressure, and maintain clarity of thought when faced with difficult decisions. I believed that by preparing individuals mentally and emotionally for the challenges they would face at sea, we could create a safer, more supportive environment for all those involved in maritime work.

At the same time, I was aware that my work could not remain confined to theory. My aim was never to stay within the walls of academic circles. I wanted to make tangible changes that would improve the safety of maritime operations in the real world. So, I began collaborating with engineers, ship designers, and maritime regulators to refine safety standards and improve operational protocols. I worked closely with these experts to ensure that our collective knowledge was applied in practical, everyday ship operations. The combination of psychological insights and technical expertise led to the development of comprehensive safety frameworks that were adopted across the industry.

As the years passed, I started to focus more on the integration of advanced technology into the operational structure of maritime systems. Specifically, I became involved in the use of artificial intelligence (AI) and expert systems, tools that could help manage and optimize the complex and ever-evolving demands of ship operations. I worked to integrate AI systems that could assist with navigation, predictive maintenance, and decision-making, especially in emergencies.

My fascination with AI began much earlier, in the late 1980s and early 1990s, when I was among the pioneers exploring how these technologies could transform maritime engineering and enhance safety at sea.

In the late 1980s and early 1990s, I was among the first in the maritime engineering field to explore how artificial intelligence and expert systems could revolutionize ship operations. At that time, the maritime industry was resistant to change, with many viewing AI as a futuristic idea rather than a practical tool. But I saw AI not as a replacement for human expertise but as a means to enhance decision-making and improve safety at sea. My work focused on integrating decision-support technologies into navigation and piloting systems—developing what we called the Piloting Advisory System. This system was a prototype designed to assist captains and pilots by providing real-time, AI-informed maneuvering strategies. It was revolutionary because, rather than simply automating tasks, the system used advanced algorithms to analyze real-time data and recommend optimal navigation routes, taking into account weather conditions, sea currents, and traffic patterns.

One of the early tests of this system occurred when I was involved in a project that took us into the narrow, busy straits of the Mediterranean. I vividly remember the moment we were nearing a particularly treacherous section, where visibility was low due to fog, and the surrounding waters were filled with a mix of fishing vessels and commercial ships. The captain, experienced as he was, found himself second-guessing his maneuvers, a rare moment of doubt. It was at this point that the Piloting Advisory System came into play, offering suggestions based on real-time data that the captain had missed or couldn't analyze quickly enough. The system guided the vessel through the narrow passage safely and efficiently, without taking the helm away from the captain, but instead augmenting his judgment with precise, data-backed recommendations.

These early successes were pivotal in proving the concept of AI-enhanced navigation. In the subsequent years, my research shifted toward integrating AI into safety systems—particularly to improve collision avoidance protocols. In one instance, I worked on an AI system designed to predict potential collision risks based on the movements of nearby ships, adjusting course and speed automatically if necessary. During a test, we simulated a situation where two vessels were heading toward each other in low visibility conditions. As the AI system analyzed the situation, it correctly calculated the risk of collision and initiated an automatic course change—proving the AI's ability to make real-time decisions faster than a human operator could react under the same conditions.

Despite resistance from traditionalists in the field, who believed that human expertise should always trump machines, I remained steadfast in my belief that AI could not only complement human judgment but enhance it. I recalled a conversation with a veteran captain who initially resisted the idea of relying on AI systems. "I've been navigating these waters for 40 years," he told me, "and I know when to trust my instincts." But after witnessing the system's accuracy in predicting potential hazards, he admitted, "It's not about replacing instinct; it's about ensuring that even the most experienced hands don't miss a crucial detail." That moment of acknowledgment marked a turning point in how the industry began to view AI—not as a competitor to human expertise but as a valuable tool to elevate safety and decision-making in maritime operations.

Looking back, those early efforts laid the foundation for the advanced AI-driven navigation platforms we see in today's ships. From collision avoidance to environmental impact monitoring and crew management, AI has become integral to the future of maritime engineering. But at its core, the work I started decades ago was always about enhancing human potential—ensuring that even in the most challenging and unpredictable environments, technology serves to protect lives, improve efficiency, and make every journey safer.

These systems could analyze vast amounts of data in real-time, providing operators with insights that might make it difficult for humans to catch in the chaos of a high-stress situation. My work in this area helped shape how the maritime industry adopted and utilized new technologies to improve safety and efficiency.

In many ways, my career was defined by my belief that technology and human resilience needed to go hand in hand. Technological innovation was an essential part of the industry's progress, but it needed to be combined with human-centered safety strategies to ensure long-term success. I wasn't just advocating for the development of new tools—I was advocating for the integration of these tools in a way that considered the psychological and emotional challenges that seafarers face.

But even as I worked to shape the future of maritime operations, I remained rooted in the lessons of my early days. I often reflected on my own experiences as a young cadet, those formative nights spent on deck, navigating by the stars. I had learned to trust my instincts and my training, but I also realized how limited our technology was at that time. We navigated with primitive systems like Loran-C and Decca, devices that could only give us a rough idea of our position. The night skies were our guide, and in those moments, we relied on our eyes, our minds, and our ability to keep calm in the face of uncertainty. It was during this time that I first grasped the true nature of the sea—unpredictable, ever-changing, and always capable of throwing the unexpected at us.

Those early experiences made me respect the sea in a way that nothing else could. They also reinforced the idea that, as advanced as we had become, the challenges of operating a ship were still grounded in the unpredictable nature of the environment. The sea was, and still is, an eternal teacher. I learned that the more prepared and precise we were, the better we could manage the risks the sea presented. But I also learned that no amount of technology or training could fully prepare us for every possibility. It was the ability to think critically, to stay calm, and to manage stress that could make the difference between success and failure.

This philosophy, this recognition of the importance of psychological resilience in the face of technical challenges, became central to my work. I didn't want to just write about it; I wanted to make sure that my ideas reached as many people as possible, especially those who could influence real change. I wrote *Maneuverability and Safety of Ships* to provide a comprehensive look at ship behavior and safety from both a technical and psychological perspective. I wanted to address the intricacies of ship operation, but I also wanted to foster a culture of safety in the industry, one that acknowledged the human element and the emotional challenges of maritime work.

When the book was published, I was amazed to see how it resonated with people beyond the academic world. Ship operators, designers, and policymakers began to take note, adopting my ideas and incorporating them into their own work. It wasn't just about understanding the behavior of ships—it was about understanding how people interacted with those ships and how the pressures of the job affected their decision-making. My work was helping create a safer, more thoughtful approach to maritime operations, one that acknowledged both the strengths and weaknesses of human nature.

In the years that followed, I saw my theories begin to gain traction globally. The preventive safety methodologies I advocated for were being adopted in various countries, integrated into regulations, and implemented by companies worldwide. I watched as the collaboration between engineers, operators, and regulators grew stronger, with a shared focus on improving safety, efficiency, and human well-being. It was a testament to the power of research and collaboration in bringing about real-world change. What started as an academic theory evolved into a movement that transformed the maritime industry.

Beyond writing and research, I became increasingly involved in international maritime conferences, where I could share my ideas and experiences with a broader audience. I was invited to speak at conferences all over the world, where I advocated for a balanced approach to technology and human-centered safety. These lectures were not just theoretical—they included vivid anecdotes from my own early career, painting a picture of the maritime world that was both educational and inspirational. I wanted to show others that the challenges we faced were not just technical—they were deeply human, and the solutions required a deep understanding of both the tools we used and the people who used them.

The challenges of ship safety were ever-evolving, but with every lecture I gave, every page of my book, I felt I was laying a foundation. A foundation that could guide the maritime world toward safer horizons, where the human element and technological advancements worked together, side by side, to create a safer, more resilient industry.

The sea, after all, is an eternal teacher. And I knew that I would continue learning from it for as long as I lived.

Chapter 11: Advancing in Academia — Becoming a Lecturer

In life, everything follows a timeline. People, things, experiences – all of them have their time, and eventually, they come to an end. Nothing lasts forever. This is a simple truth that we learn over time, though it can be tough to accept. Whether it's a person we love, a job we enjoy, or a phase in our life that feels like it could go on forever, we eventually have to face the reality that everything has an expiry date. The beauty of life lies not in its permanence but in its ability to change, renew, and offer us new opportunities with every ending.

It's easy to get caught up in the idea that things should last forever, especially when everything seems to be going well. But deep down, we know that even the most wonderful moments have to pass. Moments, though, are different from things. Moments are fleeting. They don't last forever. They live in our hearts and minds long after they're gone, but once they're over, we can never truly relive them.

Take a moment to think about a time when everything felt perfect – a day when you were surrounded by people you loved, or a time when you were in a place that made you feel at peace. It felt magical, didn't it? You didn't want it to end. But just like that, it did. And all that's left are the memories. Those moments might not exist anymore, but the feeling they gave you can stay with you forever. However, we can't stay in those moments. Life moves on. And with each passing moment, something else is bound to take its place.

Life isn't just a straight path; it's more like a journey filled with twists, turns, and different stages. There are times when we feel stuck, when we feel as though everything is falling apart. But then, we also have those moments of clarity when we realize that the end of one thing isn't truly the end. It's just the beginning of something new. Life has a funny way of showing us that what we thought was an end can be the start of something better, something we never imagined.

When faced with an ending, moving forward can often feel impossible. The weight of what we've lost, what we've had to leave behind, can make it hard to see a path ahead. But in those moments of uncertainty, it's crucial to remember that moving forward doesn't mean forgetting the past. It means carrying what we've learned from the past with us, using it as a stepping stone toward new experiences. Life doesn't ask us to erase the moments that shaped us, but rather, to honor them and keep walking forward.

Moving forward in life is not about rushing through grief or avoiding pain. It's about acknowledging the importance of what has passed and understanding that, in the grand scheme of things, each step we take forward brings us closer to where we're meant to be. Sometimes, it's not easy. It might feel like we're walking through darkness, unsure of what lies ahead. But even in those times, life is teaching us something. It's teaching us resilience, patience, and trust in the unknown.

Think of it this way: life is like climbing a mountain. At times, the climb feels steep, and it might seem like there's no way to reach the top. But with each step, you're moving forward, even when it feels like progress is slow. And when you finally reach the summit, you look back and realize how far you've come, even if the journey was difficult. It's in the act of moving forward that we find the strength we didn't know we had. It's in continuing, despite the uncertainty and the pain, that we grow.

This cycle of beginnings and endings is much like the changing seasons. Think about how the seasons come and go. Spring arrives, bringing with it a sense of newness and rebirth. The world around us seems to wake up, as flowers bloom and the air feels fresh. It's a time of hope, of new possibilities. In the same way, there are moments in our lives that feel like spring – bright, fresh, and full of promise.

Then comes summer. Summer is a time of warmth and joy. The days are long, and everything feels carefree. We spend time outdoors, basking in the sun, enjoying the simple pleasures of life. Summer reminds us of the times in life when everything feels perfect, when we are surrounded by warmth, love, and happiness. But, like everything in life, summer doesn't last forever. As much as we want it to, it eventually fades.

After summer comes autumn. The days grow shorter, the air cooler, and the leaves on the trees begin to change. Autumn is a reminder that all things come to an end. The vibrant green leaves turn yellow, orange, and red before falling to the ground. In life, autumn is often that time when we start to feel the weight of change. It can be a time of letting go, of saying goodbye to something or someone that we've held onto for a long time. It's a bittersweet time, where we start to reflect on what we've had and what we might be losing.

Finally, winter arrives. The world slows down, and everything seems to be wrapped in cold and darkness. Winter can feel like a time of emptiness, when it feels as though all life has stopped. But even in the depths of winter, there is a promise of renewal. Nature, though dormant, is preparing for the next cycle. Winter may feel like an end, but it is also the time when everything is quietly preparing for a fresh start. Without winter, there would be no spring. Without endings, there would be no new beginnings.

In this way, life mirrors the seasons. We experience moments of joy, like the warmth of summer. We go through times of reflection and change, like the shift of autumn. We face the harshness of winter, when everything seems to be at a standstill. But through it all, life continues, and eventually, a new spring arrives. Just as the seasons follow one another in a continuous cycle, our lives are filled with cycles of beginnings and endings.

The beauty of life lies in its impermanence. Each moment, no matter how brief, carries with it a lesson, a memory, or an experience that shapes who we are. The good moments are the ones we cherish, but the tough times, the endings, and the changes are the ones that help us grow. And even though we can't hold onto those perfect moments forever, we can hold onto the lessons they bring. They live on within us, shaping the way we move forward.

For over four decades, my career has been one of exploration, innovation, and a deep pursuit of excellence. By now, you know that it all began with a fascination that has shaped every aspect of my life—the sea, the ships that glide across it, and the stories they tell.

It was this early love for the sea that led me to pursue a career in naval architecture and engineering. I knew that if I was to make a real impact in this field, I would need a solid foundation in both theory and practice. To that end, I sought out rigorous academic training and earned my Chartered Engineer license by 1990. I was proud of this achievement because it confirmed my commitment to the field. It was the beginning of a lifelong journey that would span many countries and cover many fields, all tied together by my love for ships and the sea.

As my career progressed, I realized that the world of naval architecture was far more expansive than I could have ever imagined. I soon found myself collaborating on projects that took me across Europe, the USA, Japan, France, Monaco, the Bahamas, and as far away as Australia and Tasmania. The work wasn't just confined to Naval Architecture or marine engineering; it extended into environmental sciences, history, and even the arts. I became fascinated by how different cultures approached maritime challenges, and how art, science, and technology intersected in the maritime world.

One of the defining moments of my career came when I led several research and development projects focused on advancing maritime technology. These were projects that not only required a deep understanding of engineering but also a vision for the future. At the time, the maritime industry was at a crossroads, with sustainability becoming a pressing issue. I had a vision of creating ships that weren't just powerful but also environmentally conscious, vessels that could carry goods and people across the oceans without leaving a harmful trace behind.

These projects were challenging, but they were also incredibly rewarding. One of my greatest achievements during this time was establishing and nurturing a group of engineers and researchers who shared my passion for innovation. Together, we worked on solutions that would ultimately push the boundaries of what was possible in shipbuilding. Our work set the foundation for the future of eco-friendly marine technology, an area I would continue to focus on for many years.

Another important part of my career was teaching. I had been fortunate to have had mentors who guided me along my journey, and their wisdom had a lasting impact on me. I always believed that knowledge, if kept to oneself, becomes stagnant; it should be shared, passed on, and used to inspire others. This belief led me to a fulfilling chapter of my life as a professor. I had the honor of teaching in places like Naples and Genoa, Italy, Glasgow, Scotland, Melbourne, Australia, Launceston, Tasmania, New York City, and Hoboken, USA, among others, and it was a privilege to meet and work with the next generation of engineers and innovators.

One of my most memorable teaching moments occurred in 1999 at the US Merchant Marine Academy. I had been invited to deliver a lecture to a group of eager cadets, all set to embark on their own maritime journeys. The lecture, besides discussing the technical aspects of naval architecture, talked about the importance of integrity, resilience, and perseverance in the face of adversity. After the lecture, a student approached me and asked how I had reached such a high level of success. I smiled and replied, "It's not about the destination—it's about how you navigate the storm."

That moment stayed with me for years. I was not only teaching technical skills, I also had the privilege of imparting a mindset—a way of approaching challenges and overcoming obstacles that would stay with these students for the rest of their careers. Over the years, I would have had many similar moments, but perhaps one of the most rewarding was supervising students at the Australian Maritime College, where we worked on groundbreaking research in marine technology.

One project that stands out from this time, and I have talked about this in the earlier chapters, was "the Green Dream," a sustainable marine propulsion initiative that earned a government grant from the European Union. The project aimed to develop zero-emission ferries, which was a radical idea at the time. The work we did together set the stage for the future of green shipping technologies. The students who worked on this project would later go on to become leaders in the industry, and it was immensely gratifying to know that I had played a small role in shaping their futures.

While my professional journey was marked by dedication and hard work, my personal life was also filled with romance, both in the literal and figurative sense. One of the most defining personal relationships in my life occurred during my early years as an engineer, when I met a brilliant Italian engineer who shared my passion for both the sea and innovation. Though our relationship was brief, it had a lasting impact on me. She challenged me to think bigger and to dream about a world where ships could coexist with nature rather than harm it. Even after we parted ways, her influence remained with me, and I would carry it into my future work in sustainable marine technology.

As I became more deeply involved in the world of innovation, I developed a strong commitment to sustainability. I recognized that the shipping industry had the potential to be a powerful force for change, and I wanted to be at the forefront of that transformation. As the President of Futuraships, I led efforts to develop zero-emission ferries and eco-friendly propulsion systems that would revolutionize the way the world thought about shipping.

One of the most exciting moments of my career came late one night in my workshop, surrounded by blueprints and models. I was working on designs for a new generation of ships that would not only be more efficient but would also leave a minimal environmental footprint. As I was lost in thought, my phone rang. It was a major shipping company that was interested in implementing my designs on a fleet of vessels. The knowledge that my ideas could have such a far-reaching impact was a defining moment, one that I will never forget.

Throughout my career, I've had the privilege of holding leadership positions in some of the most prestigious institutions in the maritime world. These roles were not just titles or accolades but avenues through which I could influence the future of naval architecture and engineering. Memberships with the Royal Historical Society in the UK and Fellowships with the Society of Naval Architects and Marine Engineers (SNAME) in the USA, as well as the Royal Institution of Naval Architects (RINA) in the UK, were opportunities to not only collaborate with like-minded professionals but to shape the next generation of engineers and scientists.

These affiliations were deeply meaningful to me. They represented more than just recognition of my expertise—they were platforms that enabled me to mentor the next wave of innovators in the maritime industry. Over the years, I've come to believe that leadership in these institutions was about more than directing projects or making decisions; it was about creating an environment where young minds could grow and flourish, where ideas could evolve into groundbreaking technologies that would define the future of the maritime industry.

One of the most fulfilling aspects of my career has been the opportunity to share my knowledge and passion on a global scale. As a public speaker, I have traveled the world, speaking at international conferences and engaging with a diverse audience of academics, professionals, and enthusiasts. It was during these travels that I discovered my love for storytelling and how well it paired with my technical expertise.

I often found myself speaking not just on technical subjects like marine engineering and naval architecture but also diving into maritime history—stories of seafarers, explorers, and the ships that carried them across uncharted waters. These tales connected deeply with my audiences, who were captivated by the intersections of human ingenuity, technological advancements, and the natural world.

In addition to these academic platforms, I had the privilege of being a resident historian on luxury cruise ships. There, I combined my technical knowledge with my love for the sea, engaging passengers in lively discussions about maritime history and the technologies that have transformed the way we navigate the oceans. Sharing these stories with those who were sailing the very waters I had studied for years was an experience that felt both surreal and profoundly rewarding. It brought me to a full circle of my lifelong journey with the sea—from childhood fascination to academic and professional expertise.

No career, especially one as long and diverse as mine, comes without its challenges. Professionally, I've navigated complex regulatory landscapes, with the maritime industry constantly evolving in terms of safety standards, environmental regulations, and technological innovations. These changes required constant adaptation, flexibility, and a commitment to staying ahead of the curve.

However, my challenges were not limited to the professional realm. On a personal level, I have had to confront the most daunting of obstacles: my health. I underwent two kidney transplants, a journey that tested not only my physical endurance but my mental resilience. There were moments of doubt and struggle, but with each setback came an opportunity for growth. These health challenges taught me invaluable lessons about the importance of perseverance and the strength that comes from leaning on a supportive community.

I learned that while the journey might be fraught with obstacles, it is the ability to adapt, to lean on others, and to persist in the face of adversity that ultimately shapes who we are. The support I received from family, friends, and colleagues was instrumental in my recovery, just as it had been essential in the numerous projects I had undertaken throughout my career.

Now, as I look back on my career, I am filled with a deep sense of gratitude. Every chapter—every project, lecture, and collaboration—has been a vital thread in my professional journey. It's easy to get caught up in the pursuit of new innovations and the drive to make an impact, but it's important to pause and reflect on the progress made and the legacy built. My career is a story of how one person's passion for the sea and its ships can ripple through time, influencing the generations that follow.

Despite all that I have achieved, I am keenly aware that my journey is far from over. The world of naval architecture and marine engineering continues to evolve, and I remain committed to exploring new horizons, inspiring others, and contributing to the ongoing narrative of human progress.

One of the defining features of my career has been my ability to expand beyond traditional engineering practices and venture into modern technologies. With a solid foundation in classical naval architecture and marine engineering, I sought to embrace cutting-edge technologies that would shape the future of the maritime industry.

The area that has truly excited me over the years is the integration of computational fluid dynamics (CFD) and advanced materials science into ship design. These innovations have revolutionized the way we understand fluid flow around ships, improving fuel efficiency and reducing emissions. I had the privilege of working with teams across the globe on pioneering projects that explored how renewable energy solutions could be integrated into maritime infrastructure. Solar, wind, and hydrogen power—these were not just theoretical concepts but viable, practical solutions to the maritime industry's growing sustainability concerns.

Collaborating with international teams on these projects opened my eyes to the global importance of innovation in the maritime sector. Every ship we designed, every new propulsion system we tested, was a small step toward achieving a more sustainable future for the industry. It was gratifying to see the industry slowly begin to embrace green technologies, even as the challenges of implementation persisted. In these moments, I felt that my work was part of something much larger than just engineering; it was about contributing to a sustainable world for future generations.

While technology and innovation were central to my career, one of the most fulfilling aspects has been my role as a mentor. I realized early on that the success of any field, particularly one as dynamic as naval architecture, lies in the knowledge and ideas of those who come after us.

I had been fortunate to have mentors who shaped my career, and I wanted to pass that wisdom on to the next generation of engineers and scientists.

Whether through university lectures, one-on-one mentorship, or workshops at global conferences, I made it my mission to inspire young minds to tackle the challenges and opportunities the maritime sector had to offer. I encouraged my students to think beyond the textbooks, to challenge assumptions, and to approach problems from fresh angles. As I look back on my role as a mentor, I am proud to know that many of my students have gone on to become leaders in the industry, continuing the work we started together and pushing the boundaries even further.

Mentorship was not just about technical knowledge; it was about shaping a mindset. It was about teaching my students to think critically, to innovate boldly, and to navigate the challenges they would inevitably face with confidence and resilience.

The sea, as always, remains my greatest teacher. Its vastness constantly reminds me of the boundless possibilities that still lie ahead. My work is far from finished, and as I look toward the future, I am as eager as ever to explore new frontiers—both literally and figuratively. The world of naval architecture, marine engineering, and sustainability continues to evolve, and I remain committed to playing a part in that transformation.

In later years, my passion for teaching and storytelling took a new course—aboard ships once again, but not as a naval architect or engineer. This time, I returned to the sea as a Resident Historian and guest lecturer for some of the world's most respected cruise lines, including Luxury Cruise Liner Ocean, Explora Journeys, and Crystal Cruises, among others. Standing before audiences of guests from all walks of life, I shared the grand narratives of maritime history, polar exploration, and global affairs—stories drawn not only from books, but from a lifetime of lived experience. These lectures, delivered while sailing through fjords, across oceans, and into historic ports, became a deeply personal way to connect with people, to awaken their curiosity and love for the sea, and to continue doing what I've always believed in most: making knowledge not just accessible, but unforgettable.

My career has been a journey of constant learning and reinvention. It has been a testament to the power of innovation, the importance of mentorship, and the value of a community that supports you through every challenge. As I continue this voyage, I carry with me the lessons of the past and the excitement of the future, always seeking to marry tradition with modern innovation and to leave behind a legacy that resonates across time and tide.

Chapter 12: Innovation at Sea — A Journey of Discovery and Greener Horizons

The sea has always been a place of mystery and adventure, but for me, it also became a canvas for innovation. My research into hybrid propulsion systems was not just about engineering; it was a quest to harmonize human ingenuity with the timeless power of the ocean. It was a dream born from the restless lessons of the sea—patience, power, and possibility—and a vision of ships that could glide in harmony with the earth rather than against it.

The Spark of an Idea

The idea first took root during my early voyages in the late 1970s, where I witnessed the sheer force of the sea and the limitations of traditional ships. The engines roared, the fuel burned, and the air thickened with exhaust. The maritime world was a symphony of roaring diesel engines, plumes of dark smoke, and the relentless churn of fossil fuels. But as I stood on the deck of a weathered research vessel, the salty breeze tugging at my coat, I felt that familiar pull—the call to dream bigger.

Growing up in Procida's harbor, I had watched sturdy, salt-crusted vessels crewed by weathered fishermen, each journey a dance between man and nature. Yet, the modern fleets of the world seemed out of step with this rhythm. The air was thick with the scent of burnt fuel, and the waters bore the weight of pollution. I wanted to change that. I wanted to build ships that could carry the world's goods and dreams without leaving scars on the seas that had raised me.

The notion of hybrid propulsion felt almost absurd in its simplicity: what if ships could run like the hybrid cars starting to hum along city streets? What if they could blend the raw power of diesel with the quiet efficiency of electricity, switching between the two as effortlessly as the tide shifts with the moon? It wasn't just about engineering—it was about reimagining what a vessel could be. A ship that sipped fuel instead of guzzling it, that whispered through the waves instead of roaring, that left the air cleaner and the waters clearer.

Trials and Triumphs

The path was far from smooth. Early experiments were met with skepticism. "The old ways work," some argued. "Why fix what isn't broken?" But the sea doesn't tolerate stagnation. Storms change course, tides shift, and so must we.

I started small, sketching designs in a cramped office that smelled of coffee and sea air. My desk was a chaos of paper—graphs, diagrams, and notes scribbled in the margins during late-night bursts of inspiration. I wasn't alone in this quest; I was joined by a small crew of dreamers, engineers, and scientists who shared my belief that the maritime world could evolve. Together, we began building our first prototype: a hybrid propulsion system for smaller vessels, like ferries that hugged the coastlines or workboats that plied busy harbors.

The prototype was a thing of beauty, at least to us. It combined a diesel engine with an electric motor, designed to work in tandem like partners in a waltz. The system could shift OCEAN-NAVlessly between power sources, using electricity for slow, steady cruises near shore and diesel for the open water's demands. We added a rudimentary brain to it—early electronic controls that could sense the ship's needs and adjust on the fly. It was a machine that thought, in its own mechanical way, and that thrilled me.

Testing it was another matter. The sea doesn't suffer fools, and it certainly didn't care about our grand ideas. We took our prototype to the water, a modest ferry that bobbed nervously under a gray sky. The first trials were a mix of triumph and tribulation. One moment, the system hummed perfectly, the electric motor purring as we glided through calm waters, the air free of diesel's acrid bite. The next, a glitch would send us scrambling, tools in hand, cursing under our breath as we tweaked circuits and recalibrated sensors. But with each test, we learned. The sea was our classroom, and failure was our strictest teacher.

I'll never forget the day we got it right. It was a crisp morning, the kind where the horizon looks sharp enough to cut glass. We were out on a test run, the ferry slicing through the waves with quiet confidence. The electric motor was in charge, and the silence was startling—no growl of diesel, no vibration rattling the deck. Just the soft slap of waves and the cry of gulls overhead. I stood at the helm, my hands gripping the rail, and felt a surge of pride. The data was even better: fuel consumption was down, emissions were a fraction of what a traditional engine would've produced, and the ship moved with a smoothness that felt almost alive.

But dreams don't win over skeptics easily. The maritime world was a stubborn beast, rooted in tradition and wary of change. Shipowners raised eyebrows, their voices heavy with doubt. "Electric motors? On a ship? Too expensive. Too untested. What happens when the batteries fail in a storm?" I heard it all, and I understood their hesitation. The sea was unforgiving, and trust was hard-earned. So, we opened our docks. We invited the naysayers to see the system in action, to feel the quiet power of a hybrid ship, to pore over the numbers that showed fuel savings and cleaner air. Slowly, grudgingly, they began to listen.

The Human Element

What stayed with me, more than any technical achievement, were the people who made it possible. The engineers who stayed late into the night, the sailors who trusted untested systems, the dreamers who believed in a vision. Innovation is never solitary; it's a chorus of voices, each contributing a note to the symphony.

One evening, as I stood on the deck of a hybrid-powered ship, the sunset painted the sky in hues of gold and crimson. The engine's quiet purr blended with the waves, a reminder that progress doesn't have to roar. It can be as gentle as the tide, as relentless as the ocean itself.

The real breakthrough came when we started working with others beyond our small circle. We joined forces with researchers from across the globe, pooling knowledge and resources. Together, we pushed the boundaries further, weaving in renewable energy—solar panels that drank in the sun's rays, wind-assist systems that caught the breeze like sails of old. Each addition made our ships greener, quieter, kinder to the seas they sailed.

One trial stands out in my memory: a coastal ferry, retrofitted with our hybrid system, navigating a busy strait. The captain, a grizzled veteran with salt in his beard, had been skeptical at first. But as the ship responded to his commands with precision, its electric motor humming softly, he turned to me with a rare grin. "This," he said, "this could change everything."

And it did, bit by bit. Our work began to ripple outward. The data spoke for itself: fuel use cut by a quarter, harmful emissions slashed, noise levels so low that marine life barely stirred as we passed. Ports, once choked with the din of engines, grew quieter. Coastal communities noticed the difference, and so did the crews, who found their ships smoother and their work less taxing. It wasn't just about the environment—it was about people, too. Cleaner ships meant healthier waters, happier passengers, and a maritime world that felt less like a battle against nature and more like a partnership with it.

A Legacy Beyond Technology

This journey taught me that innovation is more than equations and blueprints. It's about respect—for the sea, for tradition, and for the generations to come. The hybrid systems we developed were not just feats of engineering; they were promises. Promises that the ships of tomorrow would glide through the water with less harm, that the horizon would remain clear for those who followed.

There were moments of doubt, of course. The technology was costly, and the infrastructure—charging stations at ports, better batteries— wasn't always there. But every challenge was a chance to innovate. We tinkered, we tested, we dreamed up solutions. And with each step, the vision grew clearer: a future where ships could sail sustainably, where the sea could breathe easier, where the legacy of my childhood in Procida—a world shaped by the sea's rhythms—could live on without harm.

As I look back, I see not just the milestones but the stories: the late-night debates, the eureka moments, the quiet satisfaction of a problem solved. The sea had always been my teacher, and in this chapter of my life, it taught me that the greatest innovations are those that honor the past while sailing boldly into the future.

The voyage continues, as it always does. But now, the waves carry something new—a whisper of change, a testament to what happens when curiosity and courage set sail together. As I stood on that research vessel years later, the horizon stretching before me, I felt the weight of what we'd achieved and the promise of what lay ahead. Hybrid propulsion was more than a technical feat; it was a love letter to the ocean that had raised me, a promise to leave it as beautiful as I'd found it. The journey wasn't over—there were still storms to navigate, skeptics to sway, and innovations to chase. But with the wind at my back and the sea beneath my feet, I knew I was exactly where I was meant to be, sailing toward a greener tomorrow.

Chapter 13: Into Deep Waters – Collaborating With the Major Government Maritime Agency and Collaborative Defense Research Group

It's funny how life doesn't ask for permission before changing your direction.

One moment, you're quietly working on something close to your heart. Maybe it's a project you've nurtured for months, maybe even years. Or it could be a role you've poured yourself into, or a dream that only you fully understand. It's not the kind of thing that draws a spotlight. It doesn't shout. It doesn't trend. But it's real. It's honest. It matters to you.

And in a world that often rewards noise, you keep showing up in the quiet.

You give your best even when no one's watching. You stay up late not for praise, but because you care. You make decisions that no one will ever see, but they're the right ones. Little by little, day by day, you build something meaningful. You keep going, because something inside you says, *This is worth it*.

Then, without warning, life shifts. A door opens—a door you didn't even know was there.

Sometimes, it happens in an instant. A phone call out of the blue. A conversation that lingers in your mind. A chance encounter that leads to something unexpected. In that moment, everything changes. The quiet work you've been doing suddenly connects to something much bigger. It's as if the world just caught up with everything you've been building in silence.

You might look around and think, *How did I get here?* But deep down, a part of you knows: this moment isn't random. It's the result of everything you've done up to now. Every step, every doubt you pushed through, every moment you chose to care when it would have been easier not to—it all led here.

There's something magical in that.

Not the kind of magic with fireworks or fanfare, but the kind that grows quietly, over time. The kind that builds when you're doing the work simply because it matters. When you're not trying to impress anyone—just doing your best, with intention, with heart, that kind of work carries something powerful. Integrity. Purpose. Quiet strength.

And when the timing is right, that quiet strength gets noticed.

Not always with applause. Sometimes, it's just someone saying, *Hey, I see what you're doing. It matters.* Or maybe it's being asked to take on a role you never imagined, but that feels like exactly the right fit. Or it's watching the thing you built begin to help someone else, in ways you never could've predicted.

That's when you realize: even if your original goal was small—even if you just wanted to do something good, something that felt like *you*—it had the potential to grow into something much larger. Bigger than your title. Bigger than your plans. Maybe even bigger than you.

That's the beautiful thing about staying true to what you care about. You never really know where it might lead. You don't always see the impact right away. But one day, the dots connect. The effort you gave in the dark starts to shine in the light. And suddenly, your work becomes more than just yours—it becomes a light for others.

It gives people something to believe in. A spark of inspiration. A sign that honest work still matters.

And here's the best part: when that moment comes, when the world finally sees your work, it doesn't feel like pressure. It feels like *purpose*. Like you've been preparing for this without even realizing it. All the pieces of you—your effort, your persistence, your care—finally have a place to belong.

That's a good feeling.

Sure, there might be nerves. A little fear. That's normal. Stepping into something new is always a little scary. But underneath that fear, there's something stronger. A quiet confidence. An acceptance that tells you: Yes, I've been growing into this. Yes, I'm ready to show up. Yes, this matters.

You don't need to be perfect. You just need to be present. To bring the same heart you've always brought. The same commitment. The same belief that what you're doing has meaning.

Because here's the truth: life has a way of surprising us. Sometimes, the work we thought was just for us turns out to be exactly what someone else needed. A solution. A sense of hope. A new beginning.

So keep showing up. Keep building. Keep choosing to care, even when no one sees it.

You never know when the quiet, steady work you've been doing will open a door. You never know when your journey will intersect with someone else's in a life-changing way. And you never know when the thing you created in the dark will be the exact light someone else needed.

And when that moment comes, when everything lines up and the world finally says *we need you,* you'll know:

You've been ready all along.

For me, the message came quietly. No fanfare, no dramatic phone call—just a discreet email routed through a secure channel. It was brief, to the point: "Your recent research has come to the attention of the Collaborative Defense Research Group's Science and Technology Organization. We'd like to speak with you."

It was a moment I'll never forget—not because of how it was delivered, but because of what it meant. At the time, I was finishing my year as a Fulbright Research Fellow. My work focused on maritime safety, particularly ship survivability, simulation training, and risk modeling. We had begun integrating artificial intelligence into navigation systems to reduce human error. I believed in that work deeply. Still do.

But I never expected it would open doors to the secretive, high-stakes world of military strategy. And certainly not to a partnership with two of the most formidable entities in global defense: the United States Navy and the Collaborative Defense Research Group.

Up until that point, my work had mostly lived in the civilian world. We were solving big problems—vessel routing in storm-prone areas, training for port emergencies, or creating smarter systems for cargo logistics. It was important, often life-saving work, but measured. Predictable.

This was different.

The shift came fast. Within weeks, I was invited to Brussels, where the Collaborative Defense Research Group's Science and Technology Organization (STO) hosted collaborative research efforts. At one of their think tank-style gatherings, I was introduced to a room full of specialists—defense analysts, systems engineers, policy advisors, and military officers in uniform, each representing a different country. The air buzzed with quiet intensity.

My work on AI-assisted maritime safety had landed me a place at the table. But I soon realized the stakes were much higher than anything

I'd encountered before. Here, innovation had to meet reality. Lives, missions, even national security, could hinge on getting it right.

One of the most immediate and humbling experiences was realizing that I would have to wear many hats. At any given moment, I might be called a scientist, a strategist, an engineer, or a diplomat. The military doesn't just want a good idea; they want it operational, scalable, secure, and culturally interoperable.

That meant my simulations weren't just reviewed by software engineers. They were analyzed by naval commanders, cyber-intelligence officers, and linguists trying to adapt the interface for multinational crews. We were building systems that might one day guide warships through hostile territory, respond to a chemical spill in an Arctic port, or even avert a cyberattack on a naval base.

You have to think on multiple levels: technical, human, and geopolitical. Every decision branches outward.

Walking into a room with top Major government maritime agency brass or collaborative defense research group defense strategists doesn't feel like a promotion—it feels like walking into a storm with a compass and a toolbox. You're not there to impress; you're there to contribute. Quickly, clearly, and without ego.

At one point, during a closed-door session on multi-theater logistics operations, I presented a framework for real-time threat modeling that used AI to predict the cascading impacts of mechanical failures under stress. Think of a scenario where a supply vessel loses power while approaching a tense zone—our model could simulate and recommend actions before the situation spiraled.

After the presentation, a major government maritime agency captain pulled me aside. "That algorithm," he said, "could've saved us a lot of time during a Mediterranean deployment last year. We'll need to see how it behaves with live ops data."

That's how it worked—no hype, no delay. If something was useful, it moved quickly. If it wasn't, it disappeared just as fast.

The first lesson I had to learn wasn't about AI or simulations. It was about language.

Military environments come with their own dense vocabulary—terms like "blue-water capability," "C4ISR," "threat matrix," and "force projection." It took time to understand that when someone said "asset," they might be talking about a drone, a fleet, or a team of divers. The meaning depended entirely on context.

Even the term "training" meant something different. In a civilian maritime academy, training is about knowledge transfer. In a collaborative defense research group context, it's about preparing for scenarios where you only get one chance.

Eventually, I became fluent in this world, not just in language, but in thought. I started seeing how our AI models could plug into radar systems, how simulations could mimic real weather patterns, and how ethical frameworks had to guide every technical decision.

We weren't just building machines—we were shaping decisions under fire.

Before my collaboration with the military, my team had developed a suite of AI systems for shipboard risk assessment. These systems pulled in data from sensors, weather feeds, and maintenance logs to help predict failures before they happened. It worked beautifully for cargo fleets and port authorities.

So we asked: Could the same principles be used in naval combat simulations?

We started adapting the models. Instead of forecasting engine failure due to heat stress, we modeled battle damage under missile impact. Instead of planning for storms, we planned for cyber disruptions or stealth attacks.

One of our proudest achievements came during the development of a training simulator for naval bridge officers. These are the people who steer and command the ship in tense situations—fog, heavy seas, or combat zones. Traditional simulators followed scripted scenarios.

Ours didn't.

With the help of AI, we created adaptive simulations that changed in real time, responding to the user's behavior. If a trainee made a bad call, the simulator didn't just reset—it recalibrated the scenario. It learned. We added layers: weather anomalies, conflicting orders, jamming signals, and even decoy vessels.

After the system was deployed in a trial phase with the Major government maritime agency, one officer told us, "This isn't just training. It's evolution. You've trained us to perceive the situation—not just react to it."

That single sentence is still one of the most meaningful pieces of feedback I've ever received.

Collaborative defense research group's wargaming exercises were unlike anything I had seen before. Massive simulations were conducted across air, sea, cyber, and land. Multiple countries fed data in real time. Virtual battlefields spread across five monitors. Teams in different time zones roleplayed as allied or adversary forces.

Our AI models were now playing in this sandbox. We built modules to simulate cyberattacks on naval control systems, created predictive analytics for multi-country convoy routes, and embedded decision support systems that alerted commanders to vulnerabilities before they turned into liabilities.

There were moments of awe. Watching a model we'd designed flash a warning—seconds before a simulated attack occurred—was one of them. But there were also failures. Once, during a collaborative defense research group test, one of our algorithms flagged a false positive that nearly derailed an entire exercise.

It was a humbling reminder: accuracy wasn't enough. In this world, reliability was everything.

Military projects don't follow the same rhythm as academic ones. You don't have months to refine, test, and review. Sometimes, you have days—or hours.

Once, during a collaborative defense research group emergency preparedness drill, I was woken up at 3 a.m. to troubleshoot a data integration failure. A major port exercise was set to begin at sunrise. If the system didn't work, the drill was compromised. I pulled on my boots and raced to the secure data room. We patched the code with less than an hour to spare.

In the civilian world, that might be considered heroic. In the military world, it's just expected.

With every advance came a question: Should we do this?

AI can optimize logistics, but should it also prioritize lives during a crisis? Can a system be trusted to advise on combat decisions? Where's the line between guidance and command?

These were not theoretical questions. In Collaborative Defense Research Group's briefings, we regularly debated the legal and ethical dimensions of our technology. And I'm proud of that. Our team never treated innovation as a one-way race. We always asked, "Who's affected? Who's responsible? And who decides?"

It forced me to grow—not just as an engineer, but as a citizen of the world.

Ironically, some of our most advanced defense projects went on to improve civilian life.

A risk-prediction model we built for naval convoys was later adapted by commercial shipping companies to navigate ice-prone routes. Energy companies used a training module designed for cyberattack drills to secure offshore platforms. Even our scenario-based learning systems were picked up by emergency response teams for use in natural disaster planning.

Innovation has ripple effects. You start by helping one vessel in distress, and you end up helping cities prepare for tsunamis.

If you had told me back in graduate school that one day I'd be helping Collaborative Defense Research Group model how maritime operations could hold up under the strain of war, I would've laughed. That kind of work felt worlds away from anything I imagined for myself. But there I was—standing in front of senior military officers, briefing them on resilience strategies, helping shape wargames, and contributing to training systems that would prepare crews for the toughest scenarios imaginable.

But the biggest change wasn't in what I did. It was how I saw everything.

Maritime safety had once seemed like a technical puzzle—equations, models, and simulations. But now, I saw it as something deeper. It was about geopolitics. Strategy. Ethics. Humanity. Every ship had a crew.

Every risk had faces behind it. Every decision echoed back to families waiting at home.

What truly shifted in me was the understanding that behind every tool we built was a belief—a hope—that we could make the world not just safer, but wiser. More connected. More prepared.

My role became less about systems and more about connection. Between engineers and sailors. Between data and decisions. Between civilian insights and military realities. It was about building a bridge— not of steel, but of trust and understanding.

And in that narrow space between the lab and the front line, I found something rare and powerful: a mission that felt like it mattered. A purpose bigger than any one person or project.

That bridge—fragile, evolving, essential—is the most meaningful thing I've ever helped create. Because it doesn't just carry information, it carries hope. And that's something worth devoting a life to.

Chapter 14: Bridging Academia and Industry – High-Profile Projects

If a career were a road, it would be anything but straight. It's a path filled with detours, unexpected views, and sometimes, even dead ends that force a new path. How have you navigated the winding roads of your own professional journey, especially through moments of 'holding on and letting go'.

A career isn't just a list of jobs. It's a long, winding road we walk for most of our lives. It's years of early mornings and late nights, of doubts and decisions, of holding on and letting go. It's the space where we try to prove ourselves, find ourselves, lose ourselves, and sometimes—if we're lucky—heal ourselves.

Most of us start with a mix of hope and fear. When we're young, people ask us what we want to be when we grow up. At first, the question feels like a dream. It sparkles. Maybe we say a doctor, or a teacher, or an astronaut, or a dancer. We believe in possibilities. We imagine lives full of meaning, full of magic. We don't yet understand the weight behind the question.

Then, one day, we grow up. The dream has deadlines now. Rent is due. The world is louder. We enter the workforce not always because it's what we dreamed of, but because we have to. We chase job openings like stepping stones, hoping they'll carry us somewhere safe—somewhere steady.

We try to show we belong. We say "yes" even when we're tired. We work hard, we stay quiet, we hope someone notices. There's pressure to climb, to earn more, to do more, to be more. Sometimes it feels like we're running a race and no one told us where the finish line is—or if there even is one.

A career can feel like a second home or a second prison. Some jobs give you wings. Others take your breath away. Some days you feel proud, full, and seen. Other days, you feel invisible, like no one notices how hard you're trying. You sit in meetings, wondering if this is what your life was meant to be. You get through another Monday and another year, waiting for something to change.

Sometimes, in quiet moments, we wonder: Is this it? Is this all there is?

It's a question that creeps in during commutes, during coffee breaks, during sleepless nights. It's not that we're ungrateful—we know work pays the bills, puts food on the table, and clothes on our children. But still, we long for something more. Something that makes us feel alive. Something that feels like it matters.

And then there are the jobs that do matter—the ones where your heart is in it. Maybe you can help someone. Maybe you build something. Maybe you teach, or heal, or create. Those moments can be golden. You feel like your work is an extension of your soul. Time melts away. You go home tired, but it's a good kind of tired. It's the kind that says, "I did something today."

But even meaningful work has its weight. Burnout doesn't care how passionate you are. Stress piles up. Expectations grow. People demand more. You give until you have nothing left. And sometimes, the very thing you love becomes the thing that drains you.

Over the years, your relationship with work changes. The fire you had at twenty might become a quiet flame at forty. Your dreams might shift. Maybe you realize success isn't a title or a corner office. Maybe success is being able to leave work on time and eat dinner with your family. Maybe success is having the courage to quit. Maybe it's finally saying, "I deserve better."

There's so much we don't talk about when it comes to careers. The fear. The loneliness. The way you question your worth when you get laid off. The way shame creeps in when you can't find a job. The way comparison steals your joy when you see others moving ahead faster. We scroll through perfect profiles and polished resumes and wonder, "What's wrong with me?"

But nothing is wrong with you. This is what it means to be human. To work. To try. To want something more.

Behind every job title is a person just doing their best. A person who's cried in the bathroom stall. A person who's stayed up late fixing a mistake. A person who's smiled through exhaustion. A person who's feared not being good enough.

And through it all, we grow. We learn to speak up. We learn to say no. We learn to walk away from things that hurt. We learn to mentor others, to lift them, to make space for someone else's light. We learn that our worth isn't tied to our productivity. That we are allowed to rest. That we are allowed to change.

Sometimes we change careers altogether. Start over. Go back to school. Take a pay cut for peace. Leave a "good" job for a better life. These decisions are never easy. But they are brave. They are deeply human. They say: I refuse to settle for a life that doesn't fit.

A career is a journey, not a destination. It's a patchwork of moments—some ordinary, some unforgettable. The first paycheck. The mentor who believed in you. The day you quit. The award you didn't expect. The apology you gave. The one you never got.

It's all part of the story. Your story.

So if you're tired, that's okay. If you're lost, you're not alone. If you're dreaming of something more, it's not foolish—it's human. You are allowed to want joy. You are allowed to make mistakes. You are allowed to grow.

Because at the heart of it, a career is not just what you do. It's how you show up in the world. It's how you carry yourself through struggle and success. It's the lessons you leave behind. The kindness. The integrity. The courage.

One day, when you look back, you might not remember every task, every title, every deadline. But you will remember how you felt. You will remember who you became.

And if you can say, "I tried. I showed up. I stayed true to myself," then that is enough.

That is more than enough.

And slowly, we learn: work isn't just work. It becomes personal. It touches every part of our lives. It affects our mood, our health, and our relationships. A bad job can make you sick with stress. A toxic boss can ruin your self-worth. A missed promotion can shatter confidence. And still—we get up the next day and go back, because we need to. Because survival is a kind of courage, too.

There comes a time in many academic careers when theory alone no longer satisfies. For me, that moment came not with frustration, but with a spark—a realization that the work we were doing in university labs could shape ships, ports, and shipping routes across the globe.

My transition from academic research into the heart of the maritime industry wasn't abrupt. It was gradual, natural, and above all, driven by a desire to make a difference.

From the earliest days of my career, I believed that research should serve real people in real-world situations. What good is a groundbreaking idea if it never leaves the pages of a journal? In the maritime world—a realm rich with tradition and slow to change—I saw both enormous need and enormous opportunity. Shipbuilders, regulators, and port authorities were grappling with fuel costs, maintenance delays, and weather uncertainties. It was clear to me that we could help.

Back in the 1980s and early 1990s, artificial intelligence was still considered futuristic. Most people thought of robots or science fiction when they heard the term. However, in our research group, AI and expert systems were already central to our work. While others speculated about AI's potential, we were busy applying it to cargo logistics, ship routing, and early forms of predictive maintenance. It was uncharted territory, and we knew we were ahead of our time. What we didn't know was how long it would take for the industry to catch up.

One of the first projects that made waves was our work on fuel-efficient ship design. We weren't just tweaking existing designs—we were rethinking them from the ground up. We used something called parametric modeling to test hundreds of different hull shapes in a virtual environment. We simulated how these shapes would behave in different sea conditions, with varying loads, at different speeds. Then, using AI, we could recommend the most efficient design based on specific voyage profiles. These weren't just abstract exercises; they translated into real fuel savings and reduced emissions.

I remember presenting this concept at a shipping conference in Rotterdam. The room was filled with shipowners, naval architects, and maritime regulators. I stood before them, heart racing, and explained how our AI could adapt a ship's course mid-voyage, based on updated weather forecasts and cargo balance. One shipowner stood up during the Q&A and asked bluntly, "But what happens when your AI is wrong?" It was a fair question—and one I welcomed. I explained that our models provided probabilistic outputs, not absolute answers. The final decision would always remain with the captain. That reassurance became one of the foundational principles in how we introduced AI to the maritime world.

But introducing AI and advanced modeling into an industry built on tradition wasn't easy. The maritime world is conservative by nature, and understandably so—lives and livelihoods depend on ships working as expected. Many captains, engineers, and shipowners were skeptical. They wanted proof, not promises. They wanted to see these tools working in real-time, in real conditions. So we did pilot programs. We partnered with willing companies, ran simulations, and collected performance data. We attended maritime expos and shared results. Slowly, the tide began to turn.

One particularly rewarding moment came during our collaboration with a consortium of shipbuilders in Northern Europe. The project was ambitious: design a green expedition vessel that could explore fragile environments with minimal environmental impact. I was asked to lead the integration of several advanced systems—hydrodynamic optimization, hybrid propulsion, and AI-driven weather routing.

This project was everything I'd dreamed of—a chance to apply deep technical knowledge to a complex, real-world challenge. We used computational fluid dynamics (CFD) to model how water flowed around the hull. We tested how different shapes would perform in Arctic seas, and we created smart propulsion systems that could switch between fuel types depending on the mission. Perhaps most importantly, we built AI tools that could forecast weather patterns days in advance and suggest optimal routes to avoid storms and conserve fuel.

I spent weeks in cold shipyards and chilly boardrooms, surrounded by engineers, designers, and environmental experts. I recall standing beside a full-scale hull prototype in a Norwegian dry dock, running my hand along the steel and realizing just how far our ideas had come. These weren't just models on a screen anymore. They were real.

Throughout this period, I found myself in an unusual position. I was no longer just a researcher, and not yet a full-fledged industry insider. I was something in between—a translator of sorts. I could take complex academic ideas and repackage them in a way that made sense to ship operators, regulators, and policymakers. This ability to "speak both languages" became one of my greatest assets. Before long, industry bodies and government agencies started inviting me to consultations, advisory boards, and innovation panels.

As my reputation grew, I started receiving more invitations to lead or advise on high-profile projects. Cruise lines wanted to know how AI could improve voyage efficiency. Naval architects wanted input on hybrid propulsion. Shipping regulators wanted help developing frameworks for digital navigation tools. Each new invitation was a chance to learn, to influence, and to bring real innovation to a field I loved deeply.

Yet none of this was easy. The differences between academia and industry are vast. In academia, depth and originality are everything.

You're rewarded for asking difficult questions and exploring them thoroughly. In industry, timelines are shorter, expectations are sharper, and the bottom line is always present. I often had to take years of research and distill it into simple tools—dashboards, visualizations, and user interfaces. I learned to think like a product manager as much as a scientist. This translational work was unglamorous at times, but crucial.

One recurring challenge was intellectual property. Universities have strict policies around IP, while companies want flexibility and exclusivity. Negotiating these contracts was tricky, especially when multiple stakeholders were involved. I eventually developed a model for public-private partnerships that allowed for flexible IP arrangements and shared benefits. It wasn't perfect, but it worked—and it helped keep the research flowing into practical applications.

Another challenge was the perception of AI itself. Many in the maritime sector saw it as "too smart," too abstract, or potentially dangerous. Would machines override human decisions? Could they be trusted in emergencies? I understood these fears. So we designed our systems not to replace humans but to augment them. Our AI tools didn't issue commands—they made suggestions, with confidence intervals and options. We trained crews on how to interpret and use these recommendations. Gradually, trust began to build.

Recognition came slowly, but when it did, it was deeply validating. Being elected Fellow of the Royal Institution of Naval Architects (RINA) and the Society of Naval Architects and Marine Engineers (SNAME) meant that my peers in both academia and industry saw value in the path I had chosen. Winning the UIM Environmental Innovation Award was another turning point. It wasn't just a personal milestone—it signaled that sustainability and innovation could coexist in an industry often viewed as resistant to change.

These recognitions opened even more doors. I was asked to conduct design-thinking workshops for major cruise lines. I consulted for defense agencies interested in autonomous naval systems. I sat on panels that shaped shipping safety regulations and digital standards. Each opportunity reaffirmed something I'd always believed: real change happens when knowledge leaves the lab and meets the dockyard.

During my academic leadership roles in Australia and the UK, I pushed hard to change how universities interacted with industry. I saw too many brilliant students and researchers discouraged from practical work because it didn't lead to high-impact journal articles. I fought to embed industrial placement modules in our engineering programs. I created cross-border research groups focused on solving practical challenges—port congestion, ship emissions, and crew fatigue. These were real problems, and we had real tools to address them.

Looking back, I see my journey as one long conversation between theory and practice. There were moments of doubt—times when I wondered if I was abandoning the purity of research, or compromising too much for commercial timelines. But those doubts were always outweighed by the impact we were making. When a shipping company reports fewer breakdowns because of our predictive maintenance tool, or when a port authority uses our simulations to improve traffic flow, that's real. That's the kind of legacy I want to leave.

What surprised me most along the way was how hungry the maritime industry turned out to be for innovation—once it saw the value. There was a tipping point, somewhere in the mid-2010s, when digital tools stopped being optional and started becoming expected. By then, many of our early pilots had become standard practice. AI-driven weather routing wasn't a novelty anymore—it was a necessity. Real-time fuel forecasting became embedded in voyage management systems. Maintenance dashboards replaced paper logs. The future we had imagined was now the present.

This journey taught me patience, humility, and the power of persistence. It also taught me that the best innovations don't come from lone geniuses—they come from teams. Every successful project I led was the result of collaboration across disciplines, sectors, and cultures. Naval architects, software developers, mechanical engineers, data scientists, and seasoned mariners all had a role to play. My job was often just to keep the conversation going, to make sure no one got lost in translation.

In the end, bridging academia and industry wasn't just about projects. It was about people—building trust, sharing knowledge, and working together toward a safer, cleaner, and more efficient maritime world. It was about refusing to accept that research had to sit on a shelf, and insisting instead that it belonged in shipyards, on bridges, and in the hands of those who sail the seas.

If I've contributed anything lasting to this field, I hope it's the belief that knowledge and action are not opposites—they are partners. And when they come together, remarkable things can happen.

Chapter 15: Reinventing at Sea – From METTLE to Prestige Global Bahamas LTD

Entrepreneurship is a story told in moments — small, quiet moments — more than big, flashy leaps. It's a journey full of feelings that aren't often shown in the headlines or the success stories. Feelings like doubt, fear, loneliness, hope, and stubborn courage.

Most people imagine entrepreneurship as one giant jump, a moment when everything changes — the big idea, the brave step, the instant success. But the truth is different. Entrepreneurship is more like a slow dance with uncertainty. It's not about flying in one smooth motion. It's about putting one foot in front of the other, even when your heart trembles.

That first step is the hardest. It's the moment when you stand at the edge of something unknown, and your mind floods with questions. "What if I fail? What if I'm not good enough? What if no one cares?" The fear is real, heavy like a stone in your chest.

But you take the step anyway. Because deep down, there is a voice telling you, "I have to try. This is important." That voice is hope. And hope is brave.

But the first step doesn't guarantee success. It only begins the journey. The path after that is rarely clear. It twists and turns, and sometimes, it feels like you're walking in circles. You work hard, but things don't happen quickly. You try new ideas, and some fail. You face rejection and criticism. You wonder if it's all worth it.

Doubt is a constant companion for any entrepreneur. It sneaks in during quiet moments, whispers that maybe you chose the wrong path, that you're not smart or strong enough to keep going.

It can be crushing. It can make your hands shake, and your heart ache. But it's also normal. Every person who builds something new faces doubts.

The important thing is what you do with doubt. Do you let it stop you? Or do you let it teach you to be careful, to plan better, to grow stronger?

Entrepreneurship is learning to live with doubt and keep moving anyway.

Failure is one of the hardest things to face. When things don't work, when an idea falls flat, or when money runs out, it can feel like the world is ending. You might want to give up, walk away, or pretend it never happened.

But failure isn't the end. It's a lesson wrapped in pain. It shows you what didn't work and what needs to change. It gives you a chance to try again with new knowledge.

This is where resilience matters most. Resilience is not just toughness. It's the quiet strength to get up one more time when you're tired and when your hopes feel broken. It's the ability to look at failure and say, "This isn't the end. It's part of the journey."

Entrepreneurship can be a lonely road. When you're starting, not many people understand what you're doing. Friends and family might be supportive, but also worried. Sometimes, they ask, "When will this work? When will you have a steady job?"

You carry the burden of your dream alone, and that can be heavy.

The long nights spent working while others sleep. The moments when self-doubt creeps in. The feeling that no one else sees your struggle.

But in that loneliness, there's also a deep connection to something inside you — your passion, your purpose. It's what keeps you going when the world is quiet.

Success in entrepreneurship doesn't arrive all at once. It's made up of small wins — moments that seem tiny but fill your heart with joy.

A customer's thank-you note. A problem solved after hours of frustration. A small order that feels like a victory. These small wins are like drops of water in a drought. They keep you alive and remind you that progress is real, even if it's slow. Learning to celebrate these moments is essential. They give you fuel to keep going.

Entrepreneurship changes the person as much as it changes the business. You become someone who knows how to face fear and uncertainty. You learn patience and humility. You find the strength you didn't know you had.

This growth is slow. It's not a sudden transformation. It's a series of small changes — in the way you think, feel, and act.

And it's deeply personal.

No one builds a business alone. The entrepreneurs who succeed find ways to connect. They seek advice, listen to mentors, and share their struggles.

Community becomes a lifeline. It reminds them they aren't alone. It offers perspective when they feel stuck. It gives hope when doubt creeps in.

Even a kind word or a shared story can make a difference.

In the beginning, success might look like fame or money. But over time, entrepreneurs learn to see success differently.

Success is about staying true to your values. It's about making a difference, even in small ways. It's about being proud of the work, no matter how long it takes.

Redefining success like this makes the journey richer and more meaningful.

Entrepreneurship is not a destination. It's not something you arrive at and then stop. It is a lifelong journey. A constant process of learning, growing, and trying again. The big leaps are rare. The steady, courageous steps are what matter most. What takes courage in entrepreneurship isn't the leap. It's the everyday decision to keep going.

It's waking up each morning, putting on your hope like armor, and moving forward — even when you're tired, afraid, or unsure. This quiet courage is the true heart of entrepreneurship.

Entrepreneurship is not a story of one moment. It is a story of many moments. Moments of fear, hope, failure, joy, loneliness, and growth. Moments when you choose to keep moving forward, step by step, day by day.

Looking back, I realize my story didn't begin with Prestige Global Bahamas LTD, the company many people associate with me today. No, it began much earlier, with stubborn hope, a fascination with the sea, and a deep belief that I could build something different—something better.

I've always been drawn to water. Maybe it was the vastness, the silence, the way it demands respect and inspires wonder. But my love for the sea wasn't just romantic. It was deeply practical. I wanted to understand how ships worked, how they moved, and how they could move cleaner, faster, and smarter. I wanted to challenge the systems that had stayed the same for decades.

This passion led me to start several companies long before I ever set foot in the Bahamas. Each one was a step on the journey—bold, exhausting, and deeply educational. METTLE, STR Europe, and Futuraships weren't just ventures. They were living, breathing parts of my growth as a person and a leader.

METTLE wasn't born in a boardroom—it came to life in a conversation over coffee, scribbled in the margins of notebooks, and argued into being late at night with fellow engineers. We were frustrated by the slow pace of change in marine technologies and by how hard it was to get funding for bold ideas. So, we created our own space.

The name said it all—**METTLE** was about courage, endurance, and innovation. It was our R&D think tank, a place where no idea was too ambitious. We gathered scientists, engineers, ex-naval officers, software developers, and environmentalists under one roof. Some days felt like science fairs. Other days felt like war rooms. We were obsessed with better propulsion systems, alternative fuels, and energy efficiency.

We weren't just theorizing. We consulted on next-gen naval defense projects, supported clean energy policies, and guided shipbuilders toward hybrid models years before they were popular. We proved that high-performance didn't have to mean high emissions.

One of our proudest moments was helping a northern European government design a fleet of low-emission coast guard vessels. They were sleek, powerful, and environmentally responsible. Seeing those ships launch felt like watching your kids graduate college—you never forget it.

While METTLE was a lab for ideas, STR Europe was the factory floor. It was where we rolled up our sleeves and turned vision into steel and circuits. We designed real ships for real clients, tackling real problems.

At STR Europe, we had the tools and the talent to engineer the kind of vessels that people had only dreamed about—ferries that could recharge in port using solar-assisted batteries, yachts with silent running modes powered by hybrid engines, cargo ships that tracked energy usage like athletes tracking heart rates.

Our team came from everywhere: naval engineers from Norway, industrial designers from Italy, and software coders from Eastern Europe. It wasn't always smooth—creative tension ran high. But from that pressure came some of our best work.

We became known for delivering on promises others couldn't keep. A Middle Eastern luxury client once told us, "I want a yacht that doesn't whisper—it hums." We built it with precision acoustic engineering. A Pacific ferry company said, "We need a fleet that respects our reefs." We built that too.

With that, we weren't just building ships. We were redefining what the industry thought was possible.

But the future always called louder. I couldn't help it. I wanted more freedom to imagine—not just improve, but transform. So, I created **Futuraships**, my most radical venture yet.

Here, we weren't bound by today's technology—we were guided by tomorrow's possibilities. We designed zero-emission vessels before most people knew what the term meant. We explored bio-mimicry in hull shapes, AI-assisted navigation systems, and entirely recyclable ship structures.

One of our most ambitious projects was the "Ocean Ark," a floating research and education facility powered entirely by renewable energy. It never got built. But it sparked global conversations. That was enough.

Futuraships was less about profit and more about possibility. We published papers, built prototypes, and collaborated with universities and environmental NGOs. People sometimes rolled their eyes. "You're dreaming," they said.

But I knew dreams were just blueprints waiting for the right conditions.

Running these companies wasn't easy. I didn't sleep much. I missed birthdays, lost friends, and spent too many nights in airport lounges or on conference calls. There were months when I didn't know how we'd meet payroll. Times when partners backed out, or patents failed.

But there were also moments of great pride—watching young engineers grow into leaders, seeing our designs sail the open seas, hearing from a captain that our systems saved him thousands in fuel and gave him peace of mind.

Leadership meant making mistakes. It also meant learning to trust others. I couldn't do it all myself, and I shouldn't have tried. The hardest part was letting go—stepping away from companies I'd poured my soul into. But I knew they needed room to grow without me. And I needed to discover what came next.

What came next surprised even me.

After years of tech and tension, I found myself drawn to something softer, more human: hospitality. I didn't just want to innovate—I wanted to create an experience. So I took a leap. I bought a tired old resort in the Bahamas with a faded dock, overgrown gardens, and a breathtaking view.

That was the foundation of **Prestige Global Bahamas LTD**.

Some people thought I was retiring. I wasn't. I was reinventing. This wasn't a retreat—it was a reset. I brought everything I knew about design, engineering, and marine systems and married it with architecture, service, and beauty.

We rebuilt the resort from the ground up. We added solar arrays, sustainable water systems, a yacht concierge service, and a culinary program that celebrated local Bahamian flavors. We trained the staff not just in luxury but in storytelling—helping guests feel not just pampered but connected.

I wasn't running a shipyard anymore, but I was still leading, still designing, still dreaming.

The pace was different here. Mornings began with salt air and quiet. Meetings happened over coffee by the water. Decisions weren't about specs and schematics—they were about emotions, aesthetics, and experiences.

At first, I felt lost. I missed the urgency of tech. But then something shifted. I saw guests unwind, reconnect, and rediscover joy. I saw my son sketching boat designs on napkins, asking questions I used to ask, and I saw a new chapter unfolding.

Prestige Global wasn't just a company. It was a bridge—between who I had been and who I was becoming. Between hard technology and human experience. Between invention and grace.

If there's one thing I've learned, it's that we are never just one version of ourselves. Life changes us, and we have the power to change with it. METTLE, STR Europe, Futuraships, Prestige Global—they weren't separate stories. They were chapters of the same book. They all reflected the same values: curiosity, boldness, respect for the ocean, and belief in better.

Entrepreneurship isn't a destination. It's a current you choose to swim in. Sometimes it's calm; sometimes, it knocks the wind out of you. But it always moves forward.

People often ask me: "If you could go back, would you do it all again?" And I tell them honestly—yes, but not the same way. I'd rest more. I'd delegate sooner. I'd take more walks by the water. But I'd still build. I can't help it. Builders build.

Now, when I look out from the terrace at the resort, watching the sun dip behind anchored yachts, I feel peace. Not because I've arrived but because I've aligned. My life, my work, my values—they finally feel like they're sailing in the same direction.

Prestige Global Bahamas LTD may look like the final chapter, but it's not. It's a turning point. What came before made it possible. What comes next will be shaped by it.

If the sea has taught me anything, it's that reinvention is the most courageous voyage of all.

We don't change because we have to. We change because we're still dreaming.

Chapter 16: A Double Battle – Illness Strikes Us Both

Life has a way of surprising us—not always in the joyful, unexpected-laughter way we hope for, but in the sharp, breath-stealing way that leaves us shaken. One moment, things feel normal. You're getting through the day, checking off tasks, making plans. Then something shifts. It might not even be something big. It might be the way someone speaks to you in a meeting. A message that doesn't come. A long silence on the other end of the phone. Or maybe it's just the way the sky looks a little too gray. A little too still.

And suddenly, it all feels like too much.

The truth is, even the strongest of us bends under the weight of what we carry. We smile when we want to cry. We say "I'm fine" when we're anything but. We go to work, we cook dinner, we send polite replies, all while holding back a flood inside that we hope no one sees because we've been taught to be strong. To keep it together. To not make a scene.

But life doesn't care how strong you pretend to be. It will test you. Over and over again. It will bring you to your knees when you least expect it. And in those moments, all the strength in the world doesn't feel like enough.

That's when a supportive partner becomes more than just a companion—they become a lifeline.

They are not the ones who swoop in with perfect solutions. They don't magically fix the broken pieces or make the pain disappear. What they do is much quieter—and somehow, much more powerful. They stay. They sit next to you while you unravel. They don't rush you to feel better. They don't demand that you make sense of your pain. They simply exist beside you, and in doing so, they make it a little more bearable.

They are the ones who notice the small changes. When your laugh doesn't quite reach your eyes. When you've gone quiet for too long. When you start avoiding the things you once loved. They know something's wrong not because you told them, but because they see you—not just the version you show the world, but the real, raw you.

They are the ones who offer small comforts that speak louder than any words. A hand resting on yours when your own fingers won't stop trembling. A cup of tea placed beside you, still warm, still waiting. A text that says, "I love you. No matter what today looks like." A blanket wrapped around your shoulders without asking if you're cold, just knowing that maybe today, you need it.

Support, in its truest form, isn't loud. It doesn't shout its presence. It doesn't make a big show. It whispers, "I see you. I'm not leaving." And in a world where so much can feel uncertain, that whisper can be the most grounding sound there is.

There's something deeply human about needing someone—not in a dependent way, but in the quiet way that says, "I can stand, but it's easier when you're next to me." We all have moments where the world feels like too much, when grief claws at our chest or fear tightens our throat. In those moments, having someone who doesn't flinch from your pain, who doesn't back away when you're not your best self—that kind of love can be transformative.

Because it tells you, in all the ways that matter: You are not alone.

And isn't that what we all want, deep down? Not someone to rescue us. Not someone to make everything okay. But someone who will walk beside us when things are not okay. Someone who chooses us not only when we're glowing, happy, and thriving—but also when we're quiet, lost, or falling apart.

A supportive partner doesn't always know the right thing to say. Sometimes, they say the wrong thing. Sometimes they're silent. But their presence says what words can't. They are there. They are trying. They care.

They see your tired eyes and instead of saying, "You look tired," they offer you a moment of peace. A soft pillow. A warm hug. A simple, "Let me take care of you tonight."

They hear your silence and instead of asking, "What's wrong?" they just sit with you, no pressure, no rush. Just the space to be. To feel. To breathe.

And over time, those small acts—the quiet loyalty, the patient listening, the soft reminders of love—they start to build something unshakable. A foundation that doesn't crumble when life gets hard. A connection that deepens through the storms, not despite them.

This kind of love is not flashy. It doesn't always come with grand romantic gestures or passionate declarations. It comes in the form of showing up. Again and again. It's the love that says, "Even when it's hard to love yourself, I will love you."

And sometimes, just knowing that can keep you going.

But not all stories end the way we hope.

Sometimes, even the deepest love can't shield us from tragedy. When illness comes quietly in the night and won't be reasoned with. When someone you love more than life itself fades, little by little, and there's nothing you can do to stop it.

For Corinne and me, it began quietly—without warning, without fanfare, on a gray morning in 2003. I remember the sterile scent of the dialysis room, the hum of machines, and the sound of my own breathing. My body was heavy, slow. I had just started dialysis that day, and though I'd been told what to expect, nothing could have prepared me for the exhaustion that followed.

But I didn't rest.

As soon as the session ended, I went to find Corinne. Something had been off. She hadn't been feeling well—nothing specific, just a lingering fatigue, a kind of ache she couldn't quite describe. That morning, her condition had worsened. She'd collapsed, and they rushed her to the hospital. I remember thinking, "It can't be serious." We had two young daughters—5 and 10—at home waiting for us. We had plans. She was too young, too full of life.

But when I walked into her hospital room, everything changed. The look on the doctor's face, the silence between words, the weight behind the explanation. Cancer. It felt like the walls were closing in.

I stood there, already physically drained, and tried to absorb the reality of her diagnosis. Corinne, my partner, my love, my best friend, had cancer. We didn't cry - not right away. We held hands and just looked at each other, stunned into silence.

The year that followed became a series of overlapping crises. Dialysis was a lifeline for me, but it also stripped away energy, clarity, and time. Every session felt like a battle just to make it through the day. Meanwhile, Corinne began treatment—chemotherapy, tests, consultations with specialists. Our house was filled with appointment reminders, prescription bottles, and the sound of quiet worry.

Despite everything, we tried to maintain a sense of normalcy for our daughters. We never used the word "dying" in front of them. We said things like "Mommy is sick" or "Daddy's kidneys need help." We answered their questions as gently as we could. They were old enough to feel the fear, but too young to fully understand it. I remember them clinging to us more often, seeking comfort in bedtime stories, in hugs that lasted a little longer.

There were moments of light, brief and golden. A Saturday morning when Corinne felt strong enough to make pancakes. A laugh shared over an old memory. Watching the girls dance in the living room, lost in their own innocent world. Those moments reminded us of what we were fighting for.

Through it all, I kept working. It may sound strange, but my professional life—consulting, teaching, working on international innovation projects—was both a burden and a blessing. It gave me something to focus on outside the chaos, a thread of continuity from the life we had before. But it was also a daily test of endurance. I would fly overseas, deliver a lecture or lead a workshop, and then come home to IV bags, Corinne's side effects, and my own medical routine. Every day was a tightrope walk between strength and sorrow.

In January 2004, a new door opened. A kidney became available. I remember the moment I got the call. My heart raced—not just with hope, but with guilt. How could I celebrate a second chance when Corinne was getting weaker by the day?

The transplant surgery was difficult but successful. For the first time in months, I felt my body beginning to come back to life. I could breathe a little easier, move a little more freely. It was a fragile, precious gift.

But when I returned home from the hospital, the contrast between our paths became painfully clear. Corinne was thinner. Her voice was softer. Her strength, once so bright, was flickering. I wanted to give her my new health, to trade places, to stop the inevitable. But all I could do was hold her hand, help with her treatments, and try to create moments of peace in our unraveling world.

Our home became a crossroads of healing and decline. We were surrounded by medical equipment—machines, infusion poles, and pillboxes organized by the days of the week. The girls would tiptoe around it all, their eyes wide and their questions quiet. I often found myself whispering reassurances to them at night, telling them that Mommy would get better, that we were all okay – even when I didn't believe it.

Some nights I'd sit beside Corinne as she slept, her breath shallow, the lines of pain on her face more visible in the moonlight. I would think about all the years we'd shared—the laughter, the travels, the dreams we'd built—and how everything had narrowed to this room, this moment.

By late fall, we knew. The doctors were kind, but honest. Treatments had failed. There were no more options, just time. Corinne, ever the fighter, still smiled for the girls, still found joy in their stories, still thanked the nurses and asked about their families.

Christmas came quietly. We decorated the tree with the girls, trying to pretend it was like any other year. Corinne watched from the couch, a soft blanket wrapped around her shoulders, her eyes shining with both joy and sadness. She gave the girls one gift each—a hand-written letter, full of love, memories, and her hopes for their futures. I cried when I read mine.

Then came December 31st.

While the world around us prepared for celebrations, countdowns, and resolutions, we sat in silence. Corinne's breathing had become faint. The girls were asleep in their rooms. I held her hand and watched the minutes pass, the quiet tick of the clock loud in the stillness. There were no words left to say. Only presence. Only love.

The girls believed their mom would survive, even as she lay in a coma. Every day after school, I brought them to the hospital. They'd sit by her bedside, playing cards and chatting with her as if she might wake at any moment. That day was no different. We left the hospital around 5:30 PM. On the drive home, two of her close friends called me. Their voices shook as they told me—

At 6:00 PM, she exhaled one final time.

I didn't move. I sat there beside her, watching the new year arrive without her. Fireworks echoed in the distance. Somewhere, people were cheering, kissing, raising glasses. But in our home, time had stopped.

Her death on New Year's Eve wasn't just the loss of my wife. It was the closing of a chapter we had written together with every heartbeat, every shared sorrow, every burst of laughter in the darkest moments.

In the days that followed, I moved like a ghost through our home. I cared for the girls, answered the phone, and made arrangements. People came by with food and condolences. They called me strong. But I didn't feel strong. I felt broken.

And yet, there was something else. A thread that hadn't been cut. It was love. The love we'd built, the lessons we'd given our daughters, the life we'd fought for even as it unraveled. That love didn't end when Corinne died. It lived on in me, in our children, in every memory etched into the walls of our home.

Looking back, 2003–2004 wasn't just the hardest year of my life. It was the year we carried each other. Through sickness and fear. Through dialysis and chemo. Through hope and despair. We held on.

And when the time came to let go, we did it with love.

That year taught me that strength is not about never breaking—it's about breaking, and still showing up. It is about facing the impossible and finding something worth holding onto anyway.

Corinne passed, but her spirit never left. She's in the quiet courage of our daughters, in the way I keep moving forward, one step at a time.

That year, we lost so much. But we never lost each other.

Chapter 17: Love and Loss – Losing My First Wife, Corinne

2005 began with a silence I had never known before.

The kind that didn't just fill the house—it filled me. It was the silence of drawers that no longer opened in the morning, of footsteps that no longer crossed the hallway, of a voice I would never hear again calling my name from the kitchen. After Corinne died, time didn't stop. It dragged. It limped forward, heavy and uncooperative. Every day felt like a negotiation with pain: how much could I carry without breaking?

I was now a widower. That word didn't feel real on my tongue. It sounded like something out of a book or a movie, not something you are. But I was. I was a widower at forty-two, a father to two daughters who had just lost the only mother they'd ever know, and a man with a secondhand kidney beating time in his body while his heart struggled to follow along.

Grief is a strange companion. It doesn't scream. It whispers. It hides in ordinary moments – in a coffee cup left out on the counter, in a song that comes on the radio while you're driving, in a sock that turns up at the back of a drawer. And it arrives especially loud in the quiet of the night, when the world is still and your thoughts have nowhere to go but backwards.

The girls were nine and seven. Too young for this. Too young to know how to carry a loss like this one. I watched them try, in their own ways

– one holding it all in, the other spilling tears over breakfast. I tried to be both mother and father, but I was broken too. There were mornings when I couldn't find the strength to get out of bed. But I had to. Because someone had to pack lunches. Someone had to brush hair, sign homework, show up at school concerts, and sit at the edge of their beds while they asked questions I didn't have the answers to.

"Is Mommy watching us?"

"Why did she have to go?"

"Are you going to go too?"

I swallowed my pain like bitter medicine, day after day, because there was no other choice.

Sometimes, I found myself talking to Corinne in the dark. Whispering into the pillow. Telling her what the girls had done that day, what I was afraid of, how much I missed her laugh. Her presence lingered in the house, not in a haunted way, but in the way the sun stays on your skin long after the light has faded.

I didn't know then what healing would look like. I wasn't even sure if I believed in it. But I knew I had to survive, not just for me, but for them. They had already lost one parent. I couldn't let them lose two.

So, I kept going. One breakfast at a time. One bedtime story at a time. One breath at a time.

Work became my oxygen.

In the years that followed Corinne's passing – five, ten of them – I filled every hour I could with purpose. If I wasn't moving, I was remembering, and remembering was too painful. So I moved. I said yes to everything: projects, lectures, travel, late nights, and new ventures. I built teams across continents. I mentored young engineers who reminded me, in flashes, of what it felt like to dream before loss hardens you. I gave talks in Rome, Singapore, Vancouver, and São Paulo – airports became my second home, and I started measuring my years not in holidays or birthdays, but in boarding passes and deadlines.

Professionally, those were golden years. Some of the best work of my life happened in that window. I led teams that reimagined marine propulsion systems and energy-efficient hull designs. We pushed boundaries. We won awards. My name started appearing on panels, in journals, and in conference booklets printed on glossy paper. People introduced me with words like "visionary" or "pioneer," and I smiled politely each time, knowing full well that most days I felt more like a man hiding in plain sight.

Because the truth was, I wasn't chasing success. I was outrunning grief.

At night, in the stillness of a hotel room five thousand miles from home, the applause faded. The silence returned. I'd sit by the window and stare out at whatever skyline was visible, thinking not about the day's triumphs, but about whether the girls had eaten dinner, if I'd remembered to call, if I was doing any of this right. Sometimes I'd hear

Corinne's voice in my head, quick, warm, teasing—and it would slice through me with such suddenness that I'd lose my breath.

Back home, the girls were growing faster than I could process. I blinked, and suddenly one was in high school and the other was asking to borrow my car. They were becoming strong, smart, quietly resilient. I'd like to say I was always there, fully present, but I wasn't. I was there in the way a lighthouse is there: visible, reliable, but always at a distance.

I thought I was protecting them by keeping busy. By staying strong. But there's a cost to hiding your wounds for too long. They harden. They calcify. And before you know it, you forget what it's like to feel anything fully.

Still, the work kept me afloat. It gave me structure, identity, and motion. I was building something, even if I didn't always know what. Maybe that's what kept me going, not the belief that joy would return, but the stubborn hope that, if I kept building long enough, life might one day surprise me again.

And eventually, it did.

By early 2015, I felt it, quietly at first, like a whisper under the skin.

Fatigue crept in slowly, like a tide returning after years of calm. The energy that had fueled my long days and late flights began to flicker. The clarity I relied on in meetings, the ability to process fast, speak clearly, and lead with certainty, started slipping through my fingers. I brushed it off at first. Maybe I was just tired. Maybe it was stress, or age, or grief catching up to me. But somewhere deep down, I knew.

This was something else entirely. I'd lived with borrowed time for over a decade. I'd seen my daughters grow into young women. I'd buried my wife. I'd spoken at global forums and built things that might outlive me. I wasn't young anymore. I wasn't naive. And I wasn't afraid, not in the same way.

What I felt was weariness. A deep, bone-level exhaustion, not just from the physical decline, but from the emotional toll of circling back to a place I thought I had left behind. But now I carried a different kind of knowledge with me, not just of suffering, but of survival. Not just of loss, but of what can still be found on the other side of it.

I knew what it meant to fight, not just to stay alive, but to live with meaning, with depth, with love, even when your body betrays you and life steals what matters most.

So, I didn't panic. I didn't spiral. I grieved, yes. Quietly. In my own way. I grieved the return of limitation, the loss of normalcy, the reminder that no amount of strength or intellect or success can outpace mortality. But I also resolved—again—to keep moving. To keep showing up. For my daughters. For my work. For the chance, however slim, that another door might open.

There wasn't a single turning point. No fireworks. No great epiphany. Just time—long, quiet stretches of time. Days that looked ordinary but felt different. A slow reentry into life after so much had fallen apart.

I didn't come back to myself all at once. It was a gradual return. One breath, one step, one small act of showing up. Not because I felt ready—but because something inside me refused to give up. It was less about strength and more about instinct. Survival, yes—but also something deeper. A stubborn commitment to keep moving forward, even if I wasn't sure what forward looked like.

Corinne's memory didn't fade with the years—it settled into me. Not like a shadow, but like a constant presence. A softness in the background of everything. She was there in quiet mornings, in the music I still played, in the way I spoke to our daughters. I didn't try to "let go." I carried her. And I began to realize that carrying her didn't hold me back—it kept me grounded.

The girls were growing up fast, each becoming her own kind of strong. I watched them navigate the world with a quiet fierceness, with laughter that sometimes echoed their mother's. I saw her in their stubbornness, their tenderness, the way they held space for others. And in witnessing that, I found a strange kind of peace—not closure, not the end of grief, but a new rhythm.

Life wasn't the same, and I wasn't the same man who had walked into that first storm. But I was still here. Still learning how to live with loss without letting it define me. Still learning how to give love even when I felt empty.

It wasn't a dramatic rebirth. It was more like a long exhale. A quiet permission to keep becoming. To stay open—to pain, to healing, to the possibility that maybe there was still something left in me to offer.

And maybe that was enough.

Looking back on those years, it's hard to put into words just how much they stripped away—and what, in turn, they revealed.

They tested me. Every part of me. My heart, stretched by grief and loneliness and the sheer weight of showing up day after day for two young girls who still needed their dad, even when he wasn't sure he had anything left to give. My mind, too – pushed to the edge by uncertainty, yet still expected to lead, to solve, to deliver. And my spirit, battered, humbled, but never broken.

And somehow, through it all, I didn't just survive. I softened. I slowed down. I started listening more carefully to people, to silence, to what mattered. I became more patient, less certain. More grateful, less hungry to prove anything. I started to understand that strength wasn't always about holding it together; it was often about letting go, letting others in, letting love speak where words failed.

Empathy became a second skin. I could sit with someone in pain and not rush to fix it. I could hold space for the questions that had no answers. I had learned – through fire, through failure – what it meant to truly see someone, and to be seen.

And in that space of stillness, I realized something else: I wasn't walking forward alone. Corinne's spirit was with me, quiet but constant, like a hand on my back on the days when I felt too tired to keep going. And in front of me, always, were my daughters – their lives unfolding, their futures unwritten, waiting for me not just to witness, but to guide, to bless, to be present for.

There was no triumph here, no ribbon at the finish line. Just life. Raw and unscripted. But also, somehow, more luminous than before.

And as I stood at the edge of what came next, I didn't feel afraid. I felt ready.

Ready to keep walking, with memory, with purpose, with love.

Chapter 18: Finding Strength — A New Chapter Begins

The house felt different now. It wasn't just the silence, though, that alone had grown so dense it pressed against my chest. It was the absence. Her laughter no longer echoed down the hallway, and the scent of her favorite perfume no longer lingered in the bedroom. The chair by the window—her chair—sat untouched. The stillness was not peace; it was a grief that had settled into the walls, into the air, into the very structure of the life we had built together.

Every morning, I reached across the bed — out of habit, not hope — and then I'd remember. And then it would begin again. Another day that didn't feel like anything. No momentum, no purpose. Just the familiar thud of loss landing in my chest.

I did the things I was supposed to do. Made tea, though I never drank it. Picked up books and let them sit open in my lap, unread. The radio stayed off. I couldn't bear music — not even the gentle stuff. Even soft piano felt like it might break something inside me that I was barely keeping taped together.

People tried. "Time heals." "She's in a better place." I nodded, and I thanked them. But they weren't there for the stillness of that room. They didn't see the hours I spent sitting on the edge of the bed, just... there. Not even crying. Just staring at my slippers. The air in the room felt like it was waiting too — as if it expected her to walk in, any minute.

The house made all its usual creaks, but now they sounded wrong. No voice from the hallway. No quiet laugh from the kitchen. No trace of her scent in the bathroom — the shampoo she always bought, even though she said it was too expensive. I kept expecting small things: the soft clink of her spoon in a yogurt cup, the whisper of a page turning. But the house stayed silent.

The girls were with me in the house. Our beautiful villa in Valbonne, once filled with Corinne's laughter and soft music, now felt still, as if even the walls were holding their breath. They were so young, too young to fully grasp the depth of what we had lost, yet somehow, they carried themselves with quiet courage. They tried to be strong, perhaps for me, perhaps just to keep the days moving forward.

I saw it in their small gestures, in how they spoke gently, how they played without making too much noise, how they watched me when they thought I wasn't looking. I loved them for that. And I also hated myself for not being able to meet them in that quiet bravery.

Some mornings, I couldn't speak. Other times, I forced myself to smile through breakfast, pretending things were fine, even though everything in me was fractured. But they knew. Children always do. Even at that age, they understood something had broken in the world.

We lived inside that absence together, not talking about it much, not knowing how, but slowly, carefully, we were learning how to breathe again.

Then one morning — I don't know how long it had been — I opened the curtains. Just pulled them back. I hadn't touched them since the day we lost her. I don't even know why I did it. The light that came in was too bright. It made me flinch. The world outside hadn't paused. That felt cruel. It had been weeks since light had filled the room, and as it streamed in, it caught the dust in the air, illuminating thousands of tiny particles dancing in the sun. That simple act—pulling back the curtains—felt like an act of defiance, a quiet rebellion against the darkness that had taken hold. The light didn't heal me, but it reminded me that the world was still moving, still breathing, still beautiful, even in her absence.

Still, something shifted. Not hope, not clarity. Just a twitch somewhere inside me, an urge not to disappear. I wasn't ready to "move on" — whatever that means. But I did feel a pull. A need to move. Somewhere.

I didn't feel brave. I didn't feel healed. But I was trying.

Grief is not something you move through like a tunnel, emerging into the light on the other side. It's something you learn to carry. Some days it is heavy, suffocating. Other days, it rests quietly beside you, a reminder of what was lost and what was loved. It reshapes you. It softens your voice, slows your step, and yet it sharpens your awareness of every small joy, every passing grace.

People talk about resilience as if it is a fire—bold, bright, and loud. But I learned that real resilience is often quiet. It's the moment you get out of bed, even when your legs tremble. It's making coffee even though the smell reminds you of her. It's showing up for your children, for your work, for yourself, even when every part of you is breaking. That is the strength no one sees. That is the strength that matters most.

Later that day, I opened my laptop. Dozens of emails. I scrolled out of habit. I wasn't reading, not really. Until one subject line stopped me: an old friend, now working with a sustainable resort in the Bahamas. They needed help — something about infrastructure, preservation, and local outreach. The kind of project I used to jump at.

I read the email. Then I closed the laptop. I couldn't. Or I didn't trust myself to say yes. Not yet.

Two days later, I laced up real shoes and walked to the end of the block. That was it. Just a slow loop, and back. But it felt strange. Like gravity was stronger than it had been. The air smelled faintly of lemons, or something like them. A boy rode past on a bike, shouted something, and grinned. And somehow, I smiled back.

That night, I opened the email again. I still didn't know what I wanted. But I wrote back. "I'll think about it," I said. That was all.

A week later, I was boarding a flight.

Just me. A small bag. A sketchbook. And her scarf — the soft blue one she always wore on breezy nights by the sea. I didn't even mean to pack it, but I needed her near.

Landing in Nassau was surreal. Not exciting. Not exactly sad. Just... calm. The ocean below looked like dark glass, the clouds drifting slowly, their shadows slipping over the surface. I remembered our first visit. She'd danced barefoot in the sand that night and claimed the sea held memories. I could still hear her laugh and see that ridiculous straw hat she wore for sun protection, but she insisted she hated it.

In the Bahamas, two places became sanctuaries. Nassau, with its colonial charm and rhythm of everyday life, offered me peace. I walked the historic streets near Government House, sat in quiet under the stone arches of the Queen's Staircase, and listened to the soft Caribbean waters near Potter's Cay. There, the sea spoke a different language— gentler, more forgiving. And I listened. Sometimes, I would sit for hours, watching boats glide past, letting the gentle lapping of water against dock pilings remind me of the constancy of movement and of the tides that continue no matter what we endure.

But it was Eleuthera that reached deepest. The Glass Window Bridge, where the wild Atlantic crashes into the tranquil Caribbean, became my metaphor. That raw contrast mirrored my own soul—grief and renewal. Long walks on pink-sand beaches became rituals. In that silence, I began to rebuild.

I was approached to consult on a small resort project—sustainable energy, water systems, and marine integration. The work was meaningful. Human. It bridged my mind and my heart. I remember sketching designs under palm canopies, laughing with locals, and finding comfort in the hands-on act of creation. The sea was no longer just scenery. It was collaborator, witness, and healer.

The project wasn't flashy. There was no big press release, no social media splash. Just a piece of land with memory in its soil and salt in its breeze — and a team determined to get it right. They asked if I'd consult. I said yes without hesitation.

After the Bahamas, I flew east.

Not for a project, not for business — not at first. I just needed to go somewhere that once felt like home. Somewhere that had held a different version of me, before the weight of grief settled into my bones.

Our house had been in Valbonne for many years, and although we often thought about moving, we never did—not until the girls left for university, one in the USA and the other in England. Valbonne was exactly as I remembered it, and yet somehow completely different. That's what time does. The cobbled streets hadn't changed, nor had the morning light spilling across the stone walls. But I had. I wasn't walking those streets with Corinne anymore, hand in hand, laughing about how the French serve their coffee too small. This time, I was alone. And yet... not entirely.

I went to the medieval village of Valbonne, then wandered to the bakery where we used to buy croissants and speak broken French with a kind woman named Yvette, who always gave us an extra pastry "just because." She was no longer there. Instead, a young woman—the spouse of the owner's son—stood behind the counter. She didn't know me, but she smiled warmly as if she did, and handed me a warm almond croissant along with a small paper bag of fresh, hot bread.

"You look tired," she said. "You should rest."

From Valbonne, I made my way to Sophia Antipolis, where the headquarters of my global group in Research and Development, Engineering, and Naval Architecture were located. Part of my team was based in France, another part in Monaco, and others spread across the USA, Germany, Cyprus, and Italy. The place still hummed with energy— a curious blend of ancient olive groves and cutting-edge tech campuses. It had been years since I'd set foot there, yet I could still recall the exact spot where I first pitched my sustainable transport concept to a skeptical room of engineers. I had worn a blue shirt that day—freshly ironed by Corinne.

I didn't reach out to anyone at first. I thought I'd just walk the grounds, maybe sit in on a lecture if they let me. But somehow, word got around. Emails trickled in. People I hadn't spoken to in years — some I barely remembered — asking if I had time to meet, to grab coffee, to hear my thoughts on a new marine propulsion concept or a modular urban grid prototype. I didn't know what to say at first. Part of me still felt suspended, as though I hadn't earned my voice back yet. But slowly, I said yes.

Conversations turned into whiteboard sessions. Walks turned into planning sketches on napkins. It wasn't pressure — it was curiosity. There was no deadline, no presentation looming, just that gentle nudge of innovation rising to the surface again, like a muscle remembering how to move. My mind felt awake in a way it hadn't in months. I wasn't chasing success. I was chasing questions again. The ones that mattered.

In Monaco, I stood on the harbor wall and watched the yachts sway against their lines. Their hulls gleamed in the sun, impossibly sleek, almost arrogant. I thought about what we'd dreamed of building once — not just beautiful machines, but vessels that could move through water with intelligence and humility. The world didn't need more noise. It needed grace.

I didn't stay long. Just enough to walk the old roads, to feel the weight of my own footsteps echoing against old ambitions. France had done what I hoped it would: reminded me who I was before the loss. It reminded me that I still carried that version of myself inside, quieter perhaps, but not gone.

California offered a different elegance. In Newport Beach, I saw electric yachts glide through the water—quiet, efficient, forward-thinking. I advised on hull shapes, propulsion systems, and battery efficiency. These boats weren't just machines; they were symbols of a gentler future. In their silence, I found a reflection of who I was becoming.

I walked the docks alone in the early mornings, listening to the soft hum of life beginning, remembering who I was when I first dreamed of transforming the maritime world.

Then came Miami. Always in motion.

If California was reflection, Miami was electricity. The Design District pulsed with color. Brickell vibrated with ambition. Everyone had an idea. Everyone had a prototype, a pitch, a dream. And strangely, it didn't exhaust me. It invited me in.

I walked the docks alone in the early mornings, listening to the soft hum of life beginning, remembering who I was when I first dreamed of transforming the maritime world. I sat on rooftops, consulted in boardrooms, and wandered through neighborhoods where architecture, fashion, and technology whispered to each other. I offered insights on sustainability, on resilience, on the marriage of design and purpose. It was familiar. Yet it was new.

I met with architects—young and hungry. Planners with bold visions for heat resilience, modular housing, and vertical farms. We talked about materials. We talked about smart buildings that could breathe with the climate. I didn't come with a resumé or a proposal. I just listened. And when it felt right, I offered a thought, a question, a challenge. It felt like music again—that back-and-forth of minds in motion.

Everywhere I went, people still turned to me for guidance— engineers, entrepreneurs, builders. And slowly, I allowed myself to believe: I was still useful. Still building. Still capable of shaping something that would last.

That talk turned into another. And another.

Soon, I was speaking again. On stages. In studios. Aboard ships.

I hadn't realized how much I missed it — not the spotlight, but the connection. The way a story could land with someone and crack open a new line of thinking. The way a question from the back of the room could make me rethink something I thought I knew. It wasn't performance. It was dialogue. A kind of shared building — not with steel or carbon fiber, but with words, with presence.

Teaching wasn't about handing down knowledge anymore. It was about passing along scars and the lessons they taught me. About standing in the in-between — between science and soul, between the past and what's still possible.

That's where I found my footing again.

Each day was full—not in the frantic way, but in the meaningful way. I'd wake up before dawn, walk through Wynwood as the city blinked itself awake, and let ideas drift in with the heat. I didn't feel like I was rebuilding myself. That implies you start from rubble. No. I was reweaving something—adding threads. Stronger, wiser, different.

This wasn't about chasing purpose. It was about feeling useful again. Feeling alive in the work. And knowing, deep down, that Corinne would've smiled to see me like this—curious again, engaged, with graphite smudges on my fingers and wind in my hair.

If purpose gave me ground, my daughters gave me direction.

Rebecca was the first to call — or rather, to answer when I finally found the courage to reach out. Her voice was steady, gentle. She asked how I was. I told her I was still figuring that out. She said, "That's fair."

She'd always been the cautious one. Thoughtful. Private. As a child, she'd draw trees over and over again, always rooted, always with a swing hanging from one branch. I asked her once what the swing was for. She said, "So the tree remembers to hold joy." She's like that — observant in ways people often miss.

Our bond didn't come back in a rush. It returned in silence. In long walks where we didn't say much. In texts she sent late at night: a poem, a photo of a sunrise, a recipe for lentil soup. There was pain beneath the surface. She had lost Corinne too — her lovely mother, more than just an emotional anchor. We both had to learn each other anew, not as father and child, but as two people trying to make room for one another's grief.

As the years passed, Thelma grew into her own life — strong, curious, quietly determined. Our relationship changed with her, evolving from the familiar patterns of childhood into something more tentative, more adult. We were learning how to meet each other again, this time on equal ground.

When I visited her at Hartpury University in Gloucester, England where she was working as a horse science researcher — she didn't say much. She simply led me straight to the stables. No small talk. No awkward hugs. Just: "Come see this incredible horse we're training for jumping. She showed me a sample the size of a dinner plate. "It's soft," she said, "but it can absorb twelve times more pressure than concrete."

That was Thelma in a sentence.

She didn't want me to talk about the past. She wanted to show me what she was building now. And I understood that. Sometimes rebuilding a relationship means working side by side before you speak heart to heart.

Let me tell you something about her. From her earliest steps into the stables, Thelma seemed destined for the rhythm of hooves, the scent of hay and leather, and the thrill of soaring over obstacles with elegance and power. What began as a childhood passion for animals grew into a lifelong devotion to show jumping, a sport where grace, courage, and calculation unite. Over the years, Thelma's journey carried her to arenas across France, Italy, Spain, Belgium, the United Kingdom, Ireland, and other European countries. Each competition she took part in added another chapter to a story written with sweat, discipline, and unwavering love. In every place she has competed, from sunlit Mediterranean circuits to the misty fields of northern Europe, she has brought with her not only talent but a quiet fire that inspires admiration.

I am genuinely amazed by how Thelma's strength lied not only in her physical ability but in her unique connection with her horses. She treated them not as tools for sport, but as partners, companions whose spirits she listened to and whose trust she earned. The moments before a round, when she adjusted the reins, felt the muscles tense beneath the saddle, and whispered calm encouragement, were as important as the moment of the jump itself. To watch her ride was to witness a conversation without words: the steady hand, the gentle leg, the poised body guiding an animal weighing hundreds of kilos with nothing more than confidence, kindness, and shared rhythm. Every takeoff was a leap of faith, every landing a triumph of balance, and in between lied the poetry of flight, horse and rider suspended together, as if time itself holds its breath for them.

Her competitions across Europe demanded courage. In France, she faced technical courses with their precise distances and sharp turns, where her mathematical mind transformed calculation into instinct. In Italy, she embraced the fiery energy of southern arenas, where the warmth of the crowd matched her own passion. In Spain, she soared beneath the wide Iberian skies, each round reflecting her determination to rise higher. Belgium, with its long equestrian traditions, tested her resilience against seasoned competitors. The UK and Ireland, with their deep love for horses, felt like a return to the roots of the sport itself, where she proved not only her skill but her unshakable spirit. Each country brought new challenges, yet in every arena Thelma remained steadfast: focused, fearless, and radiant in the bond she shared with her horses.

For Thelma, show jumping was more than medals or rankings. It was a metaphor for life: the courage to face obstacles head-on, the wisdom to measure the stride, the discipline to prepare, and the daring to leap without hesitation. Every refusal, every fallen pole, every setback met not with defeat but with renewed resolve, a reminder that strength is born not only from victory but from rising after the fall. Her love for animals and her deep compassion meant that she never saw herself alone on the course; there was always a partnership, a dialogue, a respect for the living being beneath her. That empathy, combined with her sharp mind in mathematics and physics, gives her an edge: she calculated angles and strides almost instinctively, but with the heart of someone who rode not only with the head but also with the soul.

There was a romance in her story, not only in the elegance of show jumping itself, with its polished boots, shining saddles, and the drama of the arena, but in the way she chose to live her life. She embodied resilience wrapped in sweetness, strength softened by compassion, and ambition guided by humility. To watch her ride was to see the essence of who she was: a young woman capable of soaring above obstacles not just in sport, but in life. She carried the rare gift of uniting science and spirit, discipline and love, power and grace. Thelma was more than a competitor; she was a vision of what it meant to live passionately, to love deeply, and to leap boldly into every horizon.

When we sat on the balcony that night, drinking tea, she leaned her head on my shoulder and said, "You seem more... calm. Less haunted." I didn't know how to respond. I just nodded and whispered, "I'm trying."

Since then, my daughters have become my compass. Not by demanding anything, but simply by being present.

Every opportunity that comes my way — a speaking invite, a design proposal, a project in a far-off place — I run it through a quiet filter now: *Will this make me a better father? Will this help me stay whole, so I can show up for them?*

They don't need me to fix their lives. They just need to know I'm steady. That I'm not drifting anymore.

And I'm not.

There was no moment of revelation. No epiphany under the stars or sudden awakening with morning light. It happened the way flowers bloom in spring—so slowly that you don't realize it's happening until one day you notice the fragrance in the air.

I had built a quiet sort of armor. Not out of bitterness or fear, but necessity. After Corinne passed, something in me closed—not harshly, but like a door gently pulled shut in a room that had gone too cold. I needed space to breathe, to grieve, to reassemble the broken architecture of my life. At first, even the thought of letting someone in again felt disloyal to her memory, as if moving forward would somehow erase what we had built.

But time and beauty have their own way of reaching you.

It began in small, almost imperceptible ways. An early morning walk along the beach in Eleuthera, the sky half-colored with sunrise. The sound of children laughing in the courtyard of a French café. The way light caught the surface of a model yacht I'd helped design in

California—pure, clean, purposeful. These weren't distractions. They were reminders. That the world still moved. That there were things still worth noticing. That joy wasn't betrayal.

One evening, after speaking to a group of young engineers onboard a ship, I sat alone near the stern and listened to the sea stretch itself into the dark. And I remember thinking—*if I can still feel this much peace, then perhaps I'm not as closed off as I thought.*

Grief hadn't left me. It never would. But it had started to change shape. No longer a sharp edge pressing into my side—it had softened into something quieter. A presence, not a wound.

And into that softened space, love made room—not by crashing through, but by waiting, patiently, like a gentle tide reclaiming the shore.

We met in Miami, though it didn't feel like the kind of place people meet for the first time. It felt like a location meant for continuation—of conversations, of ideas, of something already beginning to form.

There was a design conference at the Pérez Art Museum. I was there on a panel about sustainable waterfront development, more out of curiosity than ambition. The event was sleek, full of bright minds and polished shoes, and in the hum of voices and clink of glasses, I noticed her.

Not in the way one notices beauty. In the way one notices presence.

She wasn't trying to command the room. She was listening—really listening—to someone speak about acoustics in architectural spaces. Head slightly tilted, eyes steady. There was a calm in her that I instantly recognized. Not performance, not posturing. Just presence.

Later, we were introduced through a mutual friend—with some overlap in our work with marine spatial design. Her name was Monica, though she mentioned, almost offhandedly, that her full name was Monica. "My family still calls me that," she said with a smile that seemed to hold both stories and restraint. I didn't ask why. I didn't need to.

We talked. Not for long. But it was real. About design, yes—materials, wind flow, light. But also about rhythm. About silence. About how cities breathe when they're built with care.

She had a voice like a clear stream—low, even, but warm. And in that first conversation, I felt something I hadn't felt in a long time: I wasn't explaining myself. I wasn't performing. I wasn't protecting anything. I was just there. And so was she.

There was no follow-up flirtation. No text that night. Just a sense of... possibility. Like someone had opened a window in a room I'd forgotten was sealed.

We met again a week later for coffee. Talked longer. Walked a bit. Our pace matched, not rushed. Comfortable. We spoke about the things that mattered to us—not in the curated way people often do when first meeting, but with a kind of casual honesty that only comes when two people are ready for it.

She asked me about Corinne. Not immediately. But when she did, it wasn't out of curiosity—it was out of respect. I told her the truth, as much as I could in one sitting. She didn't interrupt. She didn't try to fix it. She simply listened. And when I finished, she looked at me—not with pity, not with longing, just with clarity.

"I think grief teaches us how to hold more," she said. "Not less."

It wasn't a dramatic moment. But it was a turning point.

Over time, we continued to meet—always with ease, never with pressure. It was never about rushing toward something. It was about recognizing what was already present.

She wasn't a replacement. And she didn't ask me to be new. She met me exactly where I was—weathered, thoughtful, alive.

And slowly, without naming it, we began something.

Not just a relationship, but a reorientation. A return to openness. To mutual respect. To emotional fluency. The kind of connection where nothing needs to be proven. Where each person holds their own ground, but chooses to walk beside the other.

As that chapter of my life began to unfold—quietly, sincerely—I realized something:

The deepest strength doesn't lie in rebuilding what was lost. It lies in being willing to begin again.

And I was beginning.

Chapter 19: Voyages of Renewal

It didn't come as a job offer. Not exactly. It came more like a ripple — soft, unassuming, and strangely familiar.

The call came from a friend, someone in the cruise industry who knew me not just by title or resumé, but by story. He had seen me through various stages of my life — as an engineer, a lecturer, a survivor — and he said something that, at the time, I didn't quite know how to receive: *"Carmine, people need to hear you. Not just what you know. But what you've lived."*

For years, I had spoken to rooms filled with experts — project directors, naval engineers, research councils. I was used to diagrams, prototypes, timelines, and equations. But this was different. This wasn't about systems or structures. This was about stories — about memory, history, the sea. I hesitated, unsure whether my voice could travel beyond the precision of engineering and into the more vulnerable waters of storytelling.

But the sea has always had a strange way of calling me back — not just to its surface, but to something deeper in myself.

I had spent a lifetime in and around ships. As a cadet navigating the Suez Canal, I had felt the pulse of global commerce. In Europe and the U.S., I had led teams in high-level innovation, building vessels that would sail through Arctic ice or carry millions across oceans. My relationship with ships had always been layered — professional, yes, but also deeply emotional. The sea was never just a workplace. It was a compass. A metaphor. A mirror.

And so, when that invitation came — an offer to join a luxury cruise as a Resident Historian — it felt less like a career move and more like an evolution. I wasn't building vessels anymore. I was rebuilding myself.

At first, the shift was awkward. I remember sitting at my desk, trying to outline my first lecture, wondering how to speak about maritime empires without sounding like a textbook. I thought of the great naval powers — Venice, Carthage, Britannia — and then paused. What was it I really wanted to say? That these ships carried gold? Troops? Trade routes?

No — what they carried was us. Our ambitions, our fears, our migrations, our mythologies.

That's when I began to understand my role not as a lecturer, but as a storyteller. A translator of time.

The sea had taught me this language — the language of movement, risk, discovery — and now I was being asked to share it not with engineers, but with travelers. People who had lived full lives, who were seeking meaning on the open water. And perhaps, like me, they were still trying to find a way forward.

So I said yes.

And with that simple word, something shifted in me.

It wasn't just about a new opportunity. I was stepping fully into all that I had become — the engineer, the historian, the survivor. The man who knew what it meant to rebuild, not with steel and code, but with memory, perspective, and presence.

I didn't yet know that this would be the start of a new life.

Nor could I have imagined that, not long after boarding that ship, I would find Monica — and with her, a kind of love I thought I had buried long ago.

But before all that, there was this moment: quiet, uncertain, and full of possibility.

The sea was calling again. And this time, I was ready to answer — not with a blueprint, but with a story.

I've always been drawn to ships — not just their architecture or mechanics, but their meaning.

Even as a young boy tracing ship silhouettes in the margins of my schoolbooks, I sensed there was more to them than steel and steam. They carried stories — not just cargo. Every vessel was a kind of floating civilization, a moving fragment of history and hope. The sea was never just water; it was memory, migration, mythology. And ships were the keepers of it all.

This was what I tried to capture in my early cruise lectures.

At first, I overprepared — charts, timelines, technical trivia. I approached those lectures as I had approached conferences for decades. But the room was different. These weren't naval architects or project engineers. These were travelers. Retirees, artists, teachers, widows. People with quiet questions in their eyes. People who weren't just here for facts. They were looking for meaning.

My first talk — on the rise and fall of maritime Venice — went... flat. I watched eyes glaze over as I dove into trade routes and naval formations. The words were sharp, but the connection wasn't there. I could feel it. The kind of silence that doesn't listen — it merely waits for time to pass.

I remember walking back to my cabin that day, feeling defeated. I knew the material. I had lived it, studied it, and mapped it. But I had missed the heart of it.

So the next morning, I started over. I threw away the slides and opened with a memory — the sound of creaking steel below deck as a young cadet, my fingers wrapped around a mug of scalding tea, staring out at the churning Mediterranean in the dead of night. I spoke about loneliness at sea. About the human cost of empire. About what it meant to be a tiny life on a vast ocean, caught between ambition and wonder.

And something shifted.

People leaned in. Eyes lit up. Afterwards, a woman in her seventies came up to me, eyes misty, and said, *"You reminded me of my father. He was a sailor. I never understood him... until today."*

That was the moment I understood what these lectures were really about.

They weren't about ships. Not really. They were about *us*. About how we move — across borders, across generations, across the unknown. Ships just happen to be the metaphor. They're the stage, but we're the story.

From then on, I spoke less like a professor and more like a person. I shared tales of shipwrecks not for the technical intrigue, but for what they reveal about resilience. I spoke of the Atlantic as a scar, tracing centuries of forced migrations and forgotten names. I spoke of the immigrant ships — leaking, overcrowded, determined — and how my own family once boarded such a vessel, searching for a better life.

And slowly, something beautiful happened. The audience began to speak back.

They told me their stories — of ancestors lost at sea, of loves found aboard liners, of journals tucked away in trunks, still stained with salt. We built something together in those rooms. A kind of oral museum. A living archive of memory, emotion, and connection.

It humbled me.

To think, after all these years building ships and systems, I had finally found the soul of them — not in a schematic, but in a story. Not on a dry dock, but in the heart of someone listening.

Ships are cultural vessels. They hold more than fuel and freight. They carry longing. They carry grief. They carry the wild, unspoken dreams of everyone who's ever stood at the edge of a shore and wondered what lies beyond.

And so, lecture by lecture, I stepped into a new kind of role — not as a teacher, but as a companion. A witness. A fellow traveler speaking across the tides of time.

This was more than work. It was healing.

And it was just the beginning.

Not all ships are created equal. That much became clear quickly.

In the early days of my speaking circuit, I accepted just about every cruise invitation that came my way. I was eager — more curious, really — to see how different companies approached enrichment programming. Some promised "cultural depth," only to deliver a half-hour slideshow between Bingo and buffet. Others had genuine intentions, but no structure — a scatter of talks with little thread, no heartbeat.

Then came the Luxury Cruise Liner.

From the moment I stepped aboard, I felt something shift. It wasn't just the quiet elegance of the ship or the thoughtfully curated art. It was the people — the passengers, the staff, even the layout of the lecture halls. There was a reverence for learning, for meaningful conversation. I could sense it in the way guests lingered after talks, the way they asked questions not to impress but to understand. These weren't just vacationers — they were seekers.

My first voyage with Luxury Cruise Liner traced the ancient ports of the Mediterranean — Athens to Valletta, with whispers of Homer and empire in every breeze. I remember standing on the deck at sunrise as we approached Santorini, the cliffs glowing amber, and thinking: *This is what I was meant to do.*

Later, Crystal Cruises invited me aboard, and that opened another door. If Luxury Cruise Liner felt like a quiet salon of scholars, Crystal felt like a ballroom of cosmopolitan curiosity. The crowd was worldly, polished, playful. There was a rhythm to the way people moved from a lecture on ancient navigation straight into a Chopin recital or a wine tasting. But even here — amid the sparkle and shimmer — people craved depth. I gave a talk on the merchant fleets of Renaissance Florence, and a woman in a sequined shawl stayed after to tell me about her grandfather's shipping business out of Trieste. "Your story felt like mine," she said, touching her heart. That stayed with me.

Then came Explora.

Explora was...different. Still new. Still finding its sea legs. But there was something raw and open about it. A kind of creative restlessness. I joined them on a southern expedition — the cold blue mystery of Antarctica. No towns. No ports. Just ice, wind, silence.

And that silence did something to me.

Out there, past the edge of ordinary, I began to feel time differently. I'd give a lecture on Shackleton or whaling stations, and then spend hours just walking the outer decks, staring at the ice floes, my breath forming ghosts in the air. It was during one of those walks that I realized: these voyages weren't just about sharing knowledge. They were about receiving it. About letting the sea teach me something new.

Each ship became a kind of mirror. Luxury Cruise Liner reflected my mind — the scholar in me. Crystal awakened my past — the part that remembered elegance, legacy, the beauty of culture shared. Explora tapped into something deeper — the part of me still being born. Still seeking.

Somewhere in those decks and dining rooms, I stopped being just a lecturer and became a participant in something larger. These weren't cruises anymore. They were chapters. Movements in a larger symphony of renewal. Of becoming.

And the guests — oh, the guests. From retired diplomats to curious college students traveling with grandparents, their stories became part of the journey. One evening off the coast of Sicily, I sat on deck with a couple from Toronto who had just scattered their brother's ashes into the sea. We said nothing for a while. Just watched the stars come out. Finally, the woman turned to me and said, *"Thank you for reminding us that the sea remembers."*

That's when I understood the deeper gift of these voyages. The ship was not just a vehicle of travel — it was a platform for memory. For healing. For legacy.

Each time I stepped onboard, I stepped into a new version of myself. No longer just the engineer or the executive. I was the storyteller. The witness. The bridge between past and present.

The right voyage, I learned, isn't about the destination. It's about resonance — the way a place, a ship, a moment, meets you where you are in your life... and moves you somewhere else entirely.

And slowly, it became clear: I wasn't just sailing toward new lands.

I was sailing home.

Monica didn't arrive in my life like a dramatic swell or a crashing wave. She came like a tide—sure, natural, undeniable. There was no grand announcement, no seismic shift. Just a quiet unfolding, as if some deeper part of me had always known she was coming.

I used to wonder what it would look like to build a life with someone after 60. After so many chapters already lived—some joyful, some scarring—how does love begin again? How does it integrate, without overwhelming what's already been built?

With Monica, I found out.

She never treated my cruise lectures or maritime projects like a sideshow to her own world. And she was never the passive companion sipping champagne on deck while I worked. She had her own fire. Her own rhythm. Monica was building something too. A career, yes—but more than that, a philosophy. Her work in design, particularly her sensitivity to aesthetics, light, and space, translated into everything she touched. Hotels, clothing lines, art, even the way she arranged a breakfast table in a rented flat in Lisbon—everything bore her signature.

So when we traveled together, it wasn't just about being "on the road." It was about layering two lives in motion, without one subsuming the other.

There were moments—many, in fact—when we'd be in the same city, yet living slightly separate lives. I'd be preparing a talk on the ship, she'd be visiting a design exhibition across town. And then, that night, we'd reunite over a simple meal, often barefoot, sometimes still jet-lagged, sharing stories like postcards from parallel journeys. I'd tell her about a passenger who wept during a talk on lost seafaring traditions. She'd tell me about a color palette inspired by antique tiles in Palermo. Somehow, it all fit.

There was one trip—we were in Copenhagen. I had just wrapped up a guest lecture series on Scandinavian naval engineering, and Monica had been working on a concept hotel built around the theme of "quiet luxury." One evening, after a long day apart, we met along Nyhavn harbor. The light was soft, the kind that makes you forgive the cold. She handed me a notebook—unannounced, unwrapped. Inside, she had sketched my lecture themes—ships, wind, sails—interlaced with her design motifs. It was like watching two minds merge on paper. I don't think I said much. Just held the book. And then her hand.

That's what love looked like for us.

Not grand declarations. Not constant togetherness. But a quiet understanding: we didn't need to be welded at the hip to be deeply bound. We were like two ships that knew how to sail side by side—sometimes docked together, sometimes apart—but always moving in the same direction.

Over time, our shared lifestyle began to feel like its own kind of art form. Airports became familiar thresholds. Port cities were chapters. Our calendar was more a constellation than a schedule—Venice, Buenos Aires, Auckland, Dubrovnik. We learned the art of reunion. And perhaps more importantly, the art of letting each other go without fear.

There were moments of friction—missed calls, mismatched expectations, fatigue. But even those became part of the rhythm. We didn't try to iron them out. We allowed the dissonance to exist, trusted it would resolve like jazz.

And somewhere along the way, without forcing it, we became co-creators—not just of a lifestyle, but of a life. My stories deepened because of her perspective. Her designs were layered with the romance of our travels. Even our silences became rich, lived-in things.

She was never "along for the ride." She was part of the map.

And I, once so fiercely independent, found that sharing the helm with someone like Monica wasn't a compromise—it was an expansion.

A life of movement can be chaotic. But with her, I found something rare: a rhythm that didn't ask me to slow down or speed up. Just to keep sailing, together.

The Eleuthera Turning Point

When the world closed down in early 2020, it felt as though someone had pulled the plug on momentum. Ships stopped sailing. Flights went quiet. Lecture halls, ports, terminals—all silent. For the first time in decades, I was still. Grounded not by choice, but by something far larger than any one life.

We found ourselves in Eleuthera almost by accident. What was supposed to be a short retreat turned into an open-ended stay. The Bahamas became a kind of cocoon—humid, bright, strangely suspended in time. Monica and I woke up every morning to the sound of wind pushing through palm fronds and the soft cadence of waves against the limestone shore. No schedules. No plans. Just breath, sun, and the slow return of presence.

It could've been a season of waiting. But we chose to make it one of building.

The resort project came like a whisper—one conversation over breakfast about sustainable tourism, another on a beach walk about regenerative architecture. Before long, we were sketching plans on napkins and driftwood, writing drafts of a dream that had waited in both of us. Not just a place to stay, but a place to reconnect—with the land, with beauty, with each other.

I took the lead on systems and infrastructure—water reclamation, solar grid design, and local materials sourcing. Monica reimagined the flow of space itself. She refused the sterile "eco-resort" cliché. Her vision was warm, grounded in texture and light. Each bungalow curved slightly to catch the wind. The guest experience was less about luxury and more about grace—how light entered a room at dawn, the soft crunch of coral stone underfoot, a library where guests could write letters and leave books behind.

The land taught us both how to listen.

There was one evening I'll never forget. We'd just finished mapping out a communal garden and were sitting by the water, our legs folded into the sand. No music. Just the hush of tide meeting shore. Monica looked at me—really looked—and said, "You've never stopped building, have you?"

I smiled, not answering right away.

And then, in a tone quiet enough to live only in memory, she whispered, "Let's build this life for real."

There was no ring. No photographer hiding in the bushes. Just two people, deeply weathered and deeply awake, choosing to make a life that made space for both of them—fully.

It wasn't just a turning point. It was a vow. Not made in words, but in shared vision. In work done together. In choosing each other, again and again, in the face of uncertainty.

That land in Eleuthera didn't just give us a project. It gave us back ourselves.

I used to think legacy was about what you left behind—projects completed, titles earned, ships launched, structures named. Something public. Something solid. Something that outlives you.

But standing in the quiet shadow of a new morning in Eleuthera, coffee in hand, watching Monica hang a hammock between two sea almonds, I realized: that's not it.

Legacy isn't the book you publish. It's the story you live.

It's not what you build for others to remember you by. It's what you build while you're still here, with full attention, with full heart.

The lectures I gave on the ships—they weren't just about naval history. They became stories of resilience, voyages of the human spirit, connections across age and culture. After a while, people didn't come to learn about hull designs. They came to be seen, to remember wonder, to feel alive again.

The resort in Eleuthera wasn't about commercial success. It was about stewardship. About designing a place where people could return to stillness. Where rainwater was caught like treasure and light was welcomed like a guest.

And Monica—Monica was never my "chapter two." She was a collaborator in my becoming. She challenged me, softened me, showed me that legacy also lives in how we love, how we support, how we give without asking to be noticed.

Now, I think of legacy as something softer. Slower. But no less powerful.

It lives in the minds you awaken, the spaces you shape, the relationships you nurture. It's built in small moments: listening instead of instructing, choosing grace over control, leaving behind not a monument—but an atmosphere. A feeling. A story that others carry forward.

I no longer feel the need to stamp my name on things. I just want to leave places—and people—better than I found them.

Legacy, for me, is now defined by nurturing.

Of minds: through teaching that uplifts, not impresses.

Of spaces: with design that honors both form and feeling.

Of relationships: by being fully present, generous, and real.

That's what the sea taught me. What Monica reminded me. And what Eleuthera anchored in me.

Not a legacy of noise, but of elegance. Not dominance, but grace.

And in that quiet, enduring presence, I finally found something that lasts.

It was just after midnight when I stepped out onto the deck. The crowd had long retired, the ship quietly humming beneath my feet as it cut through a dark, glassy sea. Overhead, the stars held their steady silence. No city lights, no noise, just the hush of ocean and the weightless pull of sky.

I rested my forearms on the railing, the salt air brushing my face like an old friend. I had stood at this edge many times in my life, first as a boy peering over cargo decks in Naples, then as an engineer counting seconds between engine cycles, later as a lecturer adjusting my mic before a talk. But tonight was different.

I wasn't looking outward for direction. I wasn't calculating next steps. I wasn't rehearsing a legacy or chasing a finish line.

I was simply here. Still. Whole.

The sea had always been my mirror. In my younger years, it reflected ambition, motion, escape. In middle age, it became a challenge, something to master, to explain, to control. Now, at this stage, it simply invited me to be. It reminded me that arrival was never really about destination. It was about alignment. About feeling myself fully in the moment I was living.

I thought of Monica asleep in our stateroom—her sketches scattered on the desk, a novel half-read by the lamp. I thought of the guests I had met earlier that evening, their stories spilling out between courses like ships docking gently into safe harbors. I thought of Eleuthera, of warm rain, of basil in the garden, of the slow growth of something worth tending.

And in the quiet, I smiled.

I no longer needed to prove anything. I no longer needed to earn the right to be on this deck or to narrate the past in order to justify my presence. Everything that mattered—love, knowledge, stillness—had already come aboard. Not as cargo, but as company.

Purpose was no longer something I chased. It sailed with me.

There was peace in that. A steady kind of joy.

As the ship moved forward into the dark, I lingered for a moment longer, eyes tracing constellations I used to memorize from maritime charts. But I wasn't mapping anything now. I was simply noticing.

A   breath.
A   heartbeat.
The deep, unwavering rhythm of being exactly where I was meant to be.

And with that, I turned back toward the stateroom—not to close a chapter, but to continue the voyage.

Intentionally. Quietly. Fully alive.

Chapter 20: Becoming a Mentor – Sharing My Knowledge

There's a stillness that comes after personal reckoning, the kind that follows when a chapter of your life closes and another begins. In the wake of my own renewal, as shared in Hoboken not long before, I found myself shifting focus. No longer the one forging forward through unknown seas, I began turning my attention behind me, to those just beginning the voyage.

The room was quiet, the kind of silence that fills the air when something important is about to happen. I was seated near the back, away from the faculty panel, trying not to be noticed. The young man at the front of the classroom, barely twenty-four, maybe, stood straight, eyes fixed on the slides he was about to present. His name was Adam, and he had chosen to defend his master's thesis on ship manoeuvrability, drawing heavily from a paper I had written thirty-five years earlier: *"Practical Calculation Method of Ship Manoeuvring Characteristics at the Design Stage."*

He didn't know I was in the room, not at first. He referenced the 1990 publication early in his presentation, calling it "the backbone" of his approach. He spoke with the kind of nervous confidence I remembered so well from my own days on the Adriatica, when I thought every sentence I wrote could shift the world of naval design, if only someone would read it. As he moved through his research, refining rudder performance under varying load conditions and simulating tight harbour manoeuvres, I could see myself in him.

The same eagerness to learn, to demonstrate, to fit in an area of study that most of the time seems too immense to ever grasp effectively. His arguments were strict, his statistics clear, but it was not his reasoning that impressed me with him: it was this strangeness, it was the fact that he paused now and then, not to take a breath, but to let an idea land. It is what you learn only when you have lived with the work a long time, so that the work becomes a part of you.

At the end of his presentation, he turned to the panel and said, "I owe a special thanks to Dr. Biancardi, whose early research gave me a foundation. I hope that I did build something useful on top of it." Somebody poked him and told him I was in the room. His face turned pink, and he glanced across helplessly, not knowing whether to smile or be sorry.

I stood and applauded.

In that instance, above all the awards or keynote speeches that I had ever given before, I understood what legacy meant. No name in a journal, title on a wall, but a flame which is transmitted, silently, without pomp, from one mind to another. Mentorship doesn't begin with a lecture. It begins with presence. With being there, watching someone else step into the work, into the uncertainty, and offering them just enough light to find their own way forward.

That morning in Hoboken, watching Adam speak my language in his own voice, I realized I was no longer the student or even the innovator. I was the one standing quietly in the back, making space. And that felt right.

Mentoring Through Flagship Projects

Mentorship didn't happen in a classroom alone. So many times, it happened alongside the front lines of actual projects, where timelines were constrained, the pressure was high, and training was conducted at full scale. I never intended on becoming a teacher, not in a traditional sense anyway. But with the expansion of our research efforts in Europe, it became habitual of me to be surrounded by young engineers, full of curiosity, with great potential looking for people to believe in their efforts.

The OCEAN-NAV project was one of the first major initiatives where mentorship wasn't a side activity, it was part of the mission. We were working on advanced modelling tools to improve ship safety and reduce environmental impact. I brought in doctoral students early, not just to observe, but to build models, present data, and challenge assumptions. Some of them struggled at first, overwhelmed by the complexity. But I knew the feeling. I remembered being in that exact place. So, I stayed close, not to provide answers, but to help them ask better questions.

Then came WAVE SIMULATOR, a far more hands-on program. We converted lab spaces into hydrodynamic test beds, with physical models and wave tanks. It was here that I saw young engineers light up. Something changes when you move from theory on a page to water moving in front of you. I encouraged them to get their hands wet, adjust the models, recalibrate sensors, repeat the runs. Mistakes weren't just tolerated, they were expected. And through those mistakes, growth came.

One of the clearest moments of this came with Mateo Varga, a doctoral student who had joined OCEAN-NAV straight from a smaller regional university. He was bright, but unsure, haunted by the idea that he didn't quite belong among the others. He'd been tasked with refining a component of the energy dispersion module, but his simulations kept failing, throwing up inconsistencies that none of us could immediately trace.

One afternoon in the Naples lab, I sat beside him while he tried yet another iteration. The fluorescent lights hummed above us, and outside the windows, the sea air drifted in, thick with the scent of salt and engine oil. He looked at me and said, "Maybe I'm just not cut out for this level." I remembered standing in that same kind of doubt, years ago, on the docks of Procida, when my father handed me the helm and told me to trust the water. "If it's easy," I told him, "you're not learning anything real." We broke the problem down, line by line, variable by variable, until the fault became clear: a misreferenced boundary condition buried deep in the model. His face lit up, not because we solved it, but because he finally saw that he could.

A few months later, he was leading a working group on energy modeling for one of OCEAN-NAV's partner institutions. His voice no longer trembled. His models held. And his ideas, his own, began influencing the design path. Watching that happen was more gratifying than any published paper. It was the work, passed forward.

One of the most forward-thinking projects we led was AURORA, focused on developing electric ferry hulls. This one brought together engineering with design, sustainability, and systems thinking. I didn't just ask students to run simulations, I asked them to propose new shapes, to argue for efficiency over tradition, to take risks that most professionals wouldn't. Some of their ideas were bold. A few didn't work. But several proved brilliant. And I made sure their names were on the results.

Several years later, I saw those same students presenting at conferences or taking on responsibilities at companies like Chantiers de l'Atlantique, Bureau Veritas, and the Port Authority of Toulon. They didn't succeed by following rigid instructions, but by learning to think and reason through complexity.

The thing that astounded me the most was not their intelligence—their intelligence to me was never in question. It was the way they saw the world and how they managed to keep a balance. They were so humble, strong, and ready to listen before making their own point. This is what actual mentorship does. Not just merely transferring knowledge from one person to another, but building their character.

And in turn? I was able to observe the future and watch it arrive, one engineer at a time.

Building an International Mentorship Footprint

My journey as a mentor was not exactly linear, nor was it constrained by geographical boundaries. My pathway led me through lectures in Naples, crossing seas to Launceston in Tasmania, up the steps of Manhattan College, and nestled itself in the restful corners of Hoboken, New Jersey. I was not just delivering lectures, I was linking the gaps between the theory and practice.

At Stevens Institute of Technology, I taught Stability and Control of Marine Crafts, a subject that, on paper, sounds dry and formulaic. But when I walked into the classroom, I didn't bring just theory. I brought stories, case studies, and actual data pulled from our own simulations. I showed students what happened when a vessel didn't respond as expected, or when a design looked perfect until it met real-world forces. They didn't just memorize equations; they learned to anticipate, to adapt, to think like naval architects in motion.

At Manhattan College, I taught Engineering and Design Management, a course that pushed students beyond their comfort zones. I would hand them live datasets from projects like THOPIC, which modelled the dynamics of docking ships, and VECTOR-GUIDE, our research on azimuth thruster control systems. We'd walk through scenarios where real vessels, under real conditions, had to respond in seconds—or face costly outcomes. The students weren't solving textbook exercises. They were stepping into problems I had faced myself, and being asked how *they* would respond.

That kind of learning changes people. Sure, it made things more challenging, but it also built their confidence. I kept seeing it play out: students who began the semester hesitant and unsure were leading group presentations by the end, answering questions clearly, even confidently.

No matter the campus or the country, one thing stayed the same. The goal wasn't just to pass on information; it was to give students a sense of power. I wanted them to walk out of the room knowing what they knew could actually matter. That they could take it and use it, to shape systems, design vessels, maybe even shift what the future looks like.

And in doing so, they shaped mine.

Teaching Through Real Systems and Data

One thing I never believed in was teaching in a vacuum. Engineering, especially in the maritime world, isn't something that lives on paper. It lives in motion, in steel, in weather you can't always predict. Early on, I made a decision: if I was going to stand in front of a class, I wasn't going to sugarcoat it. I'd give them the real thing.

That's why I started bringing live data from active, EU-funded projects straight into my courses.

These weren't polished examples or simplified case studies; they were raw, unfiltered simulations pulled straight from the field. One standout was PATHLINK, a collaborative research project focused on composite patch repairs for steel ship structures. The simulation results from that study, stress distributions, material fatigue, and thermal response under repair conditions, were used as actual lab assignments in my Advanced Marine Vehicles course.

I remember the reactions the first time I introduced those datasets. Some students were visibly overwhelmed, this was no multiple-choice quiz. But once they began working through the numbers, applying their own models, testing hypotheses, you could see the shift. They started asking sharper questions, challenging assumptions, even proposing improvements to the test protocols. That's when you know something is working.

This hands-on method did more than deepen their technical understanding. It created a rare feedback loop between academia and industry. Students weren't just learning, they were contributing. In turn, the companies and institutions involved in these projects began to take notice. Our graduates arrived on the job already familiar with the systems they'd be working on. Some had even published early findings based on the lab work we'd done together.

Over time, this approach helped position our program as a kind of hybrid space, part university, part innovation lab. It blurred the line between classroom and command room. And I believe that's exactly where real learning happens.

Institutional Leadership – Shaping a Global Ethos

Taking on the role of Director of the *International Master's in Science and Engineering of the Sea* wasn't just another professional step; it was a turning point. For the first time, I had the responsibility, and the privilege, of shaping not just what students learned, but *how* they approached the world as engineers and as people.

Coordinating a faculty of over fifty professors and researchers, spread across three continents, was no small task. There were time zones to juggle, academic cultures to bridge, and countless logistical headaches. But there was also an incredible sense of possibility. We weren't just building a curriculum; we were creating a space where knowledge could travel freely, shaped by the insights of Marseille, Naples, Hobart, and New York.

I wanted our students to graduate with more than just technical proficiency. They needed to be globally agile, equally at home designing systems for European ports as they were discussing environmental policy in Southeast Asia or adapting designs to Pacific Island infrastructure. To do that, we embedded real-world collaboration into the heart of the program. Students might run hydrodynamic tests in Toulon one semester and analyze satellite-tracked vessel behavior in Tasmania the next. They'd collaborate across borders, across languages, and often across disciplines.

But just as importantly, we talked about *why* their work mattered. We challenged them to think about safety, sustainability, and ethics, not as footnotes, but as central to the mission of engineering. Some of the most rewarding moments came not from technical breakthroughs, but from roundtable discussions where students debated the environmental impact of their designs, or how automation would affect seafaring jobs in the decades ahead.

What we built wasn't perfect, no program ever is, but it had soul. It had a heartbeat that reflected the people in it: smart, driven, and deeply aware of their place in the larger world. When I look back on those years, I don't just see lecture halls and spreadsheets. I see conversations that lingered long after class ended, emails from students who took a lesson to heart and turned it into a project, and alumni who went on to lead with both skill and conscience.

If there's a legacy I hope to leave behind, it's this: not just smarter engineers, but better ones. Engineers who know that knowledge is power, but wisdom is responsibility.

Institutional Leadership – Shaping a Global Ethos

When I took on the role of Director for the International Master's in Science and Engineering of the Sea, I didn't quite realize at the start how much it would ask of me, or how much it would change the way I thought about teaching. I'd managed projects, teams, and even whole departments before. But this was something else entirely. It wasn't just about lectures or research milestones. It was about shaping people, engineers, yes, but also future leaders, collaborators, and global citizens.

We had a team of over fifty professors and researchers. And they weren't all sitting in the same building, or even on the same continent. There were partners in Marseille, Naples, Hobart, New York... sometimes we'd have meetings where one person was just starting their day and another was finishing theirs. Coordinating across three time zones and clashing academic habits? It wasn't exactly smooth sailing. Some days, it felt like we were improvising our way through a symphony, half jazz, half logistics. But that unpredictability kept things alive. There was always this feeling, like something meaningful was just beneath the surface, waiting to come together.

Right from the start, I knew this couldn't be just a technical course with a fancy title. I wanted students to *live* the global nature of the field, to understand different contexts, and learn how to bring meaningful solutions back to wherever they ended up working. We designed it so they'd move, not just through subjects, but through countries. They might start in France, run physical model tests in Toulon, then fly to Tasmania to work on satellite data tracking. They'd meet people with different languages and different methods, and still have to solve the same complex problems. That was the point.

But we also made space for hard conversations. The kind you don't find in textbooks. What happens to traditional seafaring jobs when automation takes over? How do you balance innovation with long-term environmental risk? There was this moment during a design review, when a student raised a concern about how a hull structure might affect marine ecosystems in shallow waters. It wasn't about proving a point; what stood out was the thought behind it. They weren't just doing the math; they were thinking about the consequences.

Some of my favorite memories aren't even from the classroom. They're from those quiet moments, after a workshop, during a coffee break, when someone would ask a question that had clearly been on their mind for days. Or the email that came a year later: "I used what we talked about to pitch a new idea at my job." Those moments, for me, are the real markers of success.

The program wasn't flawless. No program is. But it had a spirit. It felt alive. And looking back, I think we built more than just a master's degree, we built a generation that understood their role went beyond the drawing board.

If I've left anything behind through that work, I hope it's not just sharper minds. I hope it's wiser ones. People who know that being a good engineer is about more than being right, it's about being responsible.

Closing Reflection – Mentorship as Legacy in Motion

Looking back now, what stays with me most isn't the titles or the projects. It's the people. The students who walked into my classroom with wide eyes and curious minds, many of them are now steering efforts I once helped set in motion.

There's a quiet pride in knowing that someone you once coached through a thesis is now heading up the hybrid ferry initiative in La Rochelle. Or that a young engineer who once struggled with thruster control algorithms is now overseeing VTMIS implementation in Bremen. These aren't just professional wins; they're living, breathing proof that mentorship doesn't end when the class is over. It continues, unfolds, and evolves.

We say a lot about legacy as though it is something that we leave behind. However, I have now realized that I couldn't be any different. Legacy goes on. It does so by talking through others. It forms itself on what we shared in the past and molds it over into something different, something twice as good, twice as smart, and twice as bold.

Many of them still write to me, some to share a technical breakthrough, others just to say thank you. And every time I hear from them, I'm reminded why this work matters. Not just because we build ships or systems, but because we shape people who can think, lead, and care.

As I once told a class during my final lecture in Hoboken: **"I was once their compass. Now they are the captains."**

Chapter 21: Pioneering AI-Driven Navigation – A New Frontier

The sun was yet to come up over the bay at Toulon. The sea air was calm and had that clear Mediterranean salty odor with just enough of a metallic tinge, which I associated with early mornings by the sea. I was on the bridge of our hybrid-electric ferry, the AURORA, leaning on the railing.

The ship moved forward without a sound. You'd have to be paying close attention to notice the slight shift in the horizon, just a small tilt as the ferry adjusted its trim. Nothing dramatic, barely visible, but real.

The crew around me didn't break stride. No alarms, no announcements, just another quiet correction as part of the system doing its job. But I felt it. Not just physically, but in a deeper way, which is hard to explain. There was something meaningful in that tiny, precise movement. The way the ferry responded, calm, deliberate, it didn't feel artificial or robotic. It felt thoughtful. Alive, almost. Like the system wasn't just reacting, but understanding.

I'd sailed these waters before. The view hadn't changed. But standing on that deck, I could feel that the ship itself had.

The AI system was working.

Without a word, without a command, the onboard algorithm recalculated the vessel's dynamic resistance based on real-time hydrodynamic feedback. Micro-adjustments were made automatically, fine-tuned corrections that even the most seasoned helmsman would struggle to notice, let alone execute with such consistency. There was no drama to it. Just precision.

For me, that moment wasn't just another demonstration of advanced maritime tech. It was a quiet, deeply personal confirmation: this was what we had dreamed about four decades ago, back when such systems lived only in sketches, code fragments, and conference abstracts. Now it was real, operational, elegant, and doing its job without applause.

No fanfare. Just function.

I didn't say anything to the engineers standing nearby. I didn't need to. Watching the system work was enough. I saw my fingerprints in the way it thought. In the logic it followed. In the instincts we had once tried to teach machines to emulate, long before anyone believed we could.

AI had arrived. And part of its DNA was mine.

Overcoming Resistance – Cultural and Operational Challenges

Back in the early days, convincing people to trust AI on the bridge was like trying to sell a compass to a man who'd spent his whole life navigating by the stars. You could show him the benefits, explain the logic, even demonstrate how it worked, but at the end of the day, trust wasn't something you could download.

In Rotterdam, I remember sitting across from a senior harbor pilot, someone with forty years under his belt, who flat-out told me, "A machine might follow rules, but it doesn't feel a ship's hesitation."

He knocked on the table with his index finger when he said it, in case I needed to be reminded that this was not some argument, but reality. At Nice, it was more diplomatic, though the meaning was the same: such systems were probably smart, but they lacked experience of what it was like to stand on a deck in a crosswind, to make a call in fog, to feel the sea rising beneath your feet.

And in Valencia, one captain asked me bluntly, "What happens when the system decides too late?" The concern wasn't whether AI could think; it was whether it could understand the moment.

And honestly, they weren't wrong to question it. That kind of skepticism wasn't just cultural, it was earned. These were people who had spent entire careers relying on instinct, muscle memory, and subtle signs: the pitch of the engine, the tug of a line, the way a vessel shifted just before wind took the stern. The bridge was sacred ground, and for good reason. Introducing AI into that space wasn't just a technical shift; it was an existential one. It made people ask, "If a machine does this, what does that make me?"

That's why, during my time at Kings Point, I shifted focus to human factors research. We needed to look beyond code and consider behavior, stress, and intuition. How does a person respond under pressure? What happens when things don't go as planned? Can a system adapt without eroding confidence or control? These weren't abstract questions; they were the heart of the matter. I remember one of our core findings, something I still stand by today: **"AI without bridge instinct is a risk multiplier."**

That line wasn't just for the paper. It became something of a personal mantra. Because if we were going to ask mariners to put their trust in these systems, then the systems had to earn it, not replace them, not override them, but *work with them*. Seamlessly. Respectfully. Quietly, in the background, like a second officer who never sleeps but never gets in the way.

That belief shaped every design choice I made after. Human-in-the-loop wasn't just a technical framework. It was an ethical stance. A compass point. It meant giving people the final say, <u>always</u>. It meant designing systems that supported instinct, not substituted it.

And I never lost sight of it.

Collaborative Breakthroughs – AI at Work Across the Fleet

No breakthrough ever happens in a vacuum. Real change, the kind that sticks, comes from collaboration, trial, and iteration. I've always believed that to bring AI into the maritime world, we couldn't just build clever systems in labs. We had to test them under real conditions, with real crews, on real water.

That mindset shaped every major project I led over the years. We worked across borders, engineers, mariners, data scientists, and regulators, each bringing something vital to the table. It wasn't always smooth sailing, but the friction often revealed what theory couldn't.

One project I still think about often is SEA-INTEL. The aim was straightforward: integrate weather forecasts into ship routing, using AI to adapt course plans in real time. What we ended up achieving was more than just smoother voyages, we cut port arrival deviations by 15%. That meant fewer delays, better fuel use, and less stress on crews. The system didn't just respond to the environment, it anticipated it. And for the captains involved, that made all the difference.

One of those captains was Captain Alain Deschamps, a seasoned navigator out of Marseille, known for his precision and a certain wariness toward anything automated. When we first introduced SEA-INTEL on his route to Bastia, he made his skepticism clear. "It's your system," he said, "but it's my responsibility." And he was right.

The test run was scheduled for early spring. The winds were moderate but gusting unpredictably; the Corsican straits can turn suddenly, and that morning was no exception. I was on board with the technical crew, monitoring system performance. Captain Deschamps stood at the helm, hands clasped behind his back, silent but alert.

As we neared the shoal markers, the AI flagged a developing crosscurrent and recommended a minor heading adjustment, just four degrees off the planned route. The suggestion came with a brief justification: "Minimized lateral drift under projected gust pattern." Captain Deschamps hesitated. He squinted at the water, then at the system readout. You could see the old habits flicker, instinct telling him one thing, the system another.

He made the adjustment. Slight. Barely perceptible. But moments later, a swell rose on our port quarter, just as the system had predicted. A small thing. Not dramatic. But it would have nudged the ferry further off course without correction. Instead, we stayed centered. No alarm. No crisis. Just a calm negotiation between man and machine.

Later, over coffee in the galley, he said, "It's like a first mate that listens more than it speaks." He wasn't sold, not entirely. But he trusted the system just a bit more than he had before. That shift, that inching of confidence, is the work.

We didn't build SEA-INTEL to replace him. We built it to support him, to see the swell before it crests, to hear what the helmsman might miss in the noise, and to offer a second opinion without ego. That's not just engineering. That's seamanship in another form.

Then there was OCEAN-NAV, which tackled a more sensitive challenge: how to safely transport dangerous goods while predicting their environmental impact if things went wrong. It wasn't glamorous work, but it was essential. The AI didn't just monitor, it learned. It could flag potential hazards based on historical patterns and real-time data. For the first time, risk wasn't a vague idea. It became something we could measure and reduce.

PATHLINK took us below the waterline. After composite repairs to ship hulls, inspectors often struggled to assess long-term integrity. With PATHLINK, we embedded sensors into those repaired areas, feeding data to an AI system that could track changes over time. If a patch began to degrade or shift under pressure, we'd know—long before it became a problem. It turned what was once a manual, reactive process into a proactive one. For maintenance crews, it was like getting a second set of eyes.

And for high-speed vessels, where margins are razor-thin and everything happens faster—we developed NAVMIND and VORTEX-PRO. These experiments laid the foundation for AI-assisted decision tools in vessels that push performance limits. Just imagine a ferry boat traveling at high speed through a narrowing channel with varying winds and currents. These systems provided quick, unequivocal, and data-supported advice.

What made all of this possible wasn't just code or hardware, it was people. Every project combined simulation with field trials, and most importantly, feedback from the mariners themselves. We'd bring the systems onboard, watch how crews interacted with them, and listen, really listen, to what they had to say. That was non-negotiable. The goal wasn't to build perfect machines. It was to build tools that worked for real people in real conditions.

Because at the end of the day, AI only matters if it earns its place at sea.

Teaching AI to Respect Seamanship – Not Replace It

From the beginning, I made one thing clear: AI is here to support the mariner, not to supplant them.

That conviction wasn't born in a boardroom. It came from years spent at sea, on the bridge, watching decisions being made in real time, judgments shaped not only by instruments or manuals, but by experience, instinct, and the subtle signals no machine can fully read.

I carried that understanding into every system we built. Yes, we were programming logic. Yes, we were training algorithms. But behind the models, there was always a deeper mission: to honor the judgment of the human being at the helm.

At a joint forum hosted by SNAME and the IMO in New York, I found myself repeating what had become something of a mantra for me:

"Seamanship is not a memory to be archived, it's a decision process to be digitally respected."

The room was filled with engineers, policymakers, ship owners, and a few veteran captains who nodded, not just out of politeness, but in recognition. They knew what I meant. Seamanship isn't just a skillset. It's a lived logic. It draws on things AI still struggles with—intuition, pattern recognition from incomplete information, knowing when to act and when to wait.

That's why I've always insisted on human-in-the-loop design. Not as an afterthought, but as the foundation. Every system we put to sea had to allow for human override. It had to be explainable, not just in how it worked, but in why it made a given recommendation. If a ship's master couldn't trust the system, or worse, couldn't understand it, it had no place onboard.

We spent as much time building trust frameworks as we did writing code. We pushed for transparency in logic pathways, clear accountability in automated decisions, and built-in ethical constraints. This wasn't about regulation, it was about responsibility.

The systems I helped develop were never meant to hand control over to a machine. They were meant to give the mariner more space to think, to reduce the noise, and to filter what matters most at the moment it matters. That's what augmentation looks like. That's what respect looks like.

Because the sea is still unpredictable. And no matter how advanced AI becomes, it should never forget who it serves.

Closing Reflection – From Sextant to Code

I still remember that night in 1978, standing on the bridge of an *Adriatica* vessel, somewhere off the coast of Tunisia, sextant in hand. The stars were out, the swell steady. I was nineteen, barely a cadet, tasked with plotting our position the old-fashioned way, by sight, by hand, by instinct. There was no GPS. No screen. Just calculations scribbled in the margins of a logbook and a sky full of silent instruction.

That moment stayed with me, not because it was perfect, but because it demanded everything. Attention. Judgment. Respect for the unknown.

Fast-forward to today. I watch a hybrid-electric ferry glide through Toulon's bay, making trim corrections on the fly, guided by an AI model I helped design. No hesitation. No noise. The system reads the hydrodynamics in real time and makes decisions a human could only approximate.

It should feel like a disconnect, but it doesn't. It feels like continuity, because beneath the surface, that same spirit of navigation remains. The same questions, the same need for clarity and choice. Only now, the tools have changed. The intuition I once trusted in my gut is now embedded in lines of code, calibrated and tested to assist a new generation of seafarers.

What I built wasn't just software. It was a vessel for wisdom, a way to carry decades of seamanship forward without drowning it in automation.

At the SNAME/IMO forum, I once said, "Seamanship is not a memory to be archived, it's a decision process to be digitally respected." I stand by that.

We didn't just teach machines how to calculate, we taught them how to listen, how to adapt, how to respect the mariner.

And now? I look at these systems and smile.

"I was once their compass. Now they are the captains."

That's the legacy I care about, not the patents or the projects, but the fact that human judgment still stands at the center of everything we've built.

Code can evolve. Tools will change. But insight, true seamanship, will always have a place on the bridge.

Conclusion: From the Edge to the Horizon

There was a time when I felt invincible. My body was like a vessel fresh from the shipyard — solid, finely tuned, ready to take on any ocean. I could cross seas without thinking twice, stand for hours delivering lectures, lead a crew in high-pressure situations, or face down a storm with steady hands. I believed my physical strength was a permanent fixture, something as reliable as the keel beneath a ship. Like the hull of a well-built liner, I assumed it could weather anything thrown its way.

You know how sometimes things look fine on the outside, but underneath, stuff is slowly falling apart? It's not sudden, not a big crash. More like little cracks you barely notice. Especially if you don't want to.

It started for me with this intense, unwavering fatigue. Even if I slept all night, I would still wake up feeling as though I hadn't slept at all. It was similar to pulling weights that no one else could see. On certain mornings, I felt like I had lost it before the day had even begun.

Then the headaches came—pounding, relentless, making even simple thoughts feel like heavy work. I knew something was off. My body was telling me loud and clear.

But when I went to the doctors, they waved it away. Stress, they said. Long hours, too much travel, not enough sleep. I wanted to shout— you're not listening. Because I knew it in my bones: this wasn't ordinary fatigue. It was heavier, darker. And the part that scared me most was realizing I was right... while no one else believed me.

After that summer trip—when I'd spent the days just dragging myself around, forcing smiles, acting like I was fine—it all finally broke. The second I got back home, my body gave out. Breathing felt thick and heavy, my head hammered, and even small movements drained me. I couldn't pretend anymore.

I drove myself to the ER, vision hazy from fear and exhaustion. The bright hospital lights, the rush of voices and footsteps, made everything feel unreal. Then the blood work came back. I caught the change on the doctor's face before they even spoke. Their tone shifted, softer, careful. That's when I heard it: my kidneys were failing.

It was the first time the truth, hidden for so long, finally stood in front of me.

I think I knew it all along, though I didn't want to admit it. There was this low hum in the back of my thoughts, warning me that something was off. I brushed it aside. I told myself to just keep going — focus on where I was headed, not every small rattle along the way. There were too many tasks on my plate, too many people counting on me.

Who has time for mystery aches and stubborn tiredness?

Eventually, though, my body forced me to listen. Routine activities started feeling like uphill climbs. A short walk left me winded. My appetite thinned, and with it, a subtle sense of myself seemed to fade. It wasn't pain that drove me to see a doctor — it was the unnerving feeling that my once-reliable engine was losing power without warning.

The tests came next. Blood work, scans, and conversations in sterile rooms that always seemed too cold. I watched the expressions of the doctors — the small furrow in the brow, the pause before speaking — and I knew before they said the words. Kidney failure.

When the doctor said it, it hit me hard. Not just the words, but the weight behind them. It felt like something heavy dropping straight into calm water. It wasn't just news about my health — it was a hit to who I thought I was.

I'd always been the one who kept going. The one who made it through, no matter the storm. The one people could lean on. But this... this was different. My body had sprung a leak somewhere I couldn't reach. And this time, sheer stubbornness wasn't going to fix it.

That day, walking out of the hospital, something had shifted. I knew now I wasn't the unbreakable ship I'd pictured in my mind. The damage had been there a long time, hiding just under the surface where I couldn't see it.

Now it had revealed itself and there was no going back to the way things were.

I left the hospital after all the scans and blood work, but the words followed me out the door. Kidney failure. I couldn't shake them. The sunlight felt wrong, too sharp, like it didn't match what was happening to me. Even breathing felt strange, like the air wasn't enough.

That night I couldn't sleep. Just stared at the ceiling, thinking over and over—what if this is it? Not years from now, not someday way ahead, but soon. Something was off. My body didn't feel like mine at all—weak, shaky, not reliable. Breathing felt harder than it should. My heart thudded heavy, beat after beat. I kept saying to myself, maybe I'm overthinking it. But the fear stayed. It wouldn't budge.

The First Battle – Dialysis and the Wait

I didn't feel sick in the way people imagine sickness. There was no fever, no sharp pain, no dramatic collapse. But the bloodwork told another story, one I couldn't argue with. Numbers don't negotiate. Within a few weeks, my days were built around a rigid routine: four hours at a time, three days a week, connected to a machine doing the work my body had stopped managing.

The treatment center became an odd sort of second home. The smell of disinfectant always met me at the door. The soft mechanical whir of the dialysis unit filled the room. Then came the sting; the needle finding its mark and the steady rhythm of blood flowing out and back again. Around me, others fought the same quiet fight. Some kept their eyes shut, some stared at the floor. We didn't trade many words, but a small nod or half-smile carried more understanding than conversation ever could. The routine became a rhythm I never wanted but couldn't escape. You learn to read the clock differently on dialysis, not in hours and minutes, but in the stretch between one session and the next. Even on the "off" days, it's there in your mind, like an anchor dragging just out of sight.

As if the shock of starting dialysis was not enough, life dealt me another blow I could never have prepared for. Almost at the same time, we learned that my wife had cancer. I remember the moment as if it were carved into me — the sterile smell of the clinic still in my nose, the hum of the dialysis machine still in my ears, when the words came: It's cancer. Suddenly, my fight for survival was doubled. I was tethered to a machine for hours at a time, my own body failing me, yet my heart was somewhere else — with her, in the doctor's office, in the hospital corridors, holding her hand through the storm. We were two patients now, each battling a different enemy, but the same fear. And in the quiet moments between treatments, I found myself wondering which one of us would run out of time first.

Then came the waiting. And waiting is its own kind of illness. At first, you think about it constantly. Every phone ring makes your chest tighten. Each unfamiliar number on the screen might be the call, the one that shifts the course of everything. For my first transplant, the wait was just a few weeks — short in time, but every day felt stretched to its limit. Even in that brief span, hope had to be measured carefully. You carry it in small doses — enough to move forward, but not so much that it crushes you if the call doesn't come immediately.

That's how long I lived in that suspended space — not fully alive, but not gone either. Always between the life I had and the one I wanted back.

And then, without warning, it happened.

When the phone rang, I almost didn't answer. I'd learned not to expect much from unknown numbers. But that day, the voice on the other end changed everything: a donor had been found. Suddenly, I was in motion — calls made, bags thrown together, a blur of hospital corridors and forms to sign.

The surgery itself was a haze. Bright lights above me, the cold bite of an IV in my arm, and then nothing until I woke up hours later, heavy and sore, wondering if the new kidney was already at work.

That's when the real test began. I spent forty days in isolation. It's hard to explain what that feels like unless you've lived it. No handshakes. No hugs. No unmasked faces. Just doctors and nurses sealed in protective layers, their voices muffled, their eyes the only part of them I could really see. My immune system had been stripped down to almost nothing; the price I paid to keep my body from rejecting the organ. Even a sneeze from across the room could have been dangerous for me during this time.

The clock barely seemed to move. That low machine hum just sat there in the room, and every so often, I'd catch the wheels of a cart squeaking down the hall. I wasn't in stabbing pain or anything, but my body felt weighed down in this dull way. Even stuff like lifting a cup, leaning a little, or trying to keep a thought straight felt like way too much.

Over time, solitude became so familiar it almost felt safe. When I finally got outside, the air felt weird in my lungs, almost sharp. I moved slowly, kind of like the ground might shift if I wasn't careful. After a while, though, I started slipping back into things — work, the ocean, regular talks that had nothing to do with test results or pills. I laughed again. Not right away, and not without effort, but I did.

I convinced myself the worst was over. For a while, I let myself believe that.

The thing about decline is that it's a slow tide, pulling you out before you realize how far you've drifted. That same deep, heavy tiredness came back — the kind that gets into your bones. My ankles puffed up, and even walking up a few steps left me short of breath. Deep down, I already knew. The kidney was quitting on me. When the doctors said it out loud, it still hit hard. They kept their voices calm, but their faces told me they'd seen this coming. The map was already drawn, and I was back on the same road I'd walked before — straight toward dialysis.

This time, the wait for another transplant was shorter. Months, not years. But in a strange way, that didn't make it easier. The first time around, I'd been ignorant of the full list of things that could go wrong. Now I carried them in my head like an inventory: rejection, infection, complications you can't pronounce. I knew the smell of the ward, the way the nights sound when you can't sleep for the beeping monitors. I knew the way hospital food turns your stomach after the third or fourth day.

There were nights when I lay there and thought, maybe this is it. Maybe I just stop fighting. The idea of letting go was tempting — no more needles, no more waiting rooms, no more pretending I felt stronger than I was. Still, a part of me wouldn't agree to quit. Call it stubbornness, or just that sailor instinct — you don't leave the ship if there's even a small chance you can make it to shore.

So I kept going to dialysis. Kept talking to people. Kept making small, almost laughably modest plans for days I wasn't sure I'd reach. I learned that survival isn't some grand, cinematic moment of triumph. It's, in fact, a chain of tiny choices. Sitting up when you'd rather stay down. Taking another spoonful of food. Hearing a different voice on the phone. When the big picture seems unattainable, small victories added together keep you going.

The second time, the wait felt different. Two years dragged on like forever. Days and weeks all blurred. Hope shrank into something small, something you keep hidden so it won't hurt as much when nothing changes. Waiting isn't just the clock moving. It's your whole life stuck in between—caught between maybe and never—trying to keep walking even when the finish line looks too far away.

The call came again — another donor, another chance. I'd been through this before, but that didn't make it any less surreal. The surgery itself was rougher this time. My body, already marked by years of treatment and the first transplant, didn't bounce back the way it had the first time. Every movement pulled at old scar tissue. Every breath seemed to remind me of what I'd already endured.

And yet, in other ways, this time felt lighter. It wasn't my first time through this. I had a sense of the rhythm — when to move, when to rest, how to notice what my body was telling me without jumping at every pang. The stretch of being shut in didn't last long. After a few days, I was back outside.

Medical advances had trimmed the edges of the ordeal, and I was grateful for every improvement. There's a strange thing that happens when you're given a second chance; you stop taking even the smallest moments for granted. The sound of footsteps in a hallway becomes something to notice. A glass of water tastes sharper, cleaner. Even the cool weight of a blanket can feel like a gift when you've spent nights in a hospital bed with scratchy sheets and constant interruptions. I found myself holding onto these details, as if collecting proof that life was still worth fighting for.

The fear was still there, of course. It always is when you've learned just how quickly the ground beneath you can give way. But alongside it was a steadier kind of faith in myself, not the naïve belief that nothing bad could happen, but the seasoned knowledge that I could find my way back if it did.

The moment I walked outside and breathed in air that wasn't filtered through a hospital ventilation system, it hit me. I had made it back. Again. The light hit me in a way I wasn't ready for — warmer, heavier somehow. The traffic noise almost had a beat to it. I found myself stopping, looking up, not for any reason — just to see that stretch of clear blue overhead.

Now I live with two transplants behind me and the visible reminders etched into my skin. Those scars carry more than medical history — they hold the quiet hours of fear, the whispered prayers, the faces of people who never got their call, and the hands of those who stood by me when I nearly didn't get mine.

The horizon's still there, shifting like it always does. I head for it each day — not thinking the storms are gone for good, but knowing now that I can ride them out and keep moving.